THE GREY WORLD

Scriptoria

The word *scriptoria* literally means "places for writing." Historically, they were writing rooms set apart in some monasteries for the use of scribes, or copyists of the community, to faithfully create or reproduce books by hand. Their efforts, through the years, preserved many important works that would have been otherwise lost, and contributed immensely to Western civilization's written treasury.

Scriptoria Books continues in the same tradition that scribes and conservators have followed through the ages. Each Scriptoria publication is an authentic reproduction of an original text. Our books are not facsimiles. They are transcribed word for word, set in a contemporary typeface, and formatted for size and readability.

Evelyn Underhill

Evelyn Underhill (1875-1941) was a renowned English author, educated at King's College for Women, London, and was Upton Lecturer on the Philosophy of Religion at Manchester College, Oxford (1921-1922). Between 1902 and 1940 she authored many works, but is most noted for the books she produced on the various aspects of mysticism.

Underhill's publications also include three novels, two books of verse, works on philosophy and religion, editions of critical essays on John of Ruysbroeck and Walter Hilton, and numerous reviews and articles. Among her writings are *The Grey World* (1904), *Mysticism* (1911), *The Mystic Way* (1913), *Practical Mysticism* (1915), *The Essentials of Mysticism* (1920), *The Life of the Spirit and the Life of Today* (1922), *Concerning the Inner Life* (1926), *Man and the Supernatural* (1927), and *The House of the Soul* (1929).

'I know . . . of no other Gospel than the liberty both of body and mind to exercise the Divine Arts of Imagination: Imagination, the real and eternal World of which this Vegetable Universe is but a faint shadow, and in which we shall live in our Eternal or Imaginative Bodies when these Vegetable Mortal Bodies are no more.'

—WILLIAM BLAKE

'Let us go forth, the tellers of tales, and seize whatever prey the heart long for, and have no fear. Everything exists, everything is true, and the earth is only a little dust under our feet.'

—W. B. YEATS

EVELYN UNDERHILL

THE
GREY
WORLD

Scriptoria

The Grey World
Evelyn Underhill

Originally published by William Heinemann, London, 1904
Transcribed and typeset by Scriptoria Books, 2009

Typeset in Garamond

Every effort has been made to preserve the text and language (English – UK) of the original publication. Minor corrections to spelling, capitalization, and punctuation were based on the period in which the work was written.

ISBN 9781448651467

CONTENTS

1   OVER THE BORDER   1

2   THE EXILE   5

3   THE RETURN TO THE ROAD   .   .   .   12

4   A LITTLE WAYFARER IS BEWILDERED   .   21

5   A DOWN-HILL STRETCH   .   .   .   30

6   STAFF AND SCRIP   36

7   MARSHLAND AND WICKET   .   .   .   43

8   THE FIRST SIGNPOST   .   .   .   53

9   A FELLOW-TRAVELLER   .   .   .   62

10   ROAD-MAKING   72

11   A BREEZY UPLAND   78

12   MAPS ARE CONSULTED   .   .   .   86

13   MR. WILLIE HOPKINSON TRIES A SHORT CUT .   95

14   BUT THE ROAD BECOMES MUDDY   .   .   104

15   A WAYSIDE SHRINE   114

16   DIFFICULT PATHS   122

17   A SHARP CORNER   129

18   INCIPIT VITA NOVA   .   .   .   136

19   THE DELECTABLE MOUNTAINS .   .   .   144

20   THE RIVER   155

21   WILLIE TRIES TO LEND A HAND   .   .   161

CONTENTS

22 CROSS-ROADS 172

23 THE VALLEY OF HUMILIATION . . . 179

24 THE PATH RUNS TO THE WOODS . . 189

25 COMMENTARIES 199

TO

ALICE HERBERT

A SMALL ACKNOWLEDGMENT OF A GREAT DEBT

CHAPTER 1

OVER THE BORDER

'Death . . . snatches us
As a cross nurse might do a wayward child
From all our toys and baubles.'

—Old Play

A CHILDREN'S hospital is not a bad place to die in: failing forest
or hilltop, perhaps, one may not easily find a better. It is clean and
airy, and there are few opportunities for the hysterical confusion of
leave-taking which gives a touch of horror and bewilderment to the
greater dignities of a private decease. The Author of the Human
Comedy, one fancies, did not pay much attention to our exits and
our entrances. They seldom strike the imagination; yet, from the
spectator's point of view, they are not the least strange or important
details of the play.

On October the 15th in the year 1878, a small boy lay in the
Princess Ward of S. Nicholas' Infirmary, dying of typhoid fever.
He was a crumpled-up bit of slum-reared humanity, a sharp mind
set in a starved frame; and being but mildly interested in his own
sensations, he found the proceeding infinitely tiresome. The bare
whiteness of the place, its uncomfortable cleanliness, and a certain
martinet method of kindness, were not pleasing to a taste that had
been formed amidst the homely squalor of Notting Dale. Being too
weak to make noises for himself, he would have liked someone else
to take on this agreeable duty; but that never happened, and the
silence and good behaviour were harder to bear than all the pains of
his illness.

Happily, however, there were occasional oases to be found even
in this desert of hygienic decorum. They were called visiting days,
and they happened twice a week. At these times his mother came
to see him, bringing with her local perfumes and phrases which
roused his dormant nostalgia to the pitch of acute desire. Her
homely figure, formed of misplaced curves, and the drooping
assurance of her hat, cheered his spirits as they entered the ward,
and, to the manifest disapproval of the nurses, gravitated to the side

of his cot. Sometimes a sticky brother or sister was with her, and
spoke to him in the beloved dialect of home, infinitely refreshing to
the ear after the frosty official English of the hospital. 'Jimmy
Rogers 'as bin 'ad up agin,' his mother would say, or, 'Yer pa came
'ome tight larst night, and I 'it 'im. Low brute!'

The child nodded approvingly, as well as his weakness would let
him, and longed for a quick return to those glorious spheres of
action. In the hospital no one was ever had up, or came home
tight, and this extreme respectability depressed him. Some
temperaments can never be reconciled to a passive world, however
virtuous its repose.

But after some weeks of luxurious boredom, and when he was
supposed to have commenced a normal and satisfactory
convalescence, his mother yielded to a maternal impulse, and
involuntarily set going the scene-shifting machinery of death. The
special lever which she selected took the form of a currant bun,
secretly administered in response to his clamouring insistence on
hunger. The results were to be foreseen—relapse, wrath of doctors
and nurses, the gradual sinking, and finally death, of the victim.
These are a fairly constant feature of hospital experience. But in
this case, for some obscure reason, these things composed not
merely the finale of the comedy, but rather the curtain-raiser of a
drama of more than fashionable length. What the apple eaten in
the garden was to Eve, that currant bun was to the small boy who
gulped it hastily down under the friendly cover of the sheet. To feel
it between his teeth was a wholly satisfying delight; but it shut him
out from the paradise of ignorance, and that, for so short an
ecstasy, was a rather heavy price.

It was on the next day that he died. Coming from a class in
which funerals were the chief and perhaps the only innocent
festivities, the idea of death was familiar to him, and not disturbing.
It was an ornamental and not always unfortunate incident which
happened to the neighbours now and then.

But his own extinction, his sudden departure from surroundings
so real, solid, and inimical to all mystery, was a very different
matter. He found it utterly incredible, even whilst it was taking
place. He was not more than ten years old, and his natural wits had
already been dimmed by the beginnings of a Board School

education. His scepticism was foolish and unreasoning, but he shared it with many reputable persons of mature age and apparent intelligence. That was a truthful if unpopular prophet who said, that the deaths of many populations do nothing to prepare us for our own.

He was distinctly conscious of the early stages of his gradual withdrawal from life. He felt pleased when the professional annoyance of the nurses became tempered with pity at the sight of his growing weakness. Then came an hour of wild struggles to retain consciousness of all that went on round him, when he felt that this alone could save him from the black and shapeless gulf which had suddenly and silently become the primary fact of existence. A sense of hopeless battle and slow fatality sapped his courage. He was fighting hard, but he knew that he should not win. He could have wept, but he had no strength to waste on tears. All was very misty round him; only he had fixed his eyes on the bright brass knob which finished one corner of his cot, and he clung to the knowledge of its existence with a desperate cunning, as if that were the last bond that held him to life.

Small street-boys of ten are not very easily frightened as a rule, but so far as he was conscious of anything, he felt now a cold terror of the grey unknown state on the verge of which he choked and trembled; and whilst the rest of the ward grew dim and wavering, he lay staring with determination at the brass knob until its swollen and shining form was burnt on to his brain. It grew very difficult to breathe after a time, but he did not mind that much. People were round him, touching him and doing things, but he hardly noticed them. The sense of touch had gone to sleep already; but in the midst of a creeping somnolence his eyes were still awake, and his ears.

'He's going now, poor little chap,' said the house-surgeon, and his voice sounded faint and distant.

'No better than murder, I call it,' answered the nurse who had been most indignant over the catastrophe; and another toneless echo replied: 'It was hopeless from the first, of course.'

The brass knob was getting very hazy; it seemed to float uncertainly in the air. If only it would not go away! He knew that as long as he saw that knob he was alive; it and he were alive together in a world that was all their own. For one short instant he had an awful unchildlike vision of his loneliness, lying there and struggling with his fancies amongst people who could not help, or enter in, or understand. He wanted to ask one of them to catch his knob for him before it was lost, but words had gone from him long ago. Then he saw that it was very close to him, after all, and shining brightly.

It seemed to smile at him, and though a thousand bells were ringing in his ears, he made an effort and smiled too.

He stretched out his hand and grasped it. . . .

CHAPTER 2

THE EXILE

'The soul, when it departs from the body, needeth not to go far; for where the body dies, there is heaven and hell.'

—JACOB BOEHME

A LITTLE ghost adrift in a strange world, from which all colour had been withdrawn. He had never heard of the Greek Hades, or it is probable that he would have thought himself there. So new and uncanny was the aspect of things that it was some time before he realized how very little had happened to him after all. He was still in the hospital ward amongst the old surroundings, but he perceived them now with the vagueness of assent that we accord to suggestions, not with the assured grasp that one reserves for indubitable facts. He had slipped into a new plane of existence, and saw the world in a new perspective—a thin, grey, unsubstantial world, like a badly-focussed photograph. Yet it was not a legendary land of shadows, but the solid ordinary earth, on which he had passed ten years of aggressively material life.

The soul of a small boy, I think, is always uncomfortable unless it is unconscious, for the human spirit takes a long time to get accustomed to its own queerness. Consciousness seemed now to be thrust upon this one as greatness upon Malvolio; and, taking rapid stock of the situation, he found himself deeply dissatisfied with the prospect. A learned spinster suddenly deposited in the midst of a Cockney beanfeast could not feel more thoroughly out of place than he in this new dimension. He was one of those brisk, sharp-witted children of the streets, whose every interest is an appetite, and whose world of joy and sorrow is bounded at either end by the Crystal Palace and the police courts. Now, wholly understanding the how or why of the matter, he was sur... all his divorced from the lean and active body which had interpre... whom pleasures, and found himself converted into a pure spir... and other the material universe was no more actual than the ... there, but it invisible gases are to living men. He knew that it v... s there, but it could no longer count for much in the scheme of things. It did not dominate the landscape.

As he got more used to the dimness and greyness, he saw his body lying in the cot where it had died, and the nurses standing round it. He knew that it was going to be taken away to the mortuary, as had happened to other children who had died whilst he was there. He felt horribly miserable then, lost and chilly; and he tried to get back to it, but some strange repulsive force threw him back every time that he drew near. Then he tried to cry out, but a queer hoarse muttering was the only sound that he made, and none of the grey people in the photograph-world took the slightest notice of it. But it brought another unpleasant point into prominence. When he heard this sound of his own cry, he suddenly realized how very quiet everything else was. In the ward there had always been a certain clink and chatter, the hurry of nurses and the play of convalescent children: now, nothing. The earthly ear had gone the way of the earthly eye; and the pleasant noises, as well as the colour of life, had left him.

The prospect was very dreary, but he was not disheartened yet. His spirit, after all, was only the essence of his boyhood; he had taken nothing into death but those qualities which he had managed to elaborate during his little life. So it was that his natural endowment of irreverence and curiosity remained unimpaired; and these spurred him to exploration, and encouraged him with cheerful thoughts. He had heard many ghost stories, some exceedingly horrid, and none without a certain fearful joy: and now he perceived, with a sudden shock of excitement, that he too had become a ghost. Visions of haunted alleys, of carefully planned tactical jokes which should make the ward untenable by nervous nurses, came to him; and he felt greatly comforted as he sketched himself a career as full of illicit delight as any embryo Hooligan could wish.

But he had no idea how to set about it, and moreover his thoughts were all very confused and weak; so that he hovered vaguely to and fro, unable to settle upon anything. Almost unconscious, he drifted out of the hospital, and got entangled in a whole network of houses, endless walls dividing up neat rooms; all much the same, like mazes built out of mist.

Nothing stopped his progress, for all the things that he was accustomed to call hard had lost their hardness and resistance, and he passed through them as easily as a bird might pass through clouds upon the hills. Often there were people in the rooms, and by fixing his attention very hard he found out that they were talking or eating or working, all in the same heavy silence. Yet, though he was amongst them, touching them, passing through them even, there was a sense of great remoteness about it all. He seemed to be looking at dim pictures of unfamiliar things .

As for haunting, if he was not doing it now, what was he doing? Yet no one noticed his presence; though he blundered through shut doors they did not creak for him, and dogs lying on the hearth-rugs refused to whine because he was there.

The solitude of the new-made ghost, especially the ghost of the child, or indeed of any other being that has depended wholly on the body for its joys, is perhaps the most terrible form of loneliness that exists. It is the real Hell, and more dreadful than any maker of religions has dared to dream of. It resembles the sick helplessness of a traveller who finds himself, tired and alone, in the streets of a foreign city. An existence is going on around him, but he has no share in it, cannot even understand it. He wanders about, and it does not at all matter where he wanders. Nothing that he sees or feels is related to him or to his desires; nothing needs him. So this dead child felt as he drifted through these comfortable little homes, past fires that did not warm him, through people who did not see him; yet to whom he longed to talk, just to escape from his terrifying loneliness. He had left off trying to cry out to them, because the sound of his own cry, echoing in the silence which he knew was not really a silence, frightened him more than anything else.

In some of the rooms were shadowy grey children, playing with impalpable toys; and he tried once or twice to grab their dolls and knock their soldiers down, before he remembered that it was useless. And it was with a horrible ghostly hunger, which hurt more than real hunger had ever done, that he fled from one nursery where they were having bread and jam for tea.

It was not until this desultory wandering had lasted for some time that a knowledge came to him of other presences in the soundless fog which formed his universe. At first he had been too dazed to do more than hang desperately on to the last fringes of life. He was no philosopher, and his discovery of the unsubstantial nature of material things had thoroughly bewildered him. He had the undeveloped but eminently cock-sure spirit of the Cockney child, and it revolted him that such signposts of reality as walls, roofs, furniture, should become a colourless sponge through which he could pass without hitting himself, and against which his most determined push accomplished nothing. He could not get used to anything so flagrantly impossible, and settled down at last on the explanation that the whole thing must be an uneasy dream, dimly connected with the currant bun. He left off trying to keep count of his surroundings, and relaxed the strain of attention which had kept him aware of the last faint remainders of his old world. It went from him like a cloud; and as it went, a new sense came in its place.

He knew, suddenly and quite distinctly, that he was not alone. The horrible silence was gone, and he heard—vaguely at first, and then with overpowering insistence—a crying and twittering, restless and very sad. In later days, the sound of seabirds crying amongst solitary rocks on the edge where the land joins the sea always reminded him of that crying on the edge between life and death: the borderlands of things have much in common.

Then he realized that he was in a crowd of other beings like himself. They passed by him in great companies, pushing, moving in an endless stream; he heard the rustling sound of their movement as a sort of undercurrent to their queer, unhappy cries. They were in and through the intangible country of life, but they did not seem to notice it at all. He thought at first that they would notice him, and that his loneliness was over; but as he drifted a little, first with one stream and then with another, or lingered in the vortex rings made by circling processions, and was jostled by immaterial crowds, the isolation of a spirit wandering amongst the living faded into insignificance beside the frightful solitude of a spirit alone amongst the dead. He came to the not unnatural conclusion that these were the souls of grown-up people, probably toffs, who would not associate with common kids; yet many kids, he reflected, died in hospitals and elsewhere, and their souls must be somewhere about. It was probable that they would be companionable, or at any rate would not show the same lordly indifference to his presence; and he set out with renewed cheerfulness to hunt for them.

Then it was that he discovered that this moving mass of spirits was hunting too; wearily searching for company, interests, something that had been made necessary to them in life, now summarily taken away. They went on, hopelessly, endlessly: the noise that he heard was the complaint which they made to the enveloping greyness because of the hardness of their quest. So he joined one of the streams, though he knew nothing of the direction in which it was going, for there was no more upness or downness for him, no boundary, and no horizon point to make for: and they travelled between other lines of searchers, each crying in his loneliness, and no one apparently caring what his neighbour cried for—all held together, like a Democratic Association, by their common restlessness.

But when they had gone like this for a little while, a sort of agreeable warmth, that nice gregarious feeling which even a strange crowd can impart, came over him, and renewed his failing self-respect. He was proud, in a vague way, of being one of the dead, just as he might have been proud of being a Londoner without getting any special benefit from his citizenship. He began, too, to feel something of the reasons that moved these spirits to sweep backwards and forwards for ever over the world. A mysterious telepathy seemed to be established, and he read deeper and deeper into the unhappy minds that were travelling beside him.

The first discovery that he made was that his soul was curiously in harmony with the general point of view. He had despised himself because he was only a child, but these people, too, were spiritually childish. They were regretting Earth and its pleasures as keenly as he was; not, perhaps, its bread and jam, but other things which were now equally wanting in substance. All their interests were there apparently—in money, friends, games, ambitions, discoveries; all the things that go to make up the fulness of life. Now this life that they had so reluctantly left was seen to be only a grey, uncertain shadow, all its beauty gone, all its realities deceptive; but still they could not kill their desire for it. They had nothing else; it was all in all to them, and their desires chained them down to it, and kept them in it though they could not be of it, and drove them

in herds on the hopeless quest of a solution through all the scenes
they had cared for once and now could scarcely recognise.

The child, with a mysterious but incontrovertible knowledge,
knew that he too was bound to that dreary trail and that aimless
search, because he was incapable of realizing any other
environment; and the prospect had that horror of dulness which
was associated in his mind with the stories that old paupers used to
tell on Sunday afternoons about the workhouse. He, then, was a
spiritual pauper, shut out from the pretty heaven which the nurses
had often described to him, and unable to enjoy the strange
changed earth that he was tied to.

He looked back now with longing to the hospital ward that he
had found so monotonous and chilly. Its little incidents were full of
the delicious homely savour of life; and the slow noise of London
used to come softly through its windows, and remind him of the
great world where existence had been quick and busy, prone to
those sudden variations of luck which leave no room for boredom.
Now London was dead and silent, and he alive in the empty
twilight.

Then, with the desire for her, came back the knowledge that he
was still in her streets; and he turned all his strength resolutely
earthwards, and saw that he was in the great broad road which ran
westward to Uxbridge, and passed close to his home. A silent,
ghostlike traffic filled it: carriages and omnibuses, big waggons, and
the tradesmen's carts that he had loved to run behind. He saw
them through the veil of rushing spirits, trotting past him in two
placid streams. It seemed horribly unjust to be deprived of all this
inexpensive amusement and get absolutely nothing in exchange.

And at that moment a man on a high bicycle flew past him down
the ghostly hill. He was leaning back in a lordly manner; he had put
his feet up. With that agreeable vision all his old instincts returned
to him violently: it had never been his custom to let bicycles go by
without a greeting, and he started in pursuit, and tried,
thoughtlessly, to put his fingers in his mouth to give tone to his
favourite whistle of contempt. The resulting failure was the last
drop in his cup of misery; the faint crying of the souls about him
drove him mad with loathing; and he flung out the whole force of
his poor little spirit in a prayer to some Force which he dreaded but

knew not, for a return, at any price, to the excitements and uncertainties of life.

CHAPTER 3

THE RETURN TO THE ROAD

'C'était un petit être si tranquille, si timide et si silencieux. . . . C'était
un pauvre petit être mystérieux, comme tout le monde.'

—MAETERLINCK

THE stucco of a western suburb received him back into life; and he
next looked out on the world from the barred windows of a fourth-
floor nursery, set in a wide brown street of reputable gloom.

It must be allowed that he had improved his position. The
atmosphere of this new home was English and domestic:
conventional therefore. Its tidy boundaries were rigid, but set in a
smiling curve. It was permeated by a cheerful fuss. Its mistress was
a Martha who did not allow herself to be troubled by the fact that
her sister Mary—an indifferent wife and a wretched manager—had
drifted into another set. The family existence rippled through a life
of happy half-tones, carefully shaded from the agitating sunlight of
truth. It drew up its blinds sufficiently high for convenience, but
always let a foot or so of lace-edged propriety show against the
upper panes. In these days of horrid publicity and bold smartness,
one must make it obvious that one possesses blinds.

The force of one strenuous wish had thrown the child back
amongst the living; but the niche thus hastily found for him was
not, perhaps, well chosen. He and his new family suited one
another but indifferently. They were of a class which is always
trivially active: he came to them overshadowed by an inconceivable
past, queer and dreamy—a fact which his mother attributed to an
imperfect digestion. Health loomed large in the assets of the
Hopkinson family, and it was Mrs. Hopkinson who kept the books
and carefully assessed the individual dividend. Very probably he
was not healthy: very certainly his marked divergence from the
family type cried for some explanation. His legs were not fat
enough, nor his hair thick enough, to please the parental eye; and
genius or disease seemed the only plausible hypotheses.

He soon took up his normal position in the household—that of
a fearful joy to his mother, who thought that he would be a poet if

she could rear him; a constant if unacknowledged irritant to his father; and an insolvable but amusing enigma in the otherwise transparent outlook of his sister Pauline. It was a pity, perhaps, that the sexes had so arranged themselves. Mr. Hopkinson could have cherished an invalid daughter; he only despised a sickly son: and Pauline, who would have been admirable as a boy, swamped her brother's weak efforts towards self-assertion in her own excess of vitality.

She was a normally wholesome child of the middle class, a girl of whom any healthy-minded parent might be proud. Born a Materialist, her High School education had concerned itself chiefly with the creation of those angles which it was afterwards to smooth away. Her opinions were positive; compromise she never understood. A rather unelastic intelligence did not permit her more than one point of view, and the one which she selected placed her brother Willie in a light which was vivid enough, but scarcely sympathetic or explanatory.

As he emerged from babyhood into a puzzled self-consciousness, in which present realities were always tempered by the memory of a confused but unforgettable past, Pauline, three years his senior, took upon herself the character of a well-meaning bogey. She was at once alarming, overpowering, and affectionate. It is difficult for a healthy animal and an immortal, if undeveloped, spirit to inhabit the same nursery in peace; and Master Hopkinson did not find his sister's disposition accommodating. Her attitude was so uncertain. He acquired, and never entirely lost, the habit of looking up at her quickly whenever he made a remark, because he was never sure how she would take it.

Constancy of environment is a necessity of happy childhood. It is only when we are old enough to perceive their absurdity that the inconsistencies of our elders cease to be distressing; and Pauline's indignant denial of imagination caused her brother many shocks, and some hours of troubled meditation.

He was a trustful little boy, naturally candid. Silence frightened him, and he was eagerly willing to converse with the whole world if he might. It was some time before he found out that his robust sister was not exactly the person to whom he might best confide his dreams and bewilderments; or the queer thoughts that came to him when he lay awake at night, and wondered where he was, and if he were alive, and if he were really a little boy as everybody seemed to think, or only some sort of tiny insect.

He sometimes had the feeling that he did not belong to the home-life at all; that he was outside of it, looking on at it, and that all the things which seemed to be happening were not happening really. This sensation he never succeeded in explaining to anyone, which was perhaps fortunate: but it continued to oppress him. He had as yet no idea that the domain of his pains and pleasures was different from that of the average child; for there was no one to whom he could apply for information, or talk out his puzzled little soul without misunderstandings.

Pauline's sensible outlook reflected the family conscience only too well. She was implacable towards fancies, and did not encourage revelations. Her brisk, 'What nonsense, Willie! Don't be such a silly little boy,' was always to be felt, like a Greek chorus, the spectator's comment on his comedy of life.

Not till he was about eleven years old, and, as Mrs. Hopkinson was fond of saying, 'Just a little anaemic, like so many London boys,' did the full weight of Pauline's temperament begin to make itself felt. Willie had brought back with him into life a keen and uncomfortable realization of the Grey World of the dead on which he had once been cast, and of its restless populations. As he grew older, and evolved his own plan of the world out of the uncertain country full of strange shapes and noises where a baby dwells, he was apt to have sudden returns to the knowledge of that dimension: vivid and uncontrollable visions in which he saw his solid surroundings fade into a sort of shadowy jelly, and heard the dreadful cry of the souls on their endless quest. Perhaps a little bit of his soul may have lagged behind there when he made his hurried re-entry into life.

Yet, in spite of these transcendental perceptions, which he hated but could not escape, he had all the practical matter-of-factness of the average urban child. His experiences had never seemed to him to be in any way odd, and it certainly never struck him that they were not shared by the rest of the family. He was so used to it all, it was so much a part of normal experience, that no doubt or question ever entered his head. Of course, no one ever talked to him about the Grey World, or acted in a way which suggested the slightest doubt about the reality of the tables and chairs or the actuality of food. He had never once heard anyone mention the strange way these things had of becoming suddenly unsubstantial and remote. This, however, he put down to that difficult science of politeness, which, according to Mrs. Hopkinson, forbade many subjects of conversation to sensible children.

He had already noticed that most of the curious and interesting things which happened every day were never spoken of at all, or apparently noticed. The bit of sky which he saw out of the nursery window, for instance, would fill itself with the loveliest cloud palaces, and knock them all down and replace them with little ships or snow mountains or flocks of sheep—all very remarkable to Master Hopkinson, and quite on the same plane of mystery as his constant neighbours the ghosts; for the joys as well as the terrors of the visionary were his. But no one took the least interest in such things, or said anything about them. When a very wonderful cloud came by, sometimes he showed it to Pauline; but she only said 'Silly little boy!' and went back to the concoction of crinkled paper lampshades and tidies—her favourite occupation.

So the cloud-world and the ghost-world were classed together in his view of the universe as subjects which were not spoken of by well-mannered persons, and were too unimportant to be noticed by those grown-up people whose lives, to eleven years old, seem compounded of the incomprehensible and the romantic. And it was really quite accidentally that he at last broke through this self-imposed barrier of etiquette, and delivered up his secret to the unsuitable custody of Pauline.

He had always a private terror of his involuntary returns to the invisible side of existence; it was lonely, it was upsetting, it took the zest out of daily amusements. He would so much have liked to forget all about it. But as he was generally alone when its presence overcame him, and his English blood had given him a certain shame of his fright, he had managed to pass through these moments of panic unperceived; and any unusual paleness or silence afterwards was laid to the account of too much chocolate or too little exercise.

But one evening after tea, as he sat with Pauline by the nursery fire before the lights had been switched on, both very amiable and lazy, the thing happened suddenly and without warning. His helpless little soul slipped its leash, the walls of sense trembled and melted, and he was back again in the horrible country of silence and mist. The old desolate feeling returned to him; he was alone in the crowd of hurrying spirits, and saw the pale grey image of the nursery fire, and the vague spectre of Pauline sitting beside it, many worlds away. He longed to hear her speak, even if it were only to snap at him; but he was in another dimension, and could not reach her. He thought, as he always did on these occasions, that he was dead, and all hope of respite over; and at that and the shock of so quick an ending, his courage fled from him in a wild yell of fright. It seems probable that the accent of that scream was not entirely earthly, for its terror infected even the stolidly unemotional Pauline, and she clutched her brother's leg, which happened to be close to her, and shrieked: 'Whatever is the matter, Willie?' in shrill and distinctly nervous tones.

The genuine appeal of her voice penetrated to the dim place where he wandered, and called him back to solid life again, a little breathless, and very grateful for such prompt deliverance.

'How I hate that noise!' he said with emphasis.

Miss Hopkinson, still rather shaken, opened large eyes of amazement upon her brother and continued her firm grasp of his leg.

'What noise?' she demanded sharply.

She was fourteen years old, and disliked being startled: her voice had a ring of semiparental authority.

But Willie was quite sure of his ground, and answered without hesitation.

'Why, the noise the ghosts make, stupid!' he said.

'The ghosts?'

Master Hopkinson was so surprised by his sister's denseness that he ventured for the first time in his life to address her in a tone of condescension.

'You know,' he said. 'All the dreadful dead people what you hear when everything gets soft and misty.'

She stared.

'Like when we were dead before we got alive again,' he concluded lucidly.

Pauline's manner now expressed cold disapprobation, and also a certain ill-temper—the natural reaction from her short attack of credulity.

'Willie,' she said severely, 'you are making things up; and you know quite well that mother doesn't allow it.'

Allegations of this kind are trying even to the least worldly temper, and Master Hopkinson's reply was delivered in a distinctly unamiable tone.

'Of course I'm not making it up,' he said. 'Why, I'm always seeing them. They're quite real, you know they are: just as real as we are. What for should I make up anything so nasty? They're here now, all about us—crowds of grey people that never stop still.'

This was outrageous, and the wrathful sincerity with which it was said roused Pauline's intolerant common-sense to fighting pitch.

'Be quiet this minute, Willie!' she cried. 'And don't tell such wicked stories, or I shall go to mother at once.'

But between his sister's extraordinary obtuseness and the undeniable truth of his own perceptions, Willie was now hopelessly confused and almost hysterical. He felt her attitude to be insulting; and her final threat, deeply mortifying to the pride of eleven years old, destroyed his last remnant of self-control. He began to stamp and whimper in a very disagreeable but reassuring way.

'I shall! I shall! I shall!' he said. 'Go and speak to mother, nasty tell-tale scratch-cat! She'll know it's true. It's you that tell stories; and I shall tell mother you were frightened 'cause I yelled!'

Five minutes later Master and Miss Hopkinson effected a hurried entrance into the drawing-room, where their mother sat silky and erect pouring out tea for several other matrons. It was her At Home day, and the air was heavy with the perfume of warm sealskin and white-rose scent.

Mrs. Hopkinson's most valued friend, the rich but homely Mrs. Steinmann, was sitting near the door. This lady had been badly translated from the German in early life, and all traces of Teutonic idiom had not yet been eradicated. For her, life held but one thing—the domestic interior. This she really understood, and into its least tempting recesses she penetrated with garrulous joy. She was one of those worthy but socially embarrassing women who are apt to change the conversation abruptly when the gentlemen come into the room.

Mrs. Steinmann, then, saw the children at once, and welcomed so congenial a reason for removing her attention from Mrs. Alcock and Mrs. Frere—superior persons who professed to know nothing of the duties of a tweeny-maid, and insisted on speaking of politics. Mrs. Steinmann was aware that their remarks were merely an epitome of the opinions of Mr. Alcock and Mr. Frere, both of whom obtained their dogma direct from the *Daily Telegraph*.

'Why, here are the dear little ones!' she said. 'How big Pauline is getting! And Willie too; quite a man! Come and kiss me, my dears.'

But the usually placid Pauline was shaken from her well-trained calm, and a strong sense of duty impelled her, with Willie held firmly in her wake, direct to her mother's chair.

'Pauline! What a dirty pinafore!' said Mrs. Hopkinson, all her senses tuned to the level of her best tea-set.

Pauline barely noticed this accusation, which was sufficiently well founded.

'Mother,' she replied in an awful voice, 'Willie's been telling horrible stories. He says the nursery is full of ghosts, and he saw them, but he was sitting on the hearth-rug all the time; and he gave the awfullest scream!'

There was a slight sensation in the drawing-room. Little Mrs. Alcock, who detested children but thought it polite to show her appreciation of them by giggling whenever they spoke, began to laugh: and somehow her empty laughter, coming so soon after his peep into the sorrowful place, outraged Master Hopkinson even more than his sister's scepticism had done. His puzzled little mind was in revolt, and he turned on her quite fiercely.

'You won't laugh when you're dead!' he observed with chilling sincerity; and Mrs. Alcock ceased to be amused.

'What a very peculiar little boy!' she said, and relapsed into uneasy silence.

The other ladies eyed him, some with nervousness, others with obvious disapprobation. Eccentricity is only tolerable when it is ridiculous, and they found the situation more uncomfortable than absurd. There was an uncanny feeling in the air. Several began to button their cloaks and get out their card-cases. But before they could say good-bye, the child, who was recovering himself, followed up his first advantage and arrested the general attention.

'Isn't it silly, mother?' he said. 'Pauline wants to make out that there isn't a Grey World, or ghosts in it, or anything. Why, I suppose you get into it often, don't you, just like I do? And anyhow, when we were dead we were there for ever so long. At least, I was, and I hated it, because of there being nothing to do. And now Pauline says I tell stories.'

The spectacle of a small boy in overalls standing in the middle of the drawing-room floor and referring casually to the time when he inhabited the unseen world is not often seen in suburban circles; and Mrs. Hopkinson, who hated anything unusual to happen on her At Home days, felt awkward and annoyed.

'Willie dear,' she said rather flurriedly, 'you've been reading some horrid ghost stories, haven't you, and got frightened?'

And she nodded to the explosive Pauline peremptory injunctions to hold her tongue.

'Oh no, mother,' answered Willie. 'The ghost stories are all wrong, you know, not a bit like the real thing; and I wasn't at all frightened. Only I got in amongst them all of a sudden, and it is so horrible; and I gave a yell, and then Pauline wouldn't believe I'd been there.'

'Pauline,' said Mrs. Hopkinson suddenly, 'what did Willie have for his tea?'

'Well, he did have one bit of cake,' replied Pauline.

The other ladies looked at each other significantly, and nodded. To those practical maternal minds the explanation was simple enough.

'You may say what you like,' observed Mrs. Steinmann, 'but with some children cake is never assimilated. I've often seen the same thing with my grandchildren. And a nervous boy like that! But put him to bed with a dose of calomel, and he'll be all right in the morning.'

'Yes,' said Mrs. Hopkinson, relieved by this congenial suggestion. 'You're not very well, Willie dear; that's what it is. Go upstairs with Pauline, and don't think any more about it. It's all imagination, you know.'

What did an Early Christian feel like when his sceptical relations treated him with contemptuous kindness, and ascribed his spiritual perceptions to dyspepsia? One hopes that he found the lions a less painful form of martyrdom. Master Willie Hopkinson, torn by disgust, astonishment, and perplexity, knew that he preferred anything and everything to Pauline, the agent of his humiliation. But whilst he was still speechless in his misery, she hurried him out of the room.

CHAPTER 4

A LITTLE WAYFARER IS BEWILDERED

'Dreams were to him the true realities: externals he accepted as other people accepted dreams.'

—GEORGE MOORE

THE adventure of the At Home day was painful to Willie's pride, but it taught him several valuable things. It developed a wariness and precocious discretion which he had not possessed before; and it made him specially careful in his choice of conversation with the family.

It was a long time before he lost the shadow which was cast by his painful efforts to review the situation and understand the intricacies of his experience; but whilst this still puzzled him, he saw that any reticence must be good which saved him from misunderstanding and humiliation, and he laid his small plans for the future very deliberately.

Most children of the normal type have their moments of mysticism, when their spirit first stirs and they wonder what they really are, puzzling over memory and consciousness and other things which elude their rudimentary language, but which they take it for granted that their elders know all about. Master Hopkinson, always acutely conscious of two worlds equally near to him, pondered perhaps less on these things, because to him they were so obvious, objectionable, and distinct. In later and more articulate years he was accustomed to say, that he came to his infancy trailing clouds which had no elements of glory. The phrase was accurate, and he did not find its literary associations disagreeable.

The Grey World was the warp on which the bright threads of his sensuous existence were spread—a strange and tiresome plan, perhaps; but to him profoundly natural, because it was the only one that he had ever known. But this sudden discovery that the rest of the family did not share his knowledge, live the same dual life, or frequent the same dim country, startled and distressed him. He had taken it for granted that he was as all other little boys; now it seemed clear that he had made a huge mistake. Instead of sharing with the others an experience as ordinary and inevitable as a cold in the head or a dose of powder, he was quite alone in his visits to the crowded country, and even in his memories of the time when he was one of its inhabitants. He had seen quite plainly that the Hopkinson family and its friends knew nothing of these things. Even his mother, that monument of infallibility, had seemed deeply astonished by what he himself regarded as his extremely ordinary remarks.

It was very bewildering, for he could really see no reason why he should be different from everybody else. He felt something of the helpless disgust of the seasoned traveller who comes home to find his truthful narrative received with sardonic smiles; or of the long-suffering chemist who tries to demonstrate radium before the hostile grins of a canny but uneducated audience.

At the same time, the human element in him was rather ashamed, and frightened by its temerity, and struggled to assure him that grown-up people must know everything; and the conviction grew that it was best to endure the slur on his veracity in silence, and only be careful in his own interests to steer clear of these complications in the future. After all, if for some inconceivable reason the rest of his acquaintances inhabited one world only, did not know where they had come from, and never dreamed of troubling about it, it was not to be expected that on the testimony of one small boy they should believe in truths which were to them both imperceptible and offensive.

And the Grey World was so monstrous, so impossible unless one had been there, that often when he was boat-sailing in Kensington Gardens, or when the jam-roly at dinner was particularly solid and good, Willie found it very hard to believe in it himself. That all the bright colours he loved: the nice flat blue poppies with yellowy-brown leaves which sprawled over the drawing-room paper, the scarlet of the local omnibus, and all the loveliness of sunshine and gaslight: should be shams which hid the horrible place of unending nothingness that lay in and through the streets and houses, and filled the air he breathed with melancholy ghosts—this would have been quite ridiculous if it had not happened to be true. So he excused Mrs. Hopkinson and her callers for their ignorance; and, half in a fit of outraged dignity, and half because he dreaded the naturalistic standpoint of Pauline, he decided to avoid all references to his own thoughts and experiences until he was quite sure that the rest of the world was likely to believe in them.

As the double life that he led rather detached Master Hopkinson from a vivid interest in ordinary boy-pleasures, and made him visionary and given to quiet delights; and as Mr. and Mrs. Hopkinson strenuously upheld the policy of only talking to the children about things that children should and could understand, this resulted in his becoming an unpleasantly silent little boy. For the grip of the Unseen on his soul enlarged as he grew older, and with it his terror of betraying himself.

So he lived for the next year or two a cautious, artificial life, and all remembrance of the At Home day episode gradually faded from the family mind. They said that he was a queer child, and hoped he was going to be clever; and as Pauline outgrew the nursery, he was left a good deal to himself.

He was certainly odd in his ways; given to long hours of brooding and sudden flashes of conviction. Dream was seldom absent from his eyes, but fortunately Mrs. Hopkinson did not recognise it under that name. He loved to read the old romances and tales of King Arthur's knights, for a peculiar inarticulate joy that they gave him: but when he tried to find out the source of his fascination, he could not. Specially the story of the Holy Graal attracted him. Though his reason told him that it and the others were as untrue, as shadowy, as the rest of life, his soul found in them some secret element which nourished it and gave it peace.

He got the habit of looking into every book that he could find, for he had somehow acquired the idea that books were real, though people, he knew, were not. One day, he found a thin volume of verse, left probably by some chance visitor—Mr. Hopkinson discouraged, without difficulty, the reading of poetry by his household; he thought it dangerous stuff. This book Willie opened, and read, amongst much unintelligible loveliness, the following quatrain:

'We are no other than a moving row
Of Magic Shadow-shapes that come and go
　　Round with the Sun-illumined Lantern held
In Midnight by the Master of the Show;'

'Then there is someone else who knows!' he thought; and went away companioned and less lonely for that knowledge. He had a constant longing to fathom the depths of the gulf which divided him from other people, though he dared not venture further confidences to discover if he really stood alone.

Sometimes he wondered if there were not other children in the same unhappy position; but he dreaded being laughed at, and the small boys at his day-school did not strike him as promising subjects for inquiry.

The solid trust in appearances which the 'grown-ups' showed, and specially his father's attitude towards life, bothered him more and more. To live in the midst of superior and authoritative persons who persistently grasp the shadow and assert that it is the substance, is aggravating to an apostle but appalling to a nervous child. Mr. Hopkinson was thought by his neighbours to be an alarmingly clever man: modern science was his god, and Huxley the high-priest of his temple, but he had a way with heretics which savoured more of theology than of reason.

Whilst Willie was still very young, he began to 'interest him,' as he said, by popular lecturettes at meal times or on Sunday afternoons, about things that the child loved to dream over, and whose beauties gave him an inexplicable delight. Perhaps it was the ugliness of his calling—Mr. Hopkinson was a wholesale tailor; Hopkinson, Vowles and Co., of Bermondsey—which developed his peculiar gift of seeing only the mechanical and ordinary in the universe, and reducing to formal hideousness the loveliest manifestations of life. But when he dissected daisies, and showed his son pictures of his own inside, and 'proved' that the magical clouds which Willie worshipped were nothing but steam and dust, and then said informingly, 'Force and Matter again! Force and Matter! That's the whole bag of tricks, Willie my boy!' Master Hopkinson found the mingled results of his father's ignorance and authority very bewildering.

He was disturbed, lonely and unhappy, and sometimes it even happened that he wished himself back in his old existence in Notting Dale, where life was always amusing and adventurous, and no one worried about turning pretty dreams into what he secretly looked upon as ugly lies.

But he kept these criticisms to himself with the rest, and listened with a blank face which his father put down to stupidity, whilst that enthusiast gloated over atoms and molecules and the physical basis of Life; and even, when his wife was out of hearing, took sideway trips into the theory of evolution. Mr. Hopkinson was fond of comparing the Universe to his own factory and himself to the Ruler thereof; and it struck him as eminently reasonable that the Almighty should secure efficiency by sacking the incompetent hands. He waited for Willie's remarks—the sharp remarks beloved of the educational parent—but they did not come; for Master Hopkinson dared not speak of the truth as he knew it, and this same knowledge shut him out from any comprehension of his father's point of view.

Pauline, on the contrary, took these things in very readily. They taught science at the High School once a week, and sometimes she argued with Mr. Hopkinson about it, which pleased him. Her questions and contentions were just sufficiently intelligent to give a fallacious air of brilliance to his own replies. She had grown into a tall, thick-ankled girl, all muscle and loud opinions; but her brother still kept pale and puny, because, said his mother, his brain was growing too fast.

'Whatever it is that keeps him back,' replied her husband, stroking the admirably-grown moustache which did not seem likely to survive his generation, 'it isn't his brain, because he hasn't got one. Not one boy in a thousand has had his opportunities of getting a thorough working knowledge of the scientific standpoint. But the lad's a regular milksop, unhealthy in mind and body, and takes no intelligent interest whatever. Goodness knows what will become of him when he gets into the City.'

It was at this propitious period that Master Hopkinson chose, for the second time, to lift the veil which hung over the realities of his life. As her children outgrew the nursery, and left more leisure at her disposal, Mrs. Hopkinson had begun to temper her household ministrations with a wider charity; and she was specially interested in a society for taking boys from the Franciscan liberty of the slums and immuring them in an institution where their morals were edited to a positively insulting extent. Willie remembered well how the young inhabitants of Notting Dale had looked upon those societies, and he did not feel very interested in the sum total of subscriptions which she sometimes announced to Mr. Hopkinson over the breakfast-table. His own collecting-card lay with the 'Boy's Own Microscope' and 'Hints on Bird-stuffing,' in a dark corner of the schoolroom cupboard.

A day dawned, however, when Mrs. Hopkinson's energies could no longer be confined to begging or secretarial work. She had always had a passion for commerce; and she now perceived that it was her duty, and incidentally the privilege of her committee, to undertake a bazaar. The remnant sales were about to begin; she had the *flair* of the born bargain-hunter. She would buy scraps and oddments offered at alarming sacrifices, confection them into sachets, baby's pinafores, and garments for the poor, and sell them to other philanthropic economists at a profit of 50 per cent. The more she thought of this idea, the more she liked it. The house was soon filled with the sound of sewing-machines and the smell of Aspinall's enamel; and Fraud, decked with the aureole of Good Intentions, became its tutelary saint.

A working-party met twice a week, and discussed a dubious morality amidst much snipping and stitching.

'Yes, dear; put that lace on it. It will do quite well. It was only three-three, but no one will notice it isn't real torchon.'

'No, I wouldn't *line* it with silk; the lining won't show.'

'Oh, is that doll's leg broken, Mrs. Steinmann? What a bother! You must give it a longer skirt to hide the join.'

These and other sidelights on ethics came to Master Hopkinson as he helped his sister to hand tea, or dived under the dining-room table to search for missing thimbles and pins. They were very ugly in their earthiness, those afternoons, and were somehow connected vaguely in his memory with a plaid flannel blouse—an unfortunate arrangement in brown and heliotrope—that his mother used to wear. Just as in art some harmony of colour or line may often suggest a link with music or with poetry, so one form of hideousness often correlates curiously with another, and stands as its eternal emblem in our consciousness.

The bazaar and all its belongings, therefore, fussed Master Hopkinson, disturbed his dreamy existence and tried his nerves. Mrs. Hopkinson thought that children should be made to interest themselves in the poor, and he was never allowed to forget that the preparations for enslaving the free-born sons of Notting Dale were going on. Having now arrived at a stage in which he remembered the days that he had spent amongst them as the only entirely happy ones he had ever known, he looked on as a rather morose cherub might have done whilst a party of elderly angels planned out Purgatory. This attitude could scarcely escape the committee, and their exalted philanthropy judged it to be wholly evil. Their little boys were chipping wood, and their little girls working laborious doyleys for the charity; but Willie had not yet come forward with any contribution.

Amongst mothers, sidelong censure of other people's children is always dangerous, but seldom resistible; and probably his deliberate languors were very irritating. At last the strain broke.

'Aren't you very glad, Willie dear,' said Mrs. Steinmann to him suddenly, 'to think of those poor little boys being taken out of the streets and put into a comfortable home?'

Passive disapprobation does not sit well on small boys, and the committee had not been alone in its growing exasperation. Master Hopkinson was pleased to have an opening for his opinion.

'No: I'm sorry for them,' he answered promptly.

A matronly chorus cried, 'My dear Willie!' and looked at each other, but not at Mrs. Hopkinson, who affected not to have heard her son's remark.

Willie felt that he was placed on the defensive, and a wild longing to shock someone seized him. Long-nourished rancours against local ideas overflowed, and abruptly demolished all his careful vows of discretion. In fact, he lost his temper—and his head.

'When I was a poor little boy,' he said, 'I liked it. It was jolly. I didn't have to be clean then. And there was lots more to do than there is here and fewer lessons, and I never heard ghosts. And you talk a lot about their drunken fathers, and all that; but drunken fathers aren't so bad. I thought mine rather amusing. I used to help get him upstairs at night. Sometimes he was awfully funny—'

Here Mrs. Steinmann's shiny dark eyes, trained to plumb the souls of her scullery-maids, began to have their effect on him. He stopped suddenly. It is never pleasant to realize that one has confided in the wrong person. Willie now perceived that he had confided in a crowd of wrong persons. Someone said, 'How remarkable!' and someone else, 'He really must have quite a vivid imagination!' His mother dropped three pins from her mouth, but found no words to fill the vacancy; and Master Hopkinson, with hot face and short breath, walked out of the room as quickly as he considered proper.

This was Willie's last serious indiscretion; and so useless and astonishing had been his fall that he never clearly understood how it came about. His wild words had left no sharp impression behind them; but they revived unfortunate memories and prejudices amongst the Hopkinson set, and confirmed the belief that he was a 'difficult child.' Some felt bound to call him clever, but all preferred to think that he was untruthful.

This he expected, and with indifference; but he was surprised in his ignorance when his mother suddenly deserted her post of family ameliorator and concealer of crime, and took the history of his outburst to Mr. Hopkinson's ears. He learnt later that Good Works rank, like etiquette and imperialism, amongst the most solemn games of mankind, and are not lightly to be smiled at. A mild irony at the expense of her pet charity will turn the most loving woman against her children, but the first time that it happens the shock is rather severe.

So Willie stood before his father feeling sick and shaky, whilst he italicized the most unpleasant aspects of the incident, and asked his son sarcastically what he meant by it. Master Hopkinson's soul, which was so familiar with the real terrors, hated his body for this ridiculous fright. He had no words, but his father had plenty—the acid reaction of his unappreciated lectures poisoned his discourse, and burnt where it fell. Willie bit his tongue hard for fear he should be tempted to speak the truth; the longing to be understood dies so slowly.

But he had learnt once for all the first rule of wisdom—never to emerge from the veil which your neighbour is accustomed to mistake for yourself.

CHAPTER 5

A DOWN-HILL STRETCH

'Education begins the gentleman.'

—LOCKE

MR. HOPKINSON, even when he was not actively annoyed by his son, felt him to be a blot upon his theory of family life; and now, disguising an act of self-indulgence in the decent mantle of parental duty, he seized the opportunity of sending Willie away to school. They were strangers to each other, these two; and worse than strangers, because mutually repellent. But Master Hopkinson was an only son, and his father could not conscientiously get rid of the British necessity of having him 'licked into shape.'

The boy was sent to a Norfolk village, where bracing air, large meals, and an athletic housemaster left little chance for meditation. Uncongenial surroundings are not always unfortunate. He was at an age when the body, if it is ever to be an efficient vehicle of mind, is bound to assert itself at the expense of the soul: and in his case loneliness, long hours spent in vague dreamy attempts to unravel the meaning of things—above all, the heavy bewilderments of a spirit that lived alone with occult realities which sapped it of all joy—had worn the body rather thin. Nature was ready for her revenge. School, to which he went as to a penitentiary, became his sanatorium; the place where he lost his life to find it—lost that isolated existence which had crushed him into savourless endurance, and found the sprightly illusions natural to his race and age. The change was sudden, drastic; and the shock enhanced its value. At Hazefield both cricket and Latin prose were serious things; but the soul was only mentioned on Sundays, and then in a purely official manner. The result was to be foreseen. At the end of six months Willie had hardened his muscles, enlarged his vocabulary, and begun to take an interest in the question of wearing his cap at the correct angle.

The slow and steady action of environment had worn away all his own convictions, and the ready-made beliefs which flourished around him slipped unnoticed into their place. He was still conscious of the shadow-side of the world, and liable to sudden moments of withdrawal when he heard its horrid noises, and lost hold of the comfortable playthings of earth. But these moments seemed to him now to be dreams and interludes; the time had gone by when he could accept them, with a faith which often verged on agony, as a part of normal experience. He did not any longer grasp them with the painful fervours of the past; there was always a mist between. Also the trend of public opinion made him rather ashamed of his visions. School-boys despise what they do not understand; and shame (with the young) is a great inducement to forgetfulness.

There followed a time when his attitude to these things was that of an Evangelical clergyman who has inadvertently read the 'Origin of Species,' and would like to forget it. He knew that the orthodox position of his schoolfellows was untenable for him; he knew that their whole idea of life was false; that the truth—the amazing, and as they would say the unnatural truth—of existence lay in his hand. But he refused to think about it: it was unpleasant, and did not fit in.

He preferred his lying senses to his inconvenient perceptions, and became sedulous in the cricket field and wholesomely casual in class. On the day when Master Hopkinson learnt the 'Psalm of Life' as an imposition, and repeated with smiling sincerity and unconcern,

> 'Life is real! Life is earnest!
> And the grave is not its goal;'

he was very nearly a normal boy. Education was doing its work. To take everything for granted, to grasp fringes and avoid fundamentals, to think only of the obvious, and to refuse to consider the unimportant incident called Death—these arts, in which our youngsters are so carefully instructed, Willie at last acquired, though perhaps less easily than his fellows.

At home during the holidays, his large appetite and slangy speech pleased his parents, astonished their acquaintances, and made Pauline jealous. He 'rotted' her and her friends in the most correct manner, was ostentatiously noisy, deliberately tyrannical, and generally displayed all the tiresomeness of the healthy male. Everyone remarked on the improvement; and even Mr. Hopkinson became comparatively genial, and began to hope that his son might be good for something after all.

'I always knew it was his health that made him so queer,' said Mrs. Hopkinson. 'Poorness of the blood—that's what I put it down to; and the bracing air of Norfolk was just what was wanted to set him right.'

Mrs. Steinmann, to whom these remarks were offered, agreed, though in rather an ungracious manner.

'Willie wanted a bit of school-life to knock the nonsense out of him,' she said. 'Tristram was just the same—moody and rather unwholesome; so different from Geraint, who was always a thorough boy.'

Mrs. Steinmann's grandsons, surnamed Levi, did not incarnate the Arthurian legend to the extent that their cultured mother had hoped.

'I often thought, you know, Mrs. Hopkinson,' she added, 'that you left Willie to go his own way too much; but of course one doesn't like to interfere. And really, considering his curious disposition, I'm thankful that the consequences have been no worse.'

The good fortune of her neighbours was a perpetual source of marvel to Mrs. Steinmann; she was always expecting Providence to punish them for the lack of that oleaginous sagacity which overflowed in her own character, and which she mistook for commonsense. Disappointment had embittered her comfortable bosom, and too often lent an acrid tone to her congratulations. She had found her daughter, the mother of Tristram and Geraint, less of a treasure than her principles had led her to expect.

This lady, whom Mrs. Hopkinson regarded with the contemptuous awe which good house-wives reserve for the intellectual of their sex, inherited from her parent a shining black fringe, a sallow complexion, but few domestic virtues. She came to maturity during the Browning period, and though carefully trained in all the ritual of Teutonic womanhood, could never be persuaded to reverence the family linen chest, or remember which was the right day to have the drawing-room turned out. Her marriage, which took place at the earliest possible moment, was more important to her as a rupture from home than as a union with Mr. Levi; an elderly widower, whose sandy hair might, she hoped, counteract her own unfortunately Oriental appearance. In this she was mistaken; and it was her painful fate to see her sons, in spite of romantic names and picturesque dresses, become more uncompromisingly Hebraic day by day. Their long necks, restless black eyes, and ferret-like expressions, offended an aesthetic sense which was nourished on Raphael and Sir Joshua Reynolds. She was best pleased when they were least in evidence, and invariably affected a refined ignorance of the less lovely details of their toilets.

It was Mrs. Steinmann—at once expert and amateur of the nursery—who, having accidentally discovered that her grandsons did not wear flannel next the skin, expressed her horror and disgust with homely directness, and took all that concerned them into her own hands. Henceforth she saw that they had their hair cut regularly, and took them to the dentist every six months. She was happier, and they were healthier, for the change; and they gave her, what she had lacked before, a criterion by which to disparage other people's children.

The little Levis, therefore, were looked upon in Mrs. Hopkinson's set as Mrs. Steinmann's peculiar property. She held them, so to speak, on a repairing lease: worshipped their unlovely bodies, quoted their uninteresting remarks, and was only successful in concealing her idolatrous state from the unsuspecting objects of her adoration. Geraint Levi, described by candid acquaintances as a born bounder, was detested by Mrs. Hopkinson for a habit he had of making love to Pauline, two years his senior.

Tristram's manners were less characteristic; his air of good breeding was a frequent source of unhappiness to his grandmother, who mistook it for ill-health.

But no Englishwoman can be expected to tolerate the comparison of her children with those of another race; and only a respect for Mrs. Steinmann's diamonds and knowledge of cookery bridled Mrs. Hopkinson's tongue when she heard her Willie bracketed with Tristram as lucky examples of the benefits of school.

'Willie was such an imaginative child,' she said. 'Always fancying things, and using his brain. He reminds me of my father, who would have written something, I'm sure, if he'd had the time, but he was always so much occupied in the—er—with commerce. Mr. Hopkinson thinks that what Willie really requires is *balance*, and we are going to put him on the modern side next term. A sound scientific training, that is Mr. Hopkinson's idea; and modern languages, which will be so useful in the business.'

Master Hopkinson went to the modern side, and it did its work well. All his old poetic fancies and love of the beautiful were eradicated, and a taste for things strange and ingenious took their place. At this period all that tickled his curiosity and gave interest to the concrete appealed to him strongly: he took in magazines which had a 'corner for curiosities,' and became keen on acrostics. The wonderful skies, cold tones, and quiet planes of the Norfolk landscape had nothing to say to him; for the message of the clouds was bound up with horrid memories of the visions of infancy, and he carried to excess the usual revolt of the adolescent from the tastes and ideals of his childhood. He grew up to be a thin, freckled youth, mediocre in talent, manners, and physical powers: moderately liked by the boys, but too indifferent to make any great friends. He did moderately well, too, in class, but scored no successes. His masters, who saw promise in the remote expression of his eyes, were disappointed by his work, which was correct but heartless. It was inevitably so. In spite of deliberate efforts to fall into line, he did not entirely 'mix in.'

At seventeen, it seemed that Willie had no decided bent in any direction, and Mr. Hopkinson formed the idea of removing this promising material to his office as soon as possible. He wished that the City might seal him with her symbolic beast before contact with a wider world had the chance of causing some inconvenient bias. There is no room for the embryo scholar or musician in the wholesale tailoring trade.

To the ideal spectator, that unemotional angel who criticises the wanderings of man, this may well have seemed the oddest, most unexpected of the stages through which Master Hopkinson passed. Here was he, an immortal spirit, and knowing himself so to be—aware of that place whence he had come, and not without a shuddering fore-knowledge of his future fate—steadily refusing his attention to all true aspects of life. He had become more animal than the animals whom he lived amongst, shared the least durable of their pleasures, was passionately credulous of the reality of their gods. He liked silly jokes and comic songs, because of the sense of comradeship that hung about them; when he was shouting a chorus with a dozen others he felt for the moment that he was one of themselves. He was redeeming his years of loneliness; and with them did his best to get rid of all that distinguished him from the other foolish, boisterous, bumptious, or otherwise wholesome young fellows who pass from school to commerce with little diminution of spirits or assumption of responsibility.

Many pass through this evolution, though few, perhaps, commence where he did. An accident checked the process as it reached its final position; he reverted to his old state of helpless perception; and the Power, fiend or angel, who had him in charge caught him once more in the fine meshes of its net.

CHAPTER 6

STAFF AND SCRIP

'These things I do,
These other things I see,
Shape not for me
Aught that I dare name true.
    Rather they seem to be
Hard riddles that, with sloth and pain,
I must again
        Undo.'

—LAURENCE HOUSMAN

WHEN he was eighteen years old Master Hopkinson caught scarlet fever; and the outward disease was the harbinger of a spiritual crisis. His childhood, though sickly, had contrived to withstand bodily stress, and it was years since he had known an illness. The psychological side of ill-health, at all events, was new to him; and as he sickened it astonished him to perceive how he withdrew into himself, and watched with timid curiosity the proportions of his environment gradually change. He wondered dreamily what was the matter, and swung between interest and dismay till at last the meaning of the thing was obvious, and he was declared to be ill.

He was the only victim, and had the school sanatorium to himself. This seemed to promise dulness, for he loved company now as much as he had once disliked it; and the pink-washed walls, bare boards, and row of iron beds, looking in their stripped and pillowless state like the skeletons of some nightmare quadruped, were not exactly cheering. Yet curiously enough they did not give him the desolate shock that he looked for; they were friendly, as the worst furniture can be if it likes. He lay and looked at them, and wondered of what they reminded him. Above all, the faint scent of carbolic acid stirred a vague memory which he could not catch. He was interested, puzzled. As yet, you see, he was not very ill, but was quite equal to a certain amount of hazy meditation. It was a change, and he enjoyed it.

But the surprises of circumstance were not over. Staring about him, he recognised one after another of the ideas and sensations that came slowly to the surface of his spirit, as one may greet old acquaintances whose names and business—all, in fact, but their unforgettable faces—have gone to oblivion. He found that he knew in advance all the ritual of sickness; the change of all human relations, even the forbidding automatonism which a nurse brings with her, did not astonish him. It was evident that he had been there before; and he roamed feverishly back through his past, hunting for the clue. But it eluded him.

Only in the middle of the third night, as he lay alone, hot, uncomfortable, and very forlorn, filled with the self-pitying miseries of the sick, did he find what he had been looking for. It was a discovery which amazed, but failed to please him. He disturbed from a sleep which had lasted for several years the distasteful and unwelcome memory of his old existences, reminding him with a shock that he was not as other boys. He had hidden them deep in that corner of his mind which we all keep for humiliating incidents, old religions, and ideals too spotless to be lived with: a corner we seldom traverse, and then with light footsteps, for fear of disturbing those inconvenient sleepers.

What he found, then, in this Bluebeard chamber of his consciousness was knowledge, accurate and indelible, of the days when he lay in S. Nicholas Infirmary—another child, sick of another fever; yet a real child, and one in spirit with the lanky schoolboy which his Ego now claimed as its home. He lived there again, and so vividly that he found it difficult to disentangle memory from reality, and to assure himself that he was not still in that narrow cot, that he was not any longer that child of the slums, that all his subsequent experience was not a dream of that illness.

Time is sequence of ideas, but when we run back upon the trail and recommence an old series, is not the interval annihilated? It all puzzled him horribly, as his mind turned from one place to the other, and groped for the landmarks and boundaries denied him by a Destiny which he now felt to be both imminent and awful.

But the Past which he had despised and neglected was waiting with a crueller revenge. When the fever reached an acute stage, and he was seriously ill, another and more disagreeable side of the subject was presented to Willie's mind. It occurred to him that, for the second time within his memory, he was very near indeed to the point of death.

For the last five or six years he had lived the god-like life of the average man, whose imagination assures him that he is immortal, although his reason tells him that he is not. Now Death became a fact, and a very disquieting fact. Its nearness annihilated the pretty draperies with which education conceals the ugly bogeys of mankind, and he saw it with primeval clearness, horrible and distinct.

It meant more to him, too, than it might do to others. He could not believe in the poetic fictions with which orthodox persons are accustomed to veil the open door. It meant a return, perhaps a permanent one, to the shadowy terrors of his childhood; an existence of crowded isolation, of hurried idleness, which might stretch into eternity or terminate with another experimental re-entry into life. Either alternative was unpleasant. Master Hopkinson was of a contented disposition, his artistic and adventurous tastes had not as yet begun to give trouble, and he felt that the prospects of his present life were tolerable. He preferred that the years should be punctuated with commas rather than full-stops.

He looked in vision on to a bright and varied world, a world full of energy and surprises and *Boy's Own Paper* pageantry. It is true that so far he had not seen much of this aspect of life, but provided that he could remain alive he might escape into it at any moment. Death offered no such allurements.

There followed on this hour of awakening a period when he was no longer capable of thought: when he battled with death, and shook the nerves of his nurses by his cries, his terrors, his entreaties. Time after time he felt as a stifling weight the perception of the shadow-land; time after time lost his grasp of solidity, slipped from the noises of earth, and heard the call of the spirits who were drawing him back to their ranks. For days he hung doubtful on the borders, and proclaimed his agony of soul. They said that he was delirious, but it is more probable that he was intoxicated with fright.

When the tide turned, the fever left him, and he knew that Horror no longer stood close by him, but had retreated to its normal place, Willie lay limp on his bed in an ecstasy of thankfulness—his poor frame as greatly shaken by the returning flood of life as it had been by the violence of its ebb. He was too weak for coherent thought at first: he was satisfied to rest in a sense of safety and well-being: and the sharpest memories of his ordeal wore off during this somnolence. So that at last, some three weeks after the crisis, he woke to a detached and placid consideration of events.

It must not be held a reproach to Master Hopkinson that he felt himself to be at this moment the centre of his own universe. Could others have seen him as he really was, they must, had they been by temperament philosophers, have held him more than usually qualified for the position. The invalid is a licensed egoist, the visionary an inevitable one; and only those who vainly desired such consolation for themselves could have grudged him his silent self-importance.

The scarlet fever convalescent has ample opportunity for thought; and this exercise, so difficult to a childhood fresh from the perceptive state, had been rendered possible to Willie by the strictly logical trend of his education. He began, therefore, gradually, slowly, and luxuriously, to think of what had happened. He thought about it in relation to the past, and, more seriously, in relation to the future. It was plain that he had been a bit of a fool. Had he died in his fever, the eighteen years of grace which he had won of life since his death in S. Nicholas Infirmary would have seemed inconsiderable enough against an eternity of boredom; and he had a clearer idea than many theologians of the black vacancy which the word 'eternal' hides. Yet this, he had no doubt, was what he had escaped from, and to this, unless he could discover some pass in the secret barrier, he was bound eventually to return. The prospect was very ghastly. He felt that he could never bear to see a funeral again. It was too evil, too ominous.

Then it occurred to him that perhaps there was some way out; that the hereafter as he knew it was curiously cruel, and, if applied universally, rather unjust. It was also at variance with the optimistic creed whose catch-words he had casually acquired, but this consideration did not affect him much.

This, then, was his problem—an acrostic of deadly import, to which he held few of the lights. This was his only chance, this earthly life to which his soul was still attached, of finding salvation from the dreary Hades that lay so near to his gates.

He had a little knowledge now of astronomy and physics, and these mingled themselves strangely with his meditations, and seemed to make the finding of a clue more hopeless than if he had only his own memories and fancies to draw on. Yet as he pondered, as he strove to link this world with that other, the conviction grew on him that some did find that salvation. In every variety of experience he had hitherto found some division into classes: people, he was told, were good and bad; events, he knew, were nasty or nice; it seemed inconceivable that amongst the dead there should not also be a few who were happy to balance the miseries of the rest.

In the black hours of his illness an unmistakable instinct had told him that he would not be one of those happy ones; that he was still bound to the trail with his old comrades, the hunters of the air. But some were not so. He was sure of it. He wondered and puzzled, and sent his soul questing for the answer; but the only result was to make him tired and restless, and his nurse cut short the hour of meditation with a sleeping draught.

Then, in a clearer hour, the truth came to him. He perceived suddenly, illogically, irrefutably, that within his own soul the solution was to be found.

> 'And by and by my Soul return'd to me,
> And answer'd "I myself am Heav'n and Hell."'

The governing mood, that was the governing fate. He saw in his mind's eye the long agony of the Dead; but saw it no longer as an unreasonable torture, rather as the inevitable result of their mental attitude. Their heaven had been the earth; they had no true existence apart from it; and thus, once parted from the body, they found no other song than a lament for its pleasures, no other environment than the shadowy outline of their once enduring homes. It was plain that one could take nothing into death but that which one had learnt during life; and a passion for some person, possession, or pursuit, such as formed the equipment of most sensible people, could not be regarded as a valuable spiritual asset once one was permanently separated from the senses and their joys.

Yet Willie had now given several years to the careful cultivation of these material interests. He shivered as he realized the narrowness of his escape. He saw his Grey World now at a new angle—not as the inevitable home of the soul, but as one amongst many convolutions of the spiritual envelope. When he reflected how various an aspect the material world assumed towards different temperaments, and even towards the same temperament when under the dominion of shifting moods, he could not doubt that subjective reality was the only one which had any meaning for the individual soul.

He perceived that the Hell of the worldly might be the Heaven of those who had nothing to regret; that those who looked up must find a different landscape from their neighbours who looked down. They, in the place of those intangible relics of life which had haunted his own wanderings, might find another outlook, and dwell before a Beatific Vision. He seemed to see the Universe unfolding dimension on dimension to the joyous eyes of some questing soul as it cast off the shackles of life and drew outwards toward the Beyond.

He looked firmly on the future, and made resolutions which had little bearing on Mr. Hopkinson's careful plans for his son's career. Earth, that dusty magnet, should no longer fetter his spirit. He was determined upon that. The claims of this world were illusory. He had always known it, but these later years, for expediency's sake, he had deliberately turned from the truth. He would learn to hold pleasure and sorrow alike with a light hand, remembering that Real Life was but one of many dimensions. He would no longer try to assume to himself that the game was a serious matter. He would refuse to care who lost or won, to concern himself about the chances of wealth or fame: would form no ties, make no terms with the enemy.

He saw Life spread out before him in gay pageant, as one may see the 'coloured counties' from the top of a hill. A pretty show he judged it to be, but dangerous. One must preserve detachment. The household at home, with its intimate cares, the wholesale tailoring business, the comments and criticisms of interested friends, vanished. One does not notice the ugliness of individual buildings when one stands on the top of a hill. And his eye was so firmly fixed on the Eternal now, that he came down to the realities of jelly and beef-tea with a start. For his body, of course, they were realities. He acknowledged that: he wished to be fair to his body. But he intended for the future to ride it on the curb.

Nor did it occur to Master Hopkinson that his point of view was open to the charge of selfishness. To the young, selfishness seems the least imminent of all the vices. It is their normal condition.

CHAPTER 7

MARSHLAND AND WICKET

'We be all Souls upon the way.'

—KIPLING

AT the end of the infectious period, Willie was returned to his family, a weedy and uninteresting convalescent. To himself, he appeared more worthy of notice than at any previous stage of his existence; but unfortunately the fact that he had realized the illusory nature of life did not mitigate the distressing angles of his figure. Only a burning faith can distinguish the philosopher under the veil of the hobbledehoy; the founders of new religions have generally been over twenty-one.

His mother met him at the station with a four-wheeler and a large rug. Her solicitude was rather irritating to a fastidious youth who knew his body to be a phantasm. He could find no comfort in the thought that the four-wheeler was a phantasm too: it placed his soul at a disadvantage. His Ego declined to assert itself in such surroundings. Master Hopkinson felt cross.

He had been looking forward to a return after sickness to the pretty pageant of life. He had meant to play the game, since it was but a game, gaily and with a light hand; forming no bonds with Earth, but hoarding amusing memories against the chances of the After-time. There were secrets, too, concerning that After-time; and it was in his intention that he would adventure to discover them.

For one who cherishes these pleasant and pagan ideals a London terminus is not an inspiriting point of departure. The cab rattled, and Mrs. Hopkinson busied herself with the windows, and asked her son how many carbolic baths he had had, because of Pauline, who was very susceptible. She added that they were very busy at home over a Café Chantant in aid of the 'Dartmoor Holiday Camps for Costers' Donkeys.'

'It's such a good idea, darling,' she said. 'Financially good, I mean; and that's everything in a work of charity. You must help at it. A man—and you're quite old enough to count as a man—is such an advantage. You'll be feeling stronger by then, and it will amuse you. And we've only got to get enough money for railway expenses, because land on Dartmoor is free, and of course the dear things will eat grass.'

She continued talking amiably on homely topics, but the conversation was rather one-sided. A slow spirit of weary disgust was creeping over Master Hopkinson. They were nearing home, and the peculiar bleakness of the London residential street struck him with a desolating force. He was born subject to that elusive emotion which hangs about the Spirit of Place—an evil gift for one who dwells in a modern city. The ugliness and arrogance of the houses, the pale and dreary desert of the road which lay between them, combined to obliterate that street-sense compounded of adventure and inclusion which narrower and less pretentious by-ways keep between their cuddled homes.

It is the narrow, winding street, with its social suggestion, its doubtful destination, which contains all the poetry of town life. Where attic whispers to attic, and pavements run friendlily beneath the walls, there is a sacrament present of the Brotherhood of Man. But the isolated villas of our wide, chill thoroughfares have nothing in common but a mutual exclusiveness. When Willie, descending from his cab, looked down the road with its rows of gray stucco boxes, wherein blameless families dwelt without remorse or discontent; its legions of painted railings whose tendency now was 'to reticence rather than greenness'; its windows without recess; and the evil pilasters about its gates; a spirit of rebellion was born in him. He had the feeling that few things were more significant, more foolish, to the visionary more depressing, than this way which society has of disposing of its homes.

Within, the impression was continued with cruel completeness. Mrs. Hopkinson had had the hall done up, and the Moorish electric-light lantern now depended from a ceiling whose Lincrusta covering simulated Renaissance plaster-work. On the walls a paper which the short-sighted might have mistaken for inferior tapestry, displayed a riot of invertebrate forms thrown together in defiance of every known rule of ornament.

Willie escaped from this, and from a minute and unpleasant inspection of his appearance conducted in concert by his mother,

Pauline, and the cook, and climbed up to his own little bedroom, where he opened the window and looked out on a twilit sky. It was the magic moment when blue fades by green into grey. He watched that heavenly transformation, and it soothed his fretted nerves. The sky, he found, had reassumed that secret power which it had for him in childhood. He had won back the world of vision in turning from the world of sense. He stood there dreaming till Mrs. Hopkinson bustled into the room to close the window, and spoke in anxious tones of the fact that the tea was standing, and night air notoriously unwholesome.

That broke the spell. He went downstairs possessed by the gnawing discomfort which a homecoming is apt to induce. Everything looked as it used to do, and no one seemed to notice his own inward change. Yet how different things were from their appearances: and how different he from the being whom his garrulous mother and sister thought that they were feeding with weak tea and homemade cake! These reflections pleased Master Hopkinson, and helped him to endure with good temper the minor trials of the evening, during which his father explained to him in detail the germ theory of infectious disease.

'So nice and homelike,' said Mrs. Hopkinson. 'All united once more round our own hearth!'

Willie arose next morning to a sense of struggle and depression such as had long been absent from his spirit. His sensitive nerves felt the weight of coming events—those small, tedious, hollow events which were going to make up the day. Things did not seem promising for his projected Game of Life: the pieces were rather shabby, and the board inconveniently arranged. He foresaw the eight o'clock breakfast, prefaced by a discussion as to what he had better eat, accompanied by annotated extracts from the morning paper, which Mr. Hopkinson was accustomed to supply for his family's mental nourishment. After breakfast there might perhaps be a tranquil interval, and later on he would be expected to go for a walk with Pauline.

For the present, in fact, Pauline seemed likely to be his chief companion. She was now twenty-one; liked a good time—in the local acceptation of the phrase—and saw that she got it; made her own blouses, held her own opinions, could talk with technical accuracy about cricket, politics, and the drama; and was generally in the front rank of Young Suburbia. But as a companion, a sister, she had her limitations. She was apt to forget that the attitude of superiority which Twelve Years Old may lawfully assume towards Nine is less suitable when the respective ages of the protagonists are eighteen and one-and-twenty. Willie knew that should he attempt to be candid, or ask for sympathy with his own view of life, she would still regard him as a silly little boy.

So it did not look well on the whole for the prospects of a pleasant life held lightly; a perpetual realization of illusion; a mind always ready to consider the spiritual aspect of things. Willie's mind was young, crude, intolerant. It seemed to him that the life of the Hopkinson family entirely lacked a spiritual aspect. Certainly, if it had one, they did not think about it. Earth for them was the one actuality; long life thereon the chief desire; quick interest therein the one duty. He saw in them potential members of the Shadowy World, and feared their slow, stultifying influence. How, in such an atmosphere, keep his own armour bright? As well try to study astronomy in a fog-bound city.

He found a way. The Fates are often kind to those who expect nothing; and six months after his home-coming they suddenly pointed out to him a road to adventure, if not to discovery. The dulness had become very desperate by this time. He did not find that the possession of special powers added anything to the gaiety of existence; on the contrary, they enlarged in an unwelcome manner a horizon which was in its dreariness already sufficiently vast. The World of the Dead in its featureless monotony is not very unlike the world of the suburbs.

He was too well assured of the illusory nature of life and the futility of its occupations. He could take no interest beyond a gentle amusement in work, play, politics, or the acquisition of knowledge. They were games, and curiously stupid ones. It never occurred to him that he had a part to play in them: duty becomes unreal when its object is known to be impermanent. But turning his eyes resolutely from Earth, he found himself confronted by a dismal nothingness. If Earth was illusion, Heaven was emptiness. So he was driven to his dreams, in default of more actual possessions, and to certain visionary books he had met with—Blake and Swedenborg and the Dutch mystics. These were congenial, if unintelligible, to him; and with them he lived—moped—drifted.

It became his habit to stroll of an afternoon through the dingy by-roads of the neighbourhood, wondering at their peculiar quality of squalor, which was neither poor enough to be excusable, nor extreme enough to be interesting. In this way he found one day a little street: a very ordinary, unlovable little street, one of those grey alley-ways which run between the cells of the human hive. There was a public-house at one corner—the Purple Elephant—and mews behind. One side of the road was bordered by a high blank wall, which cloistered the shy gardens of some villas in the next street. On the other side, a depressed terrace of yellow brick houses with unpleasant areas gave itself out as the residence of dressmakers, lodgers, and innumerable cats.

But half-way down there were shops: a pawn-broker's, a dubious dairy, a plumber's and decorator's. This last, a small tranquil establishment, was the cleanest of the three; it had drain-pipes in one window and wall-papers in the other—a symbolic display, in fact. At one side a private door, grained to imitate some rare and gaudy species of oak, led to the upper story; and by the door a repoussé copper plate bore, in vague Gothic letters, the words, 'Searchers of the Soul. Ring and walk upstairs.'

Willie stopped and looked at this inscription, with the instinct of the solitary pedestrian to look at everything that he has not seen before. It struck him rather pleasantly. He was sufficiently sophisticated to find it astonishing, sufficiently desperate to be tempted towards any promising investigation. A bad cold had left him in a nervous condition which renewed many of his worst terrors. He was like a rudderless ship, in sight of a haven which he did not know how to attain, and fearing a storm which might wreck him before he could reach it. So he did not feel justified in neglecting a chance which might lead, not only to companionship with other spiritual beings, but also to more security than he now possessed concerning his after-existences. Moreover, he urgently required an antidote to the materializing dangers of home. He looked at the copper plate, and hesitated. Then he walked on. Presently he returned, and glanced up and down the street. There was only a dust-cart in sight. He rang, and entered.

The stairs within were steep, narrow, and ill-scrubbed: three flights of them. There was time during the ascent for meditation; and Mr. Willie Hopkinson, somewhat elated on his first entrance, felt his joyous anticipations undergo a certain transformation as he clambered, accompanied by perfumes of varnish and putty from the shop below. In fact, his heart sank as his body rose; and it was in a state of peculiar nervousness that he finally knocked at the shabby door with ground-glass panels which he found at the top of the third flight.

The young woman who opened to him cured his timidity but did not raise his spirits much. Willie had a sister, and neither feared girls nor admired them; and even a slave of the sex would scarcely have been tempted to emotion by her flat face, black sailor hat, and crumpled cotton shirt. It will be acknowledged that the Searchers of the Soul had not used discrimination in their choice of a janitor.

She received him with that curious effusion, at once servile and supercilious, which the secretaries of small but earnest associations keep for possible converts. Willie did not quite know what he had come for, but Miss Toyson had no doubts about that.

'You wish to join us, perhaps?' she said. 'The movement is becoming, as of course you know, one of great importance. We are on the eve of a Spiritual Era. One feels that. It is in the air; and our Society will not be the least of its heralds. The Soul,' continued Miss Toyson, whose ready-made appearance lent a touch of unexpectedness to her lyrical speech—'what can be more important to each one of us? And the Search for it—what is more beautiful? The paths to Truth are so many; and the Society is quite non-sectarian.'

'Really?' said Willie, who repressed with difficulty a strong desire to fidget.

Miss Toyson's words might be fresh from the Gospel of Truth, but her speech displeased him. It was like hearing the Apocalypse read aloud by a stammering curate.

'Oh yes, quite. We make a great point of that; our only aim is the finding of spiritual reality. The Thing-in-Itself, you know, as—er—as a great philosopher said. Our vice-president is a believer in Shintoism—worships his ancestors, you know—and we have several Buddhists.'

Willie did not feel attracted by the faith of the vice-president. Yet, in some curious way, Miss Toyson and her Society fascinated whilst they repelled him. He was quite sure that they knew nothing about it; but their name had a glamour which he could not resist. The subscription was seven and six; he paid it. His monthly allowance was ten shillings. The meetings, said Miss Toyson, were frequent. They encouraged free discussion. It was worth something to have found a haven, however shabby, where one might dare to speak one's mind.

He went home with a lighter heart, and spoke in a deceptively prosaic manner of the afternoon's adventure. A little debating society, he said; an amusing sort of place, which would give him the opportunity of meeting other fellows.

'How nice!' said Mrs. Hopkinson. 'I'm so glad, Willie dear. Such a good plan for you to have some interests of your own. But I am sorry the meetings are in the evening, dearie. Coming out into the night air from a hot room is so very risky.'

She looked at him with an eager, half-desperate smile; hesitating as a swimmer may amongst difficult currents, yet feeling cheerfulness, however inappropriate, to be a duty to the last. There was an obscure sadness buried deep beneath Mrs. Hopkinson's stuff bodice. She found it very hard to adapt her homely love to her son's peculiar ideas and many intolerances. She was never quite sure how he would take things, and, remembering the lawful intimacies of his babyhood, she sometimes ventured a humiliating familiarity, with disastrous results. Willie was too young, as yet, to understand undecorative pathos.

In her baffled motherhood, she could only turn to her daughter for consolation: but Pauline, whose even life had never caused her to feel the need of sympathy, was entirely incapable of giving it. So it happened that Mrs. Hopkinson's existence was lonely in spite of her garrulity, and she was happiest when she was expending on a misplaced charity the ardours which her children preferred to do without.

Mr. Willie Hopkinson could scarcely expect to find the Searchers of the Soul an interest, in his mother's meaning of the word; but he did extract from this connection a certain feeling of independence, which is, after all, the chief object of youthful hobbies and pursuits.

A good many young men and maidens join societies more deleterious in order to differentiate themselves from their elders.

The first meeting astonished, the second disgusted him. There was in the atmosphere a banality, a childish affectation of occult knowledge, which he found more stifling to the spirit than the candid futilities of the home circle. But he persevered; he was not the son of a business man for nothing, and he meant to receive full value for his seven and six. He therefore went a third time, and was rewarded; for on this occasion he perceived the existence of Stephen Miller.

Mr. Miller's personality distinguished him easily from the majority of his fellow-members, whom Willie early divided into two classes—the long-haired and the beefy. He was vivid, highly-strung, physically compact. The obsession of the Aerated Bread Shop was not upon him yet. A careful observer would have perceived that this was a man who sought dreams deliberately, as an artist; did not follow them blindly, as a fool.

When he first came under the eye of Mr. Willie Hopkinson, Stephen was striving to assimilate the frothy periods of Mr. Verrian Spate, the expounder—in minute detail—of a new doctrine of reincarnation, elaborated by himself. Novel theories of the Future State were a speciality of the Society. Willie, who had grown accustomed to apathy, here found himself plunged into a world of wild conjecture. He listened with growing amazement whilst Mr. Spate—he was the President of the year, and belonged to the beefy class—vigorously defended the dogma of Successive Incarnations, and turned a battery of heavy facetiousness on his opponent, exploiting the rich resources of the subject as a fountain of personal abuse. Nor was he less astonished when Mr. Spate's remarks, which had been received with great favour, were succeeded by a convincing exposition, by his anaemic *vis-à-vis*, Mr. Norman Dawes, of the hypothesis that the human spirit must of necessity return to its Mother the Sea after death.

A genial tolerance of anything that was improbable seemed to be the distinguishing characteristic of the Searchers of the Soul; yet as Willie looked round the ring of faces—weak, wistful, or dogmatic —lit to cold pallor by the incandescent gas, he knew himself farther from spiritual progress than he had been for many months. With knowledge lying so close to their doors; with the emblems around them of an unstable, impermanent world, which he knew to be ready to rock and dissolve at the first blow dealt upon the portals of sense; with phrases on their lips which constantly touched edges of the Truth; it seemed incredible that these people could continue so profoundly earthly, so desperately dense, making game in their happy ignorance with the secret beyond the veil. He felt that annoyed astonishment which is often induced in persons having the sentiment of Religion or Art when they are confronted by the immutable limitations of the Philistine or the Atheist. He knew that should he rise to relate his own experiences, his fellow-members would be pleasantly excited by his originality, and ask him to go on the committee. But they would not believe in him, because that would prevent them from believing in all the others, and so rob the Society of half its charm.

But Stephen Miller was different. To Stephen the objects of the Society were no pretence, though its methods might be. His sincerity was manifest in his disillusion. Willie looked at him, and in the infallible knowledge with which spirit meets spirit in the invisible place, knew that if that virile brain once perceived the truth of his story, his years of loneliness were over, and he had found a friend.

He woke from his meditation to find that Mr. Dawes' remarks were drawing to a close.

'Yes!' he was saying, as his voice penetrated to Mr. Hopkinson's consciousness—'yes, in the beautiful words of Browning, it is our aim when we meet together here

> '"To bring the Invisible full into play!
> Let the visible go to the dogs—what matters?"

That is our desire, that is the ideal we set before us! And if each can contribute a little quota to the grand total of Truth, we shall indeed be amply rewarded!'

He subsided amidst murmurs of admiration, and at the same moment Mr. Miller rose abruptly and left the meeting. Pleasure had died from his face and been succeeded by a tired disappointment as the speaker slowly dragged his theory from the heights of poetic speculation, and forced it into the sticky by-paths of suburban argument. Mr. Willie Hopkinson also had ceased to be interested or even amused, so he went out after Mr. Miller, following him without thought, as a needle after a magnet, and they spoke together on the door-mat.

They were very young—under twenty—an age when the founding of a friendship seems always the first page of a romance. They looked at each other, and the miracle was done. It was a case of love at first sight, a phenomenon rather absurdly supposed to occur only between persons of opposite sex. They were both excited. The horrid gulf which yawned between the title and transactions of their Society had disgusted but not yet discouraged them. They saw each other, and through each other the trend of the event, hopefully, with the air of explorers who have found the justification of their journeyings. The seal was loosened upon Willie's lips, and even at that early moment he held back confidence with an uncertain hand. Stephen, who had the quickness of a spirit sensible of mystery, that longs to look in the face of the unknown, perceived some secret behind the strangeness of their attitude. To one of his temperament, that was more than enough. Each went home that night the richer for a friend, though less than a dozen words had passed as yet between them. Willie had at last made one step forward.

CHAPTER 8

THE FIRST SIGNPOST

'Nous nous sommes dit bien peu de choses. Mais nous avons pu voir
que nos deux vies avaient le même but. . . .'

—MAETERLINCK

IT was Mrs. Hopkinson's dearest hope that her son should become
a cultured person. Culture had made strides in their suburb since
the days when studious tastes were considered effeminate in a man
and immodest in a woman. Girls now read translations of Russian
novelists in the intervals of home dressmaking, and sneered at their
parents: and these commented caustically in reply on the headaches
which visited the victims of unaccustomed learning. They had not
yet reached the depths at which a local Debating Society becomes
imperative. A little further westwards, where the omnibus gave
place to the tram, that came as a matter of course; but the district
which was served by the Inner Circle accepted membership of the
London Library as a certificate of intellect.

Mrs. Hopkinson, therefore, felt that as Willie did not seem likely
to develop into either a useful or a popular young man, it was
desirable that he should be known as a clever one: and, looking
about her for an acquaintance who would start him in the right
direction, and turn his indolent attention towards fashionable fields
of knowledge, she suddenly perceived the peculiar merits of Mrs.
Hermann Levi.

Elsa Levi, as has already been remarked, was the only child of
Mrs. Steinmann. Her garments—which they considered to be
indecently suggestive of a dressing-gown—gave scandal to her
mother's friends, and kept them, to her delight, at a sufficient
distance. They sometimes brought their country cousins to call on
her, thus bridging the gap between the attractions of the Zoo and
South Kensington Museum; but such visits were based more on
curiosity than approval. On these occasions Mrs. Levi, who was
too self-conscious to dislike admiration, however strange its form,
received her visitors cordially, and made a point of saying

something a little bit shocking before they left. It was expected of her, and she could not neglect so obvious a duty.

She was at this time a slender and alluring person of thirty-eight; and the uncomfortable tendencies of her soul made her liable to brief joys and long periods of boredom. She had a superficial knowledge of many things and a great respect for efficiency; her friends thought that she was artistic, her enemies said she was soulful. In reality she was a woman who lived, by predilection, close to the tree of knowledge, but was not quite tall enough to reach the apple which she ardently desired for her own.

When she first married Mr. Levi, Elsa had suggested that he should change his name to Darcy. Mr. Levi refused; what was worse, he did so in an intolerably good-humoured manner, and thus convinced his wife, even sooner than she had expected, that he was utterly incapable of appreciating either her talents, her aspirations, or her soul.

'Mr. Levi,' she would say, 'is a Materialist. He does not perceive the beautiful part which Symbolism plays in the lives of the spiritually intelligent.'

The curtain now lifts to disclose Willie Hopkinson taking tea in the drawing-room of Mrs. Hermann Levi. They were alone. She had arranged, without ostentation, that this should be the case. For two people, the room seemed empty. There was an absence of small tables, and the walls, except for a boldly designed frieze by Walter Crane, were barely coloured. There were only two pictures. One was a small and evilly-restored Madonna, which Mrs. Levi in her more sanguine moments attributed to Perugino; the other a grubby and obvious Degas. She had friends amongst the extreme right as well as the extreme left of the artistic parliament, and each by turns dictated her always admirable taste. This arrangement had only one disadvantage—Elsa never finally decided which picture she really liked best. But with two such works of art, a little fumed oak, and the poems of Emile Verhaeren in a Niger morocco binding, any room, she considered, was adequately furnished.

She leaned back now in the corner of the settle, and carefully placed her dark head against a cushion of violet silk. She wore a soft dress of subdued and cloudy blue, and Willie, who was in a happy and impressionable mood, thought of the Bride of Lebanon.

Mrs. Levi also was contented with the atmosphere and the hour. It was her hobby to act the Sybil to interesting young men, and the fact that Willie's family found him difficult to deal with inclined her to place him in this class.

He was shy, but his hostess was experienced. A less subtle woman would have tried to make him talk about himself, and failed lamentably. Elsa, on the contrary, assumed towards him a confidential air which was at once flattering and instructive. She said little beyond generalities, but her manner gave the impression that she was baring her soul to his gaze. Under its influence his petals uncurled rapidly. He looked into her eyes, which were brown and pathetic, and knew for the first time that other persons beside himself had spiritual griefs.

They talked of Art, a subject which young Mr. Hopkinson had seldom heard mentioned. Though his father, he knew, disliked it—a fact clearly in its favour—it conveyed to him no more than a suggestion of strange cretonnes and bound volumes of *Academy Notes*. But Art, he now gathered, was an important thing; a secret and mysterious power, and also a pleasing one. It was spelt with a capital letter. From the vague and reverential way in which Mrs. Levi spoke of it, he inferred that it stood somewhat on the same plane as religion.

'Where should we be,' she had said, 'if it were not for the Arts? In the Neolithic cave, perhaps, or even the ancestral tree. It is this which raises us from the market-place, and leads us to the skies. I am sure we think alike on these subjects, do we not?'

Willie prudently remained silent, but his expression was rapidly becoming one of adoration, and his hostess did not, like Mark Antony, pause for a reply.

'Yes,' she said, 'Art is the real language of the soul. I am convinced of it. How else can we explain its existence? It is the link with the Beyond.'

At this point Willie, whose attention had wandered from Mrs. Levi's words and fixed itself on the fascinations of her person, suddenly became interested. The matter seemed to have some personal application. His alert but puzzled air attracted her.

'Have you never felt the spell of Ultimate Beauty?' she murmured.

He had not, but it was obvious that he would like to; and she saw prospects of conversion ahead. Your convert is always the best disciple. Elsa liked her followers to be tame and appreciative, and she warmed to her work.

'Beauty,' she said, 'is the only thing really worth having. You will know that when you have found it. Beauty in poetry, Beauty in form, Beauty in life.'

'But—'

She would not hear him.

'I tell you,' she said, bending forward and looking exactly like Rossetti's 'Astarte Syriaca'—'I tell you that all the banners of Empire and powders of the merchant weigh as nothing in the scales of Eternity against Durham Cathedral or the Samothracian Nikè.'

These words suggested little to Mr. Willie Hopkinson beyond a sense of welcome change from the atmosphere in which he daily dwelt. But his eye, though untrained, was sensitive. He recognised an essential peace in the simple graces of Mrs. Levi's decoration which was lacking amongst the photograph frames and antimacassars of home. He saw himself, a creature of infinite capabilities, evidently able to interest so brilliant a woman as this, placed by Fate amongst cruelly inappropriate surroundings. He remembered his old dreams of a delicious, free, unconventional life; saw that some people at least might realize these bright ideals; and felt very sorry for himself.

'My father,' he remarked bitterly, 'thinks that nothing is of serious importance that has not some bearing on practical affairs.'

'You must not blame your father,' answered Mrs. Levi, and the gentle pathos of her tone was itself a delight. 'It is not his fault that he is born a Materialist. You and I have windows that look out on Eternity, but his are turned towards the earth. It is sad for him, poor man! though he does not know it. My husband is just the same. He thinks Titian's "Flora" a fine woman, but he has never got further than that. Of the life-enhancing qualities of Art he knows nothing—nothing.'

In this particular Willie was in much the same position as Mr. Levi, but he did not say so. The conversation languished; both were thoughtful, he gazing dreamily at his hostess, and trying to piece together the chief elements of the gospel which he was sure that her scattered remarks must contain.

'Do have another cup of tea!' she said presently.

Willie drank in new courage with his tea. He was certainly having an exciting, astonishing, ever-to-be-remembered afternoon. The Searchers of the Soul had shaken his belief in spiritual possibilities; but Mrs. Levi had revived his faith, and even augmented its strength. It is a curiosity of youth that those who turn a blank wall of reticence towards their families are often most ready to confide in the first sympathetic nature that they meet. Elsa's dexterous use of conversational opportunities convinced him, as more open flattery could not have done, that for once he was really understood. He longed to tell her all, but refrained, which was prudent.

She, on her side, saw a neurotic, perhaps a clever, boy; awkward and ill-educated, full of fancies, rather absurd in the little airs of equality which her careful encouragement was leading him to assume. It would be amusing, she thought, to detach him from those horrible Hopkinsons, and show him something of the ideals which she loved, or thought that she loved. She pined for intelligent admiration; and to train up one's own admirer is one way to success. She perceived possibilities in Willie. She was sure that he thought her handsome, and felt her to be sympathetic. He was a nice lad.

The conversation revived, and took a more intimate turn.

'The beautiful in life,' said Mrs. Levi—'that is what we must look for, and refuse to see the uglinesses in our path.'

'It is so difficult.'

'One must persevere.'

'The uglinesses discourage,'

'Even though one has a friend to help one?' asked Elsa softly.

Willie searched for a suitable reply to this intoxicating utterance, but the cool deliberation with which he was apt to regulate dialogue in the home circle completely forsook him. He could only look at her, and encouraged by the expression which he thought that he saw in her eyes, ventured at last to press her hand—that soft and manicured hand with its strange rings of olivine, chrysoprase, and enamels. He experienced in the act a new sensation, compounded of terror and daring, which assured him that he had yet much to learn.

And whilst he still held it, the goddess spoke again.

'Life is really very beautiful!' she said.

They had not heard the hall-door bang loudly beneath them, or subsequent feet upon the stairs; so that when the electric lights were switched on in a sudden click both started in astonishment, and stared at each other with dazzled eyes which had grown accustomed to the discreet shadows thrown by firelight on a dusky room. Mrs. Levi, who had been growing curiously younger during the past hour, immediately resumed her rightful years. Willie drew back, feeling dreamy and insecure. Before he had recovered himself, the door opened with unnecessary amplitude and fuss, and Mr. Geraint Levi, red-tied and frock-coated, entered noisily.

'What ho, mater!' said he; 'been sitting in the murky? I've just got back from the shop. Lively day at the House. Lollies are softening; makes the boss feel quite sick. Lollies and Babas are his principal nutriment at present.'

Mrs. Levi offered no remark. Willie, horrified by this too natural climax to their idyllic afternoon, also remained silent. Geraint, unconscious of offence, retained control of the conversation.

'Saw your governor, Hopkinson,' he said. 'Had a chat with him going down in the Underground. Same old bun, Science and Sewing.' He paused, and showed some amusement at his own epigram. 'I suppose they'll be setting you on to the trouser-stitching soon. What a lark!' He helped himself to a cup of stale tea, grumbled at it, drank it; ate four pieces of thin bread-and-butter in two mouthfuls, kissed his mother suddenly on the nose, missed entirely her glance of candid dislike, and went out of the room as noisily as he had entered. 'I'm just going out to get this week's *Tuppenny Tips*,' he shouted from half-way down the staircase.

There seemed to be a chill in the air after Geraint's departure. Elsa, whom he always irritated, was particularly vexed that so disastrous an illustration of her precepts should have been brought to Willie's notice at this early stage of their acquaintance. She felt herself a partner in his vulgarity, and knew that it imperilled her influence. He was as bad as a poor relation.

Willie, whose point of view was vague, but already very serious where Elsa was concerned, feared to intrude on what was certainly an annoyance and probably a sacred grief. But he reflected that a father like Mr. Hopkinson was almost as great a trial to a spiritually-minded young man as a son like Geraint could be to Mrs. Levi. It was a bond between them. His assurance returned, and he would have taken her hand again, but she gave him no opportunity. Even in moments of sentiment, she managed to steer clear of bathos.

Presently she remarked in a new tone:

'I suppose your father means to take you into the business? Shall you like that?'

He had nothing to say. He only looked at her, felt a new power clutch at his throat, and wished that he could go away without more words. He had been having tea in Paradise, and now she was helping him back to earth. But she was merciful. She saw that he did not possess the agility which allowed her to drop to fresh conversational planes without shock or disaster.

'You are sad,' she said. 'Geraint has spoilt the moment for you. You must not mind; in life things always happen like that. Beauty, you see, presupposes ugliness, and would hardly be noticeable without it.'

'Oh, but why is life so horrid?' said Willie. 'And why are all the real things mixed up with hideous shams? If only I could know what life meant! But it is so difficult.'

Mrs. Levi smiled at him, and nodded appreciatively.

'I think sometimes,' she said, 'that perhaps this world is a sort of pantomime for the angels. If one can only get far enough away it is really very amusing. And after one of the great tragedies of the universe, when a splendid star has burnt itself out to a dark cinder, or gives up its life in fragments to the planets that are its sons, it must do them good to laugh at us for a little.'

She forgot Willie's presence for a moment, and laughed herself, but not very mirthfully. 'Oh, but it's all very ridiculous!' she said.

He was charmed. Here at last was a person who put his own ideals into practice, and held life with a light hand. He was sure that Mrs. Levi perceived their essential sympathy, and found him attractive. He did not know that the attraction consisted in his own ignorance and fundamental simplicity. He was an empty and rather well-shaped vessel into which she could pour the ferment of her restless thoughts; but he imagined himself to be the wine as well as the pitcher. He went away feeling that, with two such friends as Stephen Miller and Elsa Levi, the future, which had once seemed repellent in its nakedness, was amply draped. How happy she, he thought, in such surroundings; lovelinesses springing up about her at her will! No doubt she knew hundreds of interesting spiritual people; for he had learnt that afternoon that such people existed, and might even be more interesting than he was.

He forgot what she had said about her husband; he found it impossible to remember that Geraint was her son.

Mr. Willie Hopkinson reached home in a flushed and excited condition; happier than he had been for months, and less tolerant of his environment. Life was a charming game, and Mrs. Levi the most accomplished of players. But there was beefsteak with onions for dinner; his father was a hearty eater, and his spirits fell.

*　　　*　　　*　　　*　　　*

Elsa was a woman who found conversation, even with uncongenial persons, a necessity of existence. There is a certain luxury in laying pearls before swine; and she was never more appreciative of her own jewels of speech than when spreading them at her husband's feet. The process was soothing and self-explanatory, and there was seldom any fear that his replies would eclipse the brilliance of her own remarks.

'That boy of the Hopkinsons',' she said to Mr. Levi during dinner, 'has been here this afternoon. He affects me curiously. I detect a strange element in him. I must have him to tea again.'

'He's an odd chap, certainly,' replied Hermann, half occupied by an excellent omelette. 'Do well with music or the stage, I should think. Fancy he's an annoyance to Hopkinson, who expected him to turn out differently. That fellow seems to think that he can breed boys like puppies, with any points he likes. But kids are queer; you can't depend on 'em! Look at Connie!'

Mrs. Levi did look at Connie, whose portrait hung near the fireplace; and she sighed. She would have given much for a share in that form of queerness. It was beautiful and Bohemian; attributes specially dear to her ill-fed emotions.

Connie had brought with her into life one valuable asset—an exquisite skin, moulded on to a form of Grecian purity. Her swarthy but extremely respectable family looked on the matter as one of no moment, they only wondered whom she took after; but at fifteen Connie, already conscious of her charms, chanced upon Browning's 'Lady and the Painter.' The life it pointed out was easy, lucrative, and adventurous; and in her case, curiously enough, it remained reputable. She is famous in many studios, vainly desired in many palaces, and her portrait adorns the galleries of both worlds.

'Yes,' admitted Elsa, after a brief reflection on Connie's career, 'kids *are* queer! But I don't think Willie Hopkinson will be an actor, dear; he's too thoughtful. I fancy he will develop into a mystic; he has that point of view.'

'No good,' said Mr. Levi decisively; 'no money in that. Hopkinson wouldn't stand it. All right as a hobby, of course. But a lad must have some serious employment.'

'And is not the search for Ultimate Truth a serious employment?' asked Mrs. Levi rather warmly. Her controversial manner was apt to be feverish, the temperature rising without warning in sudden spasms.

'Of course it's not,' said her husband, 'except for the nincompoops who can't do anything else! Very pretty and all that, but it don't pay. It's no use glaring, Elsa my dear, or sitting on your chair as if it was a pin-cushion. I never saw the mystic yet who could pay your dressmaker's bill.'

He carefully lighted a large cigar; and Mrs. Levi, who found it convenient to dislike tobacco, fled to her boudoir, where she smoked cigarettes in solitude for two hours, and thought of Willie Hopkinson in a mood which she wrongly imagined to be maternal.

CHAPTER 9

A FELLOW-TRAVELLER

'Those obstinate questionings
Of sense and outward things,
Fallings from us, vanishings;
Blank misgivings of a creature
Moving about in worlds not realized.'

—WORDSWORTH

THE influence of Mrs. Levi on her disciple was soon perceptible. She raised his standard of taste, without conferring a corresponding benefit on his morals. The result was of doubtful advantage to a person who still lacked the power of omitting ugly externals from his visionary field. In effect, Mr. Willie Hopkinson became more dreamy, and even less agreeable to his neighbours than of old.

His mind had passed from the condition of boredom to that of unrest. It hungered for Elsa's society, and for the stimulus of her disturbing ideals; excluding her from the verdict of hollowness which it passed on the rest of creation. She was the one fixed point of his universe, and wandering from that he felt lost. He cherished her occasional letters, and valued the touch of her hand, with an inconsistent materialism which he realized but was unable to kill. He forsook the old dull poise of disillusion, but found no new one.

He began to grow, too, with a spiritual growth, painful and spasmodic; for his soul, though always conscious, had developed little since the childish times when it first woke to its own existence. Its powers, beyond those of mere panic, were immature. It perceived, but could not co-ordinate. It was still the baby spirit, the troublesome precocious child, which takes notice easily but holds nothing in a comprehensive grasp. Its little fits of fear, its glimpses of the Veil, and shuddering acknowledgments of the Grey Country where the Dead search the fields of life for something to love, were cast in petty lines. Lacking as yet the Great Companion, Willie walked only with the dim reflection of his own mean little soul.

It was under the direction of his Egeria that he now began to brood upon artistic problems, to read the *Studio* and the *Artist*, and to pay secret visits to the National Gallery. From these he returned ill-tempered and disconsolate, tired out by uninstructed efforts to appreciate Medieval Art. He found little which accorded with his preconceived idea of the Beautiful. Mrs. Levi, perhaps overestimating his intelligence, had directed his attention to Memlinck and to Gherard David, to Duccio and to Botticelli; and he spent puzzled hours before masterpieces as far beyond his apprehension as he was beyond that of his relations. Only the quiet of the place pleased him and compelled his respect; speaking as silence will of the Idea which lies beyond appearance. He had been in other years with his mother and Pauline to the Academy; and he remembered the discord with which the pictures seemed to shout from the walls. Here there was the peace of mutual courtesy. So, coming for Art, he stayed for Serenity; and still influences began their slow civilizing work upon his soul.

Stephen Miller, in another direction, gave a helping hand to the extrication of his spirit from the marshlands of vegetative life. Their friendship grew, slowly and carefully. Both youths suffered from family criticism; they had been led to think their most ordinary actions eccentric; and this gave a coyness to their early advances. Even immortal spirits dislike being laughed at. The emotion conceived on the dim stairway of the Searchers of the Soul could not at first endure a cold and unbecoming daylight.

Not, indeed, till he had been introduced into Stephen's family circle, did Willie discover how valuable were the peculiar qualities of his friend. They seemed to have been prepared for one another by a good-natured and discriminating Providence. Stephen had been reared, like himself, in an atmosphere of overpowering solidity. But his home was opulent: there were wide passages, and two footmen. Circumstances were easier for him than they had been for Mr. Willie Hopkinson, though scarcely more inspiring. His father was a thin, radiant old gentleman, who seldom gave himself the trouble of rebuking his son: who read *Punch* through carefully every Tuesday night, and the *Referee* on Sundays, smiling silently at every joke. He refused to give any serious attention to the eccentricities of the young.

'Stephen,' he said to Willie in the course of his first visit, 'has run through all the religions, and now he's reduced to the freaks.'

This, as Willie later discovered, was an exaggeration. Mr. Stephen Miller had retained the fragrance, if not the dogma, of the cults by which he had passed; and morsels culled from the Upanishads, the Book of the Dead, and the *Acta Sanctorum*, embellished his view of the world. Each new religion, he said, gave him the sight of a fresh angle in the polygon of Truth; a figure of which old Mr. Miller, safely established in the pawky materialism of middle age, probably doubted the existence.

Stephen and Willie, however, were little bound by the limitations of their elders. Each obtained early, if vague, assurance of the other's interest in spiritual things, and bridges were soon established between them. Superior young persons often pride themselves on isolation whilst they pine for comradeship. The flattering comprehension of an elder woman still leaves gaps to be filled. Willie had room for Stephen; and Stephen, whose spiritual life was dominated by a lively and eclectic curiosity, eagerly desired the exploration of his friend's soul.

But Mr. Willie Hopkinson preserved a certain reticence. Stephen, he saw, followed every occult clue, however bizarre the colours of the thread; and seldom refused his hand to an unproved proposition. He did not wish his own story to take rank with these experiments. Stephen's spirit, greedy for truth and sensible of its nearness, looked towards him hopefully; but though it seemed sad that so intelligent a person should share the delusions of the rest of the world, he avoided its contact.

Stephen argued his way toward the light by intellectual effort; did not perceive as Willie did, naturally and irrationally, the Grey World folded in the shadow-world of sense. One could not conceive of his giving to spiritual presences the same cool assent that he accorded to the tables and chairs. Yet as realities they were equally substantial. His universe was still a concrete affair; his diligent dreams no more than the expression of an aesthetic unsatisfied mind. He wished to know the Beyond as children wish to see fairies; because he believed it to be strange, beautiful, exciting.

They went together fairly regularly to the meetings of the Searchers of the Soul. Each had a secret hope that the absurdities of that Society might one day draw from the other an indignant protest, and incidentally confession of faith. It seemed a flint on which, at any moment, one might strike out the spark of truth. And it was, finally, in some such way that they did actually come to understand each other.

It was an evening in which the tone of the meeting had been one of great intellectual, as well as atmospheric, stuffiness. The dogmatism of the Dark Ages, wedded to the unbridled speculation of the present, had exalted the imagination, and paralyzed the intelligence, of the Society—'The heirs of all the ages in the foremost ranks of time' as Mr. Vincent Dawes had happily observed in his eloquent speech. Table-turning, astrology, and divination by coffee-grounds, had all been called in to provide a facile solution to the great conundrum. Willie and Stephen, escaping at last from the fumes of gas and the sounds of aerated oratory, stepped from that squalid stairway, with its suggestion of putty and cheap lodgings, straight into the austere pageant of the night.

They stood upon the threshold, amazed and comforted by the purity which the west wind blows from a dark sky. It was such an abrupt change as Dante felt when he came out from Hell '*a riveder le stelle.*' The moon rode high above London. Little clouds, hurrying across the heavens, became opalescent poems as they approached her—faded to grey prose as they rushed away. Bathed in that milky radiance the town, coiled in massy folds of black and of ashy grey, hid its shameful outlines as well as it might. In the great west road, electric lamps blazed with an angry blue fire, trying to put out the splendours of the sky: but the moon looked down on them serenely and was not afraid. Under that heaven, so secret and so white, one seemed to imagine wide spaces of quiet and happy country at rest; and the black shadow of London—man's ugly attempt to build himself a world—lying like a blot in the midst, yet sharing in the same merciful dispensation of darkness and light. The spirit of London was awed, too, by the guardianship of this cold and gracious moon, as never by the brightness of the sun. Even the traffic went with a muffled tread. Cities dream on a moonlit night; and in their dream they smile and become beautiful.

'On a night like this,' said Stephen, 'so magical and still, one is almost tempted to wonder if anything is real. These streets are not the same streets now—their essence isn't the same—as in daytime. And who's to say which is the Real street?'

'It's we who are different,' said Willie. 'And so we see another world.'

'I wonder? Do you think the other Searchers of the Soul will see what we see now?'

Willie laughed.

'Quaint persons, those,' he observed.

'Quaint? Horrible! They make me ill! Always making a pretence of wanting to know, talking of the powers of the spirit and all that—words they don't even know the fringe of. Want to know! I want to know—you want to know. We're in earnest. But they only want to gabble.'

'They used to disgust me at first,' answered Willie, 'because I had expected them to be genuine. Don't you understand? One's always hoping for companionship; it seems incredible that everyone should be blind. But now they rather amuse me. Most burlesque is built on the ashes of tragedy. I like to sit and listen, and wonder what would happen if one got up and told them the truth.'

'They would say that they couldn't accept it without investigation, and that the Vice-president's hypothesis was more in accordance with their spiritual intuitions.'

'Probably it is.'

'Oh,' said Stephen suddenly and violently, 'look! look at the wonder and the mystery of it all! The great stars and the darkness; and the strange, careless, cruel earth. It must be different really; more ordered, more sane. Will one ever find the thing itself?'

'Better not. You're happiest in the searching.'

'How can you tell? Think! somewhere, perhaps, there's an inconceivable glory, if only our eyes were clear.'

'Yes; but in searching for that you may find the horror.'

'The horror?'

'Yes: that comes first. It's not so difficult to find it. But the other—the real secret—is hidden, if it exists.'

Stephen looked at Willie rather oddly.

'Don't *you* begin to talk rot, Hopkinson,' he said. 'I've always felt that you were very different from those chattering fools we've just left. I believe you're as keen to find the truth as I am; but it's not to be done by telling each other fairy-tales.'

'Fairy-tales! Good heavens! A moment ago you knew yourself, for a minute, that all this funny dazzling bewildering world is nothing but a fairy-tale. What could be queerer than the things our senses show us? Things that simply don't exist in the forms under which we see them.'

'But do you know that?' said Stephen. 'If I knew that much, it would be something.'

'Something?' answered Willie—'something! It would be Hell! If only I didn't know! Ignorance is the real happiness, after all.'

He stopped. He was astonished at himself. He wished that he had not spoken with such picturesque force.

Stephen was looking at him through half-closed eyelids, with a strange, concentrated expression. His hand, it seemed, was on the latch; and he leaned forward, directing all his will towards the words which hovered between them.

Then Willie began to speak; quite slowly, in a curiously level voice. He had always known that he would tell Stephen the truth about his life: it seemed only fair to do so, where the knowledge would quiet a searching mind. But he did not specially desire the moment. Their superficial comradeship had not ceased to satisfy. Now some hand touched a spring that was not of his adjusting. He was impelled to candour.

He spoke about his life in the slums as he remembered it, and of his death in the hospital. His manner was rather matter-of-fact; not interesting. He described—this in a lower key, for it was still a present dread—the Grey World, and what he had endured whilst it held his spirit. His account was circumstantial, full of small detail; he spoke in the present tense. Stephen gradually realized that he was describing something which he saw, and which only his own imperfect vision prevented him also from seeing. He quietly demolished the hedgerows of conventional experience, and exposed the desolate uncharted country through which life runs, a faint and wavering path. But the subject, in his hands, seemed insusceptible of glamour. It was coldly real; as real as a dried flower, and as unimpressive.

Stephen, on his side, remained quite quiet. It seemed to him that
he was hearing a very ordinary tale; an addition, merely, to the
sordid aspects of life. It corresponded more or less with other
theories that he had heard of, and had dismissed for their sterile
quality, which did not please his active synthetic mind. He did not
realize the tremendous significance it possessed, as belonging to the
World of Fact, and not the World of Idea. Those solid pavements
on which they walked; the scuttling hansoms; the hoardings with
their insistent presentation of food, tobacco, and amusement as the
real interests of life; dulled his imagination, and he was not
conscious of the transformation of his universe which Willie's slow
sentences involved.

Mr. Willie Hopkinson felt disappointed. He was making the
great revelation of his life; chiefly, he thought, out of kindness to
Stephen; and he did not appear to have produced much effect. He
had hoped to see a friendly spirit start to life at the touch of
truth—to communicate some of the wonder and the fear, and find
a companion on the lonely road. But Stephen was impassive,
unexcited; he seemed to be brooding. To Willie, now, the
atmosphere was full of dreadfulness: by force of his own words he
was turned towards the dark, and had lost himself in the hateful
desert of infinity. He forgot the great blurring shadow which life
casts for the living. He was alone in space with Stephen, and
Stephen gave him no comfort. He saw no star. Friendship had
been a false beacon. The glow of narration died, fright came
instead; his story dwindled and ceased.

Then Stephen spoke.

'Is it true?' he said.

Willie only looked at him.

'You know,' continued Stephen in the same placid, even tones, 'I
don't want it to be true. It's too ugly. If it isn't true—if the other
country isn't here, at the back of appearance, as you say—I may
forget it, and go back to my beautiful lies. Of course they're silly
and deceptive, but each new one makes me hope I am going to find
the Real. If this is the Real—'

'It's my Real,' said Willie.

He spoke sulkily, but with decision. Stephen, by contrast,
seemed to falter. Now that the strain of listening was over, dim

ideas were beginning to surge up in his mind and constrict his utterance.

'You and I, as we look to each other now, aren't real,' continued Willie. 'All this city that you see isn't real; colour isn't real, or sound. There's only space and silence, really; and the living who have one dream, and the Dead who have another. What we call reality is only a sensation that we throw outside ourselves. Don't you see that? We each make our own universe—or let other people make it. But I've made myself a world in four dimensions, and that's why I can never rest in three.'

'It's wonderful!' said Stephen slowly. The thing had filtered into his consciousness at last. He fidgeted uneasily. 'And no one else has it! Just you! Why can't we all know, if know? If it's true, one ought to find it; but no one has.'

'I've thought sometimes,' said Willie, 'that perhaps I am the first of a new régime. A trial piece, you know; an experiment. It's about time something new was evolved from the race, isn't it? And isolated specimens aren't usual in nature. Which is lucky; it's not nice to be one. That mixture of fatigue and foolishness which the first man who stood upright must have felt, when he limped and stumbled amongst the four-footed things, is just what I feel now. That want of incentive for tree-climbing, weakness and lostness in forests made for creeping and leaping creatures, which he must have had—shame for his state mixed with secret knowledge of his new powers—all that is just a parable of my life, going with new perceptions amongst people who instinctively resent the light.'

'But *is* your world the True?' answered Stephen. 'It can't be. It must only be another illusion wrapped inside this one. This can't be all—can't be the end—this Grey Horror that you talk of. It's too mad, too evil, too unjust.'

'I have that feeling, too, sometimes,' said Willie. They had reached the inner core of his mind now, and he was impelled to confess it. 'I seem to know, then, that there is a better country hidden away for people who are not tied to the earth-side of dream. But I can't find it yet. The other is the beginning anyhow. Always here—always there—and for most, it's the end: I've proved that.'

Stephen shivered. He felt lonely without the pretty, iridescent dreams which he had woven for himself from varied psychic material. Willie's cloud-land descended as a fog, and choked him.

'Oh, but I will find a way back to beautiful thoughts!' he said.

*   *   *   *   *

He parted from Willie on the doorstep, and went into the house. Mr. and Mrs. Miller were dining out, and the drawing-room felt cold and lonely. Stephen went up to his own den, turned up the lights, tried to remember the words that Willie had said to him. But he could not think very clearly: the house was so horribly still.

Presently he found himself looking nervously about the room. In spite of the stillness, the air seemed full of inaudible sounds. He stood up, sent quick glances towards the door. He thought he would like to go downstairs again, and find companionship: he felt cold, breathless. Solitude ceased to be a fact, and became a dreadful person robed in chilly winds, who stood close to him. He had still sufficient self-control to wonder at himself, to ask his muddled brain the meaning of its frenzy; but it could not answer him. It referred him to a more cloistered inhabitant—to that Dweller in the Innermost whose calm vigil he seldom disturbed; for Stephen's activities were largely intellectual, though he loved to give them spiritual names.

It was, then, the tremor of his soul whose reflection he now felt in physical wretchedness. Whilst his reason doubted and argued, setting its teeth in the framework of Willie's vision, it had perceived. It had been roused by familiar accents, and now reminded him of the dark places in which he stood. It had pushed out suddenly into the transcendental world, dragging his weak consciousness in its wake. He could not hold it back.

Material life is only made possible by material faith: by a childlike acceptance of appearances. Stephen's belief in appearances had been rudely shaken. The texture of his world had become thin, unsubstantial: he thought that he could see through it the shadowy outline of another landscape. Old landmarks slipped from him. He grabbed suddenly and nervously at the nearest chair, longing for solidity; but his senses turned against him, and he could not assure himself that it was hard and durable to his touch. He was not even clear about the floor that he stood upon. The brightness of the electric light terrified him; it seemed to be veiling awful darks.

He had lost the sense of bodily existence, of visual reality. He was

'Far from the shore, far from the trembling throng
Whose sails are never to the tempest given'—

alone and immaterial in an illusory and immaterial world. No sound, no sight, no Real, between him and grey nothingness. He stood and shivered, choking with horror, and powerless to move, because he had lost the sense of space.

Suddenly he heard a distant cry, a rustling sound.

Then blind terror brought its own relief. He fainted.

CHAPTER 10

ROAD-MAKING

'Indentures and Apprenticeships for our irrational young; whereby, in due season, the vague Universality of a Man shall find himself ready-moulded into a specific Craftsman.'

—THOMAS CARLYLE

MRS. STEINMANN was giving a little dinner. It was at her own house: at restaurants, she said, one never knew what one was eating. Margarine, she felt sure, was used freely; whereas in her own kitchen she could rely on honest dripping and clarified fat.

Both dinner and conversation were solid, but easy of digestion. There were no insidious entrées in either department. This was a comfort to Mrs. Hopkinson, whose husband had lately suffered from dyspepsia, and still required diplomatic supervision at his meals. She had sent a note to her hostess in the morning, asking that he might be given toast instead of bread, and some weak whisky-and-soda in a champagne glass. Mr. Hopkinson, when he discovered these attentions, revenged himself on Fate by taking two helpings of fried potatoes, and avoided the supplicating glance which his wife directed towards him from the other side of the table. He was sitting next to Mrs. Alcock, who had developed with years a childish, appealing manner, which made her popular with the husbands of other women, and now impelled Mr. Hopkinson to give her carefully diluted information on several subjects with which she was already acquainted.

Elsa Levi, judiciously dressed for her mother's eye in a tight-fitting frock of modest ugliness, surveyed him from the opposite seat, and compared him—as she always did all suitable specimens —with her own husband. Mr. Hopkinson was of the military-commercial type; a thick moustache, square shoulders, an assertive shirt-front. He appeared to have been created to show off his own manufactures. Mr. Levi, whose sandy hairs fringed a bald pink dome, and who insisted on retaining the whiskers of his early youth, seemed to find evening-dress less *chic* but more comfortable. Elsa concluded that there was little to choose between them; Hermann ate his soup less noisily, but Mr. Hopkinson's complexion did not become shiny as the evening advanced. She balanced these advantages of sight and sound for a little while, but could come to no practical decision.

A sideway glance at Mrs. Hopkinson's uninspired profile set her wondering how Willie came to be mingled with this strangely unsuitable family. She had seen a good deal of him; and discovered that though he tended more towards weak amativeness than she considered desirable, he was capable of amusing, even of interesting her. His rather effusive gratitude made her feel unselfish, which was pleasant. She was naturally self-indulgent, and knew it; but she liked to foster the illusion of altruism. Also, the vacuous state of his mind in respect of fashionable culture gave scope for her ideals of education: and there was never any fear that he would think her ridiculous.

When the ladies returned to the drawing-room, she sat down near Mrs. Hopkinson and talked to her in a gentle, rather pathetic voice. It was her policy to make friends of the parents of her disciples.

'I love to be loved by the loved ones of those whom I love,' she had said one day.

'I am so interested in your boy,' she now observed. 'He is rather like you, is he not?'

'Well,' said Mrs. Hopkinson, 'I've always thought so, though it's never been noticed. My dear father, you know, had a vivid imagination; I've often heard mother say that he would wake up in the middle of the night screaming with terror—though he always dined early, and never took meat at supper, only savoury eggs, or fish cakes or something light like that—and I dare say that's where Willie gets it from.'

'No doubt,' said Elsa. 'Heredity is *so* wonderful, isn't it? But your son, I think, has great gifts. With a little training in the right direction, he ought to do well.'

Mrs. Hopkinson was pleased. One may think one's own duckling ugly and ill-tempered, but it is not disagreeable to hear other people call it a swan.

'Mr. Hopkinson thinks,' she answered, 'that Willie might start at the Factory at the beginning of the year. He's had a long holiday, and is quite strong now; and training is just what he will get there, being kept constantly under a father's eye.'

'I fancy, do you know?' said Elsa, 'from little things he has let drop now and again—not that I should think of encouraging him in any ideas of that kind—that business does not attract him altogether. It seems a pity, doesn't it?'

'Oh, Willie's full of high-flown fancies,' replied Mrs. Hopkinson. 'He has got into rather idle ways, I'm afraid, these last few months; always staring at pictures and mooning over books. You see, he's clever. But his health has got thoroughly established, which is the main thing, and now he must begin to learn what life really is.'

'Ah! which of us knows that, dear Mrs. Hopkinson?' answered Elsa softly. 'And do you think Willie is likely to find the solution in Bermondsey?'

'And then, by the time he's ready to marry and settle down,' continued Mrs. Hopkinson, busy with her own idea, 'he can be taken into partnership.'

'And that is to be his future?'

'Yes: such a comfort, isn't it, to feel that he's so well provided for? It's getting quite difficult to find any opening for boys. If only he takes to the business! But he's easily unsettled. That young Stephen Miller, I'm afraid, does him no good.'

'Stephen Miller?' said Mr. Hopkinson, who, being bored by Mrs. Alcock's mechanically receptive manner, had arrived in the hope of detaching Elsa from his wife's neighbourhood and demonstrating to her that the art of flirtation was not confined to aesthetes. 'An idle, loafing sort of lad. He often comes in of an evening; eyes Pauline and talks gibberish to Willie. I sometimes wish him further. But they're well connected people, the Millers. Miller's Sapoline, you know—a very old-established firm.'

Elsa did not know much of Stephen, but such details as she had heard from Willie did not please her. Spiritualism was out of date; besides, he was a possible rival, and she hated strangers in her own line of business.

'I'm afraid he's rather a foolish youth,' she said.

'Glad you agree with me,' replied Mr. Hopkinson. She had only done her duty, but he liked to be kind to women.

He sat down by her on the sofa, and intimated that he was willing to converse. He thought her a fool, she called him an animal; but they were not too narrow-minded to find amusement in each other's deficiencies. She had a small waist—a thing he seldom saw at home—and her husband's financial position lent a golden glow even to her most irritating follies. Mr. Hopkinson's claim to tolerance was, perhaps, less obvious; but he was a man as well as a materialist, his eye was appreciative. Amongst Mrs. Steinmann's commercially solid and mentally woolly friends, he shone as the least polished tin will do when surrounded by duller metals.

They warmed to one another perceptibly.

'So you are going to put Willie in the business?' said Elsa. She was really good-natured, and wished to deliver the boy from the dragon which awaited him; seeing herself in the position of a strong-minded princess, coming to the rescue of some helpless and neurotic S. George. 'It seems difficult to believe that he is old enough!'

She looked at Mr. Hopkinson—a look which suggested both incredulity and admiration, and pleased him.

'Why, goodness, yes!' said he. 'The boy's close on twenty—a year younger than your Geraint, if I remember right. You mustn't judge age by your own appearance, Mrs. Levi.'

Elsa sighed.

'I'm getting an old woman,' she answered, 'and beginning to take an old woman's interest in young people.'

Mr. Hopkinson gave a laugh composed of polite scepticism and quite honest embarrassment. He began to perceive that the conversation had some more serious aim than after-dinner dalliance; and he distrusted and disliked Elsa's serious edges.

'How's your second boy getting on in Paris?' he said.

'Tristram?' said Elsa. 'He is perfectly happy. The life of an art-student, I think, is an ideal one for a young man. Technique and aspiration hand in hand. I feel that he is learning to love familiar beauties.'

'Very probably,' replied Mr. Hopkinson. He had some knowledge of underground Paris.

'It seems so sad,' continued Elsa, 'so unjust, does it not? that all who feel the spell of loveliness should not be able to tread the higher paths. Now your Willie—'

'Willie's path leads to the Factory,' said Mr. Hopkinson, 'and I hope the influence of environment will soon knock the nonsense out of him, when he gets there.'

'It may do, of course. A young soul is so easily blunted by contact with earth—' She slid a little farther back on the sofa: its pink and grey damask covering gave sharp contrast to the lines of her figure, and she knew that Mr. Hopkinson was secretly enjoying her pose. 'But I don't think he will ever be a successful business man,' she added.

'Don't you indeed?' said Willie's father, without demonstration of astonishment.

He had no illusions about his son, and looked forward with mixed feelings to the prospect of Willie's daily presence in his office. A long experience had taught him the signs which distinguish an efficient clerk from a useless one.

'No,' said Elsa. 'And all his faculties; those which make him so different from the ordinary young man of his class—how wasted they will be, will they not? His imagination, for instance.'

'Not at all,' replied Mr. Hopkinson. 'He can design the new models. There's a great deal to be done in that way; and more to be made out of it than most of these artists make out of their pictures, I can tell you. Something the public wears, and something it wears out—that's the thing to make money by. Now, pictures must always be a fancy article, and jolly lasting too: some of these Old Masters, I understand, have been going for hundreds of years, and are still quite fresh. But clothes—we must have 'em; and as long as men are born naked, there'll be a living to be made out of trousers and coats.'

'I do not think,' answered Elsa, 'that Willie will make it. He does not seem to have inherited your talent for practical matters.'

'Well, there it is,' said Mr. Hopkinson, modestly evading the compliment. 'The place is ready-made for him, and what can we do but put him in it?'

'I think,' replied Mrs. Levi, 'that he has rather a fancy for one of the artistic trades.'

She had, which came to the same thing. Tea and twilight would secure Willie's acquiescence. But Mr. Hopkinson looked at her with surprise and some resentment.

'What! retail?' he said.

'Oh, no!' explained Elsa hurriedly. 'I don't mean that at all. I ought to have said handicraft, not trade.'

'Thought you meant Art Furnishing.'

'No, bookbinding, you know, or jewellery, or metal-work —something of that kind. The creation of really beautiful things, as the medieval craftsmen used to do. That's so very delightful; and all the most cultivated people are taking to it. It's paying, too, I believe. They get enormous prices for these things.'

'Do they indeed?' said Mr. Hopkinson. He seemed more interested.

'Yes. I know several girls who have gone in for enamelling and bookbinding and so on—'

'Oh, girls! That's very different.' He employed female labour, and did not wish to see its value in the market increase.

'Not really,' answered Elsa. 'And Willie is just a little effeminate, is he not? And surely, what a woman can do well, a man is sure to do better?'

She smiled at Mr. Hopkinson. He temporarily forgot that she was only an ingenious compound of molecules, and owed her sinuous charms to Pre-Glacial ancestors.

'You have interested me very much,' he said kindly. 'I shall think of what you have been saying. Of course, I saw long ago that Willie would never make a smart man of business.'

'I'm sure he'd fail at it,' answered Elsa. 'And that would be such a pity.'

'Oh, we'll hope he wouldn't quite come to that,' said Mr. Hopkinson. 'I'm proud to think that so far no member of my family has ever had to file his petition. There's plenty of capital to fall back on.'

He bade Elsa good-night with elephantine gallantry; and on the way home, having lowered both windows of the four-wheeler for fear of infection, he gave his shivering wife a summary of their conversation. From this she easily gathered that such original features as it possessed had been entirely of his creation.

CHAPTER 11

A BREEZY UPLAND

'All kinds of skill are gifts of the Holy Ghost.'

—TAULER

IT is a disability of the hurried children of Time that—make as they may an illusion of the hours—the boundary of each moment is for them firmly set. The Angels, whose day is timeless, do not feel this. Theirs is the delicious leisure of eternity, and that is why they sometimes judge our omissions rather harshly. They cannot understand that time given to the outer, is taken from the inner life; that to earn one's living it is often necessary to pauperize one's soul. They would laugh were they told that in modern life, no hour has been left for revery: that it has been given, perhaps, to physical culture, or chip-carving, or local politics. Rational religion, the Broad Church, and other expressions of our spiritual state, do not claim rights for meditation. It is hustled out of sight to make room for more useful hobbies, and the eye of the soul becomes dim in consequence. So the spirit is drowned in the luxuries that the restless brain and dominant body have earned it, as the Duke of Clarence in the butt of Malmsey wine.

These matters occurred vaguely to Mr. Willie Hopkinson during the ensuing days, when his future career came to the family bar and was kept waiting for judgment. They suggested to him reasons why the wholesale tailoring trade should not be allowed to swallow up his existence. As opinion leant towards a career which would bind all his hours to the City, he felt the Grey World grow more immediate. Fifty years of moderate affluence would ill prepare him for the eternal penury of that dimension. He longed to say, 'These careers that you speak of are all *Maya*, illusion. The necessity is that my body shall be placed in surroundings which will help, and not stunt, the soul, which is real.'

He could not think Bermondsey consistent with the transcendental life. There would be no intervals for readjustment. It seemed impossible that its enervating atmosphere could do other than weaken his grip of the Unseen. He would fall back into the power of the crowded country—a citizenship both he and Stephen Miller had sworn to escape.

He had lived nearly twenty years in the knowledge of a dreary and apparently inevitable Hell, yet had taken no valid step toward his own salvation. Once immersed in a business life, hope would be over; he would be held for ever in the general stream.

Considerations of this kind, though unintelligible to the rest of the family, were to him a great means of resistance. The fear of material illusion which they induced strengthened him for the struggle which Mrs. Levi had ingeniously set on foot. So it was that after hours of stagnant opposition, when parental authority met youthful determination in drawn battle; after long chilly days of silent disapproval on one hand and stubborn indifference on the other; after scornful counsel from his father, and the tearful administration of Bovril and good advice by his mother, his first conflict with the powers of the earth was won.

It was decided that he was not to follow the wholesale tailoring trade. Elsa's secret encouragements, his own detestation of commerce, a carefully fostered idea that the professions vaguely known as Arts and Crafts approach the higher life, had armed him for a triumphant charge against prejudice and family inertia. Hopkinson, Vowles and Co. would look elsewhere for their junior partner. It even seemed possible that Mr. Geraint Levi might one day occupy that position. Elsa thought that the exchange would be excellent, and her opinion was, for the moment, in power.

But matters went less smoothly when she was not present. Tradition is not upset in a moment, and Mr. Hopkinson had fierce reversions to his original point of view. The sacrifice of prospects was what struck him most. Willie would never earn more than a bare competence, he expected, at bookbinding—the craft he had chosen—whilst the Factory was always good for a solid two or three thousand a year. But the boy, who had no ambition towards clothing his fellow-beings, adored books for a permanence of thought which they possessed; and extended his love of literature with odd inconsequence to the leather which dressed it:—as young and ardent lovers will sometimes confuse chiffons and soul. As to the money, it did not trouble him. Having scarcely in all his life wished to buy anything, he did not understand the pleasure or importance of wealth. Few of the things that he loved were offered for sale in earthly markets; for the stuff that dreams are made of is not sold by the yard.

It was Elsa, proud of her triumph but fearful of a sudden sally from the enemy, who found the bindery where he should begin his career. She persuaded Mr. Hopkinson to pay the fees for a twelve months' training in advance, representing this course in its economical aspect. Mrs. Hopkinson—whose meek comments were now seldom audible by her husband—thought that she perceived a certain rashness in the proceeding. If the work did not suit Willie's health, or he caught cold going to and fro in the winter, it would be very awkward. But knowing that women always make mistakes when they speak of business matters to their husbands, she went to bed for two days with a headache, and said nothing.

An artist of the newest school, whose output included pictures, altar-plate, and bedroom furniture, had told Mrs. Levi that the work of the bindery was beautiful and individual; and was patronized by several wealthy book-collectors, who paid—with a cheerfulness unknown in husbands—high prices for the luxurious dresses of their pets.

It was situated at Turner's Heath; that new, well-named, artistic suburb of the north-west. It did not call itself a bindery; that would have been too obvious. Reticence is the note of the artistic crafts. Above the doorway, a sign swung on wrought-iron hinges. It bore two pierced hearts, and said, in Kelmscott-Gothic characters, 'Atte ye Signe of ye Presse and Ploughe.' Underneath, in case the public might not understand this cryptic phrase, there was added in English type the information, 'Books bound Artistically and Inexpensively.' On each side of the entrance a strip of tired grass was kept within bounds by primitive oak palings. Within, a vestibule, whose grey canvas walls were relieved by pleasant but ordinary Japanese prints, led to the workshop. This long, well-lit building of galvanized iron was sharply corrective of the feeble aestheticism of the front door. Benches and presses were its furniture; but at one end a 'show-case' held specimens of the best work the bindery had yet turned out. On the walls, racks of tools, shelves piled with folded leather, designs for future work, studies of plants, of lettering, of curves and scrolls, gave a strangely combined impression of industry and 'artiness.' The floor was not clean; but numerous snippings of paper, leather, and cloth, took the edge off its griminess.

Willie made his first entrance to the workshop to the cheerful sound of many hammers. Mr. Tiddy, the superintendent, was trying to teach his two apprentices, Miss Brent and Miss Vivien, to 'back' a book. From the other end of the room an elderly workman glanced at them occasionally, in the intervals of removing superfluous glue from the backs of a pressful of books. He seemed to be amused, but not pleased. His name was Carter; and he was the real instructor and mainstay of the bindery, though this position officially belonged to Mr. Tiddy.

Mr. Tiddy was short and dark: his razor was scarcely efficient. A complexion like that of an Old Master before it has been restored was not enhanced by the collarless shirts of coarse blue linen which the example of more celebrated craftsmen compelled him to wear. Yet such is the power of sex, that in spite of these disabilities the girl apprentices were obviously pleased should he happen to speak a word to them in passing, and were incapable of looking unconscious when he leaned over them to criticise their work. He and Mr. Carter, neither of them gifted with a talent for conciliation or an appreciation of tact, often created for themselves situations of some difficulty; which alarmed, when they did not amuse, the apprentices. But the position of each depending to some extent on the approbation of the other, they relapsed, after abortive explosions of mutual contempt, into a condition of armed neutrality.

Willie, arriving for his first lesson, stood in the midst of the workshop uncertain what to do. He was nervous, confused, slightly disappointed. He perceived much noise and muddle, but few signs of that higher life which Mrs. Levi had led him to expect. There was tension in the atmosphere, and no one noticed him. He looked at the girls and their teacher. The book upon which Mr. Tiddy was operating slipped several times during his attempt to put it in the press, and he became annoyed. He gave the unhappy volume a vicious blow with the hammer. Old Carter at the other press was watching him carefully.

'That'll *do*, Mr. Tiddy,' he said presently. 'Remember it's a book you're 'itting.'

There was a silent interval, but Carter was a power in the bindery. Tiddy removed his book from the laying-press, and carried it away. Carter cast a look of disgust after him.

'Mr. Tiddy is a gentleman and all that,' he observed to the shop in general, and the two girls in particular, 'but he don't know much about backin'. I've bin learning how to back books for forty year, and I haven't finished yet. But Mr. Tiddy, he took a six-months' course, and now he starts on at the teachin'. When I was a lad,' continued Mr. Carter slowly, ''twas seven years' apprenticeship, and learnin' all your life. I don't like to see you young gents and ladies as come 'ere, hurryin' and scurryin' and hurtin' of the books like you does.'

He fitted a fresh knife to his plough, and turned silently back towards the cutting-press.

Willie was early drawn to Mr. Carter, whose illusions seemed to him less noisome than those of the persons amongst whom he had been reared. A dwindling memory of the time when he also was a child of labour helped him to understand the limitations of his class, and placed him easily on the footing of friendship.

This was the first happy and honest workman whom he had met—the first who extracted the soul of labour from its outer shell by his attitude of steady reverence towards his craft. The relation of a City man to his ledger, of a factory hand to his machine, is not lovely: but there was a sincere and beautiful connection between Carter and his work. With him it was a manual religion, faithfully followed without any sordid thought. He felt slovenly work to be a sin towards his material, as well as towards the master who paid him. He hated the showily-finished bindings of cheap polished leather and facile tooling which visitors to the bindery thought so very artistic.

'Fancy stationers' stuff,' he said contemptuously.

Carter liked Willie Hopkinson because he worked without excitement and did not hurry. He waited quietly whilst glue dried, and did not spoil a promising piece of work by a sudden hour of impatience. Possessing the deliberation of the idealist who looks to process not to completion for his pleasure, and knows reality to consist in anything rather than material results, he found each stage of the work as important as its end. The girls were always straining towards the finishing-point, incurring Mr. Carter's wrath by their indifference to the more solid portions of the craft'; and Mr. Tiddy only ceased to be languid when construction gave place to ornament. But Willie saw a symbolism even in the paste-pot, and Carter began to hope that he would train one master-binder before he died.

They conversed much together in the intervals of work, and the reaction of homely intuition on convinced idealism made them mutually interesting. Willie would describe books that he had read, and quote bits that pleased him, receiving earnest and unexpected criticisms in exchange.

'I read somewhere the other day,' he said one morning, as he worked by Carter's side at the finishing-bench, 'a bit that would make a nice motto for a bindery. It was this—"We are each of us a book in ourselves, but we only see the bindings of each other." Rather true, isn't it?'

"'Tis,' replied Carter sententiously, 'but it's not always the best readin' that's put up in polished levant, Mr. Hopkinson.' He moistened his finger, tested the heat of his tool, and continued: 'I've known the works of Samuel Smiles, or the "Pilgrim's Progress," or fine writings such as that, brought in 'ere, and all that's asked for is half-roan sprinkled edges. And then people comes and orders inlay and best tooling and all, for books of poetry as to my mind it's barely decent to leave lyin' on the table.'

'Yes, I suppose that is so,' answered Willie doubtfully. He had begun to feel the technical obsession which weighs so heavily on craftsmanship, and found it difficult to believe that any book could be more important than its binding. Minor poetry, printed on Japanese vellum and morocco bound, seemed to him as desirable as pocket classics in plain cloth.

'Of course that's so,' said Carter. 'Insides and outsides all to match—that 'ud be one of God Almighty's own bindings; and even He don't often manage it. Take care with your toolin', Mr. Hopkinson. You haven't done that last line very nice.'

Willie rubbed the superfluous gold-leaf from his book-cover, and looked with blind pride at the rather uncertain pattern of hearts and lilies which he had impressed upon it.

'It's effective,' he said.

'But 'taint effect you're 'ere for, Mr. Hopkinson,' answered Carter. 'It's good toolin'. And that work's not solid. Look at them corners: you haven't mitred them neat. You don't want to do your fmishin' shop-window style; you wants to do it so as it looks right when it's held in the 'and after it's bought.'

'Oh, I can't do it over again!' said Willie.

'Then you ain't no workman, Mr. Hopkinson,' answered Carter.

In spite, or perhaps because, of this tonic discipline, Willie found his daily life so happy that he was not often tempted to impatience or haste. He wished to savour each moment of his day, and felt sad when the time came for leaving the quiet bindery, and going out into the windy world. There was a flavour of past ages about the workshop; and the tram which took him home, took him also into another and less peaceful century. He learnt here for the first time in his life the meaning of his hands, and discovered their use. They gave his soul a new and inexplicable pleasure. Regular manual occupation steadied him, drawing off his earth energies and leaving his spirit clearer.

As he sat at the sewing-press, or mechanically pared the edges of leather for the covers of his books, he meditated. Busy hands and dreaming soul balanced one another, and he felt sane, alive, untrammelled. Though the future was still blank to him and the outer world an unsubstantial chaos, he caught the fringes of a larger hope. The symbolic rightness of quiet work justified to him the existence of his body, and sometimes allowed him a glimpse of the gateway which leads to the Heaven of the Industrious.

Behind labour, he felt, there was Something—a spirit or power which blessed. The misty disease of unreality and confusing presence of the Grey Dimension, never attacked him when he had a tool in his hand. That forced him to singleness of outlook. And persons who did their work lovingly and honestly, for rightness, not for profit, might hope for a happier eternity, he fancied, than the earth-bound populations of the Sorrowful Country whose presence still shadowed his daily life. He told some of these thoughts, but not all, to Elsa, who approved them.

'He has quite the Medieval tone of mind,' she said.

But Miss Mildred Brent and Miss Janet Vivien, the apprentices, who had felt the arrival of a young man in the bindery to be a possibly significant incident in their lives, were disappointed. They perceived with acid astonishment that he saw them as Persons, not as Girls; and decided that he was very odd.

CHAPTER 12

MAPS ARE CONSULTED

'Then the Divine Vision like a silent Sun appear'd above
Albion's dark rocks: setting behind the Gardens of Kensington
On Tyburn's River.'

—BLAKE

THE grief of knowledge is the gain of sympathy. From the moment when Stephen shared Willie's vision, a link, stronger than that of friendship, was forged. Each now held by the other for support, and found the immaterial world which bathed existence less awful for the presence of his friend. To each, the other was a rest and a point of reference in the difficulties of his conflict with experience and with fact.

There came a day, however, when divergent ideals strained this invisible fetter, and each of its prisoners drew away from the other as far as he might. There was surprise on both hands, and some sadness, but temperament the bond-breaker had its way. It was impossible that the ethereal roads on which Willie was destined to travel should suffice for Stephen's more human and adventurous tread.

There is a path in Kensington Gardens which, running north and south, is good to walk along at sunset-time. Its western boundary shows trees and sky in nice proportion, and a glint of water to the right. On a seat arranged for the enjoyment of this landscape Mr. Willie Hopkinson and Mr. Stephen Miller were sitting about four o'clock of a November afternoon. There were few people about. It was still too light for lovers, and most of the babies had gone home to tea.

There had already been a change in their relation. Since Willie entered the bindery, he had become more patient, less assertive towards existence. But Stephen, his eyes once opened upon the uncharted country, could not think of it peacefully. Willie, learning slowly—almost unconsciously—to treat his work as a sacrament which bore some mystic relation to truth, lost the constant itch to step from his path, and hunt for solutions to the Great

Conundrum. He had an inner content, equally removed from piety and despair, which anaesthetized his spirit.

Stephen had recently been placed in the office of an architect, whose terra-cotta palaces, majolica facades, and miracles of plate glass and iron girders, had done something toward the introduction of humour to the City streets. He found little nourishment for his imagination in the details of plan, measurement, and material, there placed before him. Thus he turned naturally and vehemently from the atmosphere of the drawing office to that of the transcendental world—searching, with a fever that was the index of his helplessness, for some clue to the tangle, and some escape from the dread, to which Willie had introduced him. Each time they met he had some new theory to offer; but Willie, braced by the tonic society of Mr. Carter, often gave him an attention more repressive than enthusiastic.

Sitting now in Kensington Gardens, feeling very near him the delicious contours of the trees and sorcery of the sky, he listened rather languidly to Stephen's talk. He felt dreamy, disinclined to occult discussion. He began to discover that a disciple can be very boring. Mr. Stephen Miller had been thinking hard, he said, about Appearance as distinguished from Reality. His black hour had passed; he was in a cheerfully credulous mood, treating the shadow-side of the universe as a fluid medium in which he could swim and splash at will. He hinted at results which might interest Mr. Willie Hopkinson.

Willie was not pleased. It seemed to him inappropriate that Stephen, groping in the dark and only aware of the darkness through his friend's magnanimity, should take upon himself the propounding of theories and hopeful exploration of the Unknown. He was unique—a consoling fact. He did not desire a partner. He was very willing to save Stephen, should a way of salvation ever appear to him; but he found his behaviour in working his own way towards the light ungracious and objectionable. It constituted a failure in the duties of comradeship. Friendship had done nothing to disturb his cold, deliberate egoism. He liked his friend; he liked more the sense of power which affection gives to its object. His flattering intercourse with Mrs. Levi did not offer this. But Stephen cared more for him than he for Stephen—a desperate condition.

The spirit of Mr. Stephen Miller was exalted. He fidgeted; his eyes flashed; his phrases, though meaningless, possessed a Celtic glamour. Willie, to whom work and his own personality now appeared as two fixed lights in the midst of a shifting illusion, was irritated by this contradictory optimism. He judged it, as he judged everything he disagreed with, to be materialistic. He suggested to Stephen, in crisp sentences devoid of charm, his own industrial standpoint.

'Work,' he said, 'is the thing. Any kind of work, so long as you do it thoroughly. Nothing else gives the same satisfied feeling. Only, of course, one must not forget that work is only part of one's dream.'

'But,' said Stephen, 'there must be something that isn't only part of the dream—that is a persistent element right through the real and the illusion. Learn to know that, and you will learn the secret of existence.'

'How is one to learn it?' answered Willie. He was cross, but he could never resist an argument. 'To learn anything that really matters seems impossible; everyone is so busy teaching games. But one can learn to work, and that has a meaning, however useless the material work may seem in itself. Sometimes I know there is something behind—a world far more lovely, which saves from the colourless place. But we have not got the key.'

'We have,' said Stephen, 'and I have found it.'

Willie was excessively surprised.

'What is it?' he asked rather brusquely.

He was not prepared for Stephen's reply.

'It is love.'

'Rubbish!'

'Oh, I don't expect you to believe me,' answered Stephen. He appeared confused, though his tone was dogmatic. 'But I have found it out lately, and I know it's the truth. Someone has shown me—but I needn't go into that. When you know what love is, you will have found out everything you want to know. It is beautiful, which is enough for me; but it is more than that. It is the only thing that lights up the Real behind the dream. Oh, Willie, that will save you from the horror of the afterwards. It is the people who have never known love who cannot escape the Grey World. They are held there hunting for the best part of themselves.'

'That,' said Willie, 'is nonsense. Life means more than getting fond of a girl.'

'So does love.'

'Oh!'

'It does. It means everything. One finds one's soul in a woman. I have found mine, so I am sure. That is what we are here for—to find ourselves in loving one another. Those who don't, are lost.'

Willie was filled with a helpless disgust. The contempt which the passionless person feels for love is of an acrid kind. To him, it appeared a sickly and unpleasant thing: he did not know that it existed apart from kisses and engagements. In the Hopkinson family it was not referred to in a manner which left room for reverence. Elsa avoided the subject; prudence was born in her when she approached the frontier of genuine feeling, and thanks to her tact he had never analyzed the vague sensations which moved him when he touched her hand or came unexpectedly into her presence.

It followed that to make Love the pivot of the Universe was a monstrous and revolting proposition. Stephen had said, when truth first laid siege to his dreamland, 'I will find a way back to beautiful thoughts!' This utterance had remained with Mr. Willie Hopkinson, and inspired a happy vision in which he and Stephen won their way by transcendental paths to the high cold splendour of some Ineffable Reality. But it seemed that a Lover's Lane was the path Stephen had chosen; and Willie, astonished and disappointed, declined to believe that it led to the top of the hill.

Stephen, meanwhile, was speaking sketchily of the miracle which he believed to have occurred to him. It was not a common love affair: it was a spiritual experience peculiar to himself. He was certain of that. The greater part of the ecstasy seemed to have taken place in his own heart, without other incentive than that supplied by his busy imagination. But it was none the less life-enhancing.

'Even to know her,' he said, 'is enough. I don't ask more than that.'

There is a Maeterlinckian flavour which steals over Kensington
Gardens as the sun goes down—a sense of secrets hidden in the
trees. The white walks become magic pathways which converge on
the Ivory Gate; the Round Pond a haunted pool, where Melisande
might lose her crown. As Stephen spoke, therefore, Willie looked
at the dreamy scene before him; and his mind being occupied with
what he was hearing, it did not intrude itself on the simple vision of
his eyes. He saw the row of trees which were near him, very black
to the last filmy twig stretched out from the earth. They were
exquisite in their delicate strength. And in the sky behind—the
shining, mystic sky of autumn after rain—a faint pink cloud, just
visible, threw one tree into fresh tone-relations with the rest. On
the horizon, distant trees were blue. Behind all, that sky, strangely
transparent—like a face whose apparent candour veils an
unfathomable soul.

The magic of this vision removed him many worlds from
Stephen's sentimental commentary on life, and led him to think
dreamily and luxuriously of the Beautiful. He thought of the pro-
ducts of the bindery, praised with strange adjectives by Mr. Tiddy
and appreciative visitors; of the performances of other craftsmen
which he had been bidden to admire—angular furniture set with
strange ornament, clumsy metal-work, deliberately barbaric jewels.
The effortless masterpiece of nature now before him revealed these
things as ugly and unskilful. All the nobility they possessed came
from the industry which created them; the hours spent without
impatience on the slow journey towards a craftsman's ideal.

'The Grey World,' he said abruptly, 'is the Purgatory of the
inefficient.'

'Oh yes, that's just what I meant,' replied Stephen happily. 'And
it is love that helps us to climb and struggle and perfect ourselves.'

This was not at all what Willie had meant. But he perceived that
argument was useless, and waited with a patience born of the sunset
whilst Stephen extracted, with some diffidence, a messy manuscript
from his coat-pocket.

'I have written a little thing about it,' he said.

Willie knew that his friend practised literature in secret, having
sometimes helped to buy stamps for the return postage of his

ineligible efforts—a matter of several pounds in the course of the year.

'Where are you going to send it?' he asked, as he noticed the action, and the extreme slimness of the work produced.

'This is not for publication. I have written it for a friend, and because I think it is true. One should write down a bit of truth when one finds it; it helps one to remember. But I don't care to pour out my soul on paper for a lot of idle women to flick over between a muffin and a yawn.'

He was pleased with this sentence, and looked toward his friend for appreciation. But Willie was again entranced by the sky. It was fading to dim silver and transparent grey, making him feel melancholy and very quiet. Allegories of his own vivid ideal of life, which time was changing to greyer tints, occurred to him. He enjoyed the sadness of these sensations, taking them to be the hallmark of a superior soul.

He suddenly woke from his revery to find that Stephen had commenced the reading of his story. The opening paragraphs had already gone by, and he took up the thread in the midst of a sentence.

' " . . . So Pan left the happy nymphs and the little dancing fauns; and he sat down alone by the waters of Lethe, and took some red earth from the river-brink to play with. And whilst he played the clay began to take shape beneath his fingers, until at last a rough red image lay in his hands.

' "Then Pan took his pipes and blew on them softly, and the image moved and stood upright on its feet.

' " 'See!' he cried, 'I have made a man.'

' "But his Master looked down from the mountain and said:

' " 'Nay, friend, not so fast. More than red clay and wild music go to the making of Man.' And his breath, coming gently over the river, fell on the figure, which opened its mouth and spoke.

' " 'This is a fine toy we have made,' said Pan.

' " 'It must be made better yet,' his Master replied.

' "Pan was annoyed: he had been proud of his skill.

' " 'It is good enough,' he said. 'I can carve it no finer, for I have no tools. Also, the clay is fragile, and easily crumbles away.'

'"But the Master answered: 'It needs no tools; from the weakness of the earth and the virtue of my breath shall come its beauty. A day of toil and a night of rest, and Man will be perfected.'

'"Then he set the image on a very dreary hillside, and he marked a rough path before its feet; and Pan and his Master sat down to watch their toy. Some time they watched him, but he did not move—he stood on the hill where the Master had placed him, a helpless figure of inanimate earth.

'"'We must urge him on,' said Pan; and he took up his pipes again. The air he played was fierce and plaintive, and at its sound the Man started forward, savage eagerness and cunning on his face. Pan laughed as he laid down the pipes.

'"'It is a mighty march,' he said. 'I do not know a better! Hunger is the tune that moves the world!'

'"Searching for food, and struggling with the beasts whom he hunted, the Man moved upwards slowly; for his limbs were feeble and his eyesight dim. He stumbled very pitifully on the stony road, and often missed his way.

'"'Poor wretch!' cried Pan; 'he cannot see. We must give him better eyes.'

'"But the Master said: 'No: if he saw what was before him he would have no courage to climb. Truth is for the gods alone.'

'"So Pan refrained, and the toy was left in his blindness. But presently dark clouds came up from the mountains and hid the sun, and a bitter wind blew across the river and made sad sounds amongst the rocks. Then heavy shadows fell on the pilgrim's path, his steps flagged, his energy diminished; and at last he bowed his head in complete despair.

'"'We have tried him too hard,' said the Master. 'He is only red clay after all: he needs to be companioned on his way.'

'"His hand caressed the rock which edged the pathway; and suddenly a figure of mist and sunlight stood by the lonely traveller, and shed a radiance on the darkened road. But Pan, who cannot love an ethereal essence, viewed the newcomer with great disdain.

'"'What use is a creature like that?' he growled. 'He cannot hew wood or hunt game. At most he will only draw foolish pictures, or tell lying tales.'

' " 'What of that, if he make the hills seem shorter?' said the Master. 'It is more than you could ever do.'

' "So Art was born.

' "Now the Man stepped out more bravely, and always his comrade was by his side to whisper sweet stories, and point out new beauties in sky or earth; so that his search for food grew languid, the pleasures of Art absorbed him more and more, and he lost the strength of body born of his arduous life.

' " 'Aha!' cried Pan, 'you have spoilt your toy; he grows soft and idle. We must find him a better friend than this dreamy fellow—a mate, for whom he will work.' And taking red earth, he made another image, smaller and softer than the first, and placed it at Man's side. But he looked without joy at the Woman thus committed to his care, and heeded her not.

' "Then the Master said: 'Oh, Pan, thou foolish god! will earth strive for earth, or clay suffer for clay?' and he turned the brightness of his face toward the Man and Woman, so that they shrank back, dazed and awed. But they saw each other, in that bewildering moment, illuminated by the light of Love.

' "So side by side they started up the path, falling amongst stones, in the sun and the rain, each helping the other and working for the common good. And presently, as they climbed, evening fell, and the summit was nearly reached.

' " 'Courage, dear heart!' the Man whispered, as he bore the Woman up the last steep slope. 'Night comes, we shall sleep!'

' " 'It has been a long day,' said Pan, 'and the clay wore well. The hardships of the way have even improved its form. What reward shall we give our toys after all their toil?'

' "But his only answer was the sigh of the night-wind, as it cried upon the hills—

' " 'Oblivion!' " '

Stephen folded the manuscript with elaborate carelessness, and stuffed it untidily into the outside pocket of his overcoat. Then he waited; rather proud and very expectant.

'It's a bit high-flown,' said Mr. Willie Hopkinson.

Stephen blushed, but did not answer.

'Rather pretty, though,' added Willie. He had been, to his surprise and annoyance, uncomfortably touched by the concluding phrases. It was no part of his programme to permit himself to be weighted by these earthy emotions.

'Pauline thought it beautiful!' said Stephen.

But Willie did not hear him. The spell of narrative was broken, the cold magic of the sky had called him back, and he missed the astounding information which Stephen's last words conveyed.

CHAPTER 13

MR. WILLIE HOPKINSON TRIES A SHORT CUT

'A friend is a person with whom I may be sincere.'

—EMERSON

THE things which are called little are oftenest those which put persons in the disposition to act. They spur the emotions gently but sufficiently: the great event presses too heavily upon the soul, and results in inertia.

The story of Pan and his Master left an impression on Willie's mind. Like most boys who possess sisters and lead a sequestered life, he did not tend easily towards love. Pauline, who had provided Stephen's inspiration, was to him no more significant than the other furnishings of his home. But a natural ear for literature had been struck by the note of sad sincerity in the conclusion of Stephen's clumsy parable, and now inclined him to look upon girls in a manner strange to him, if normal to mankind. It seemed to him that work, in its spiritual aspect, might gain an added value, were it linked with a friendship more equable than the fevered service which he offered Elsa, more romantic than the affection he now felt for his fellow-traveller Stephen. He had no thought of marriage, only of an idyllic comradeship. Matrimony, he supposed, was a purely utilitarian measure.

These ideas crystallized in his consciousness as he strolled one morning from the tram to the bindery, and perceived Mildred Brent, the less significant of the lady apprentices, walking before him.

She was a small, neat, mouse-like person; and, by the fact of her unsuggestive face, seemed the living negation of her own temperament. Hair turned smoothly back from a forehead of ordinary mould, brown eyes of a certain intelligence carefully veiled, ready-made clothes and a London accent—these tell no tales. But a fire and a coldness lived side by side in her heart: a fire for the future, a coldness for the present. She hated grey walls and monotony, and the mingled art and commerce of the bindery. She longed to escape to those higher circles of handicraft which are celebrated in the art magazines. Yet a sense of humour, running on disastrously commonplace lines, kept her from the appearance of aestheticism which would have best expressed her inner state. Picturesque dress was only possible to her in the best materials. She had two ambitions—to become a member of the Arts and Crafts Society, and buy her clothes at Liberty's. These seemed unattainable. She was content that they should be so. But she would not offer herself the consolation of a cheaper success.

She had her secret pleasures. As she walked now in front of Willie, she noticed with appreciation the white glitter of some raindrops caught on the bare twigs of a plane-tree; and was glad to find herself capable of these artistic enjoyments. Mr. Willie Hopkinson perceived the touch of assurance which this sudden contentment gave to her pose, silhouetted for him against a red-brick villa still in the flamboyant stage of architectural infancy. It pleased him. He knew that she had seen some unobtrusive loveliness; and to him also landscape could impart a peculiar ecstasy. The lights of London, her crown of topaz and opal, flashed into instant existence on a wintry afternoon, or the sudden vision of trees folded in blue mist, revived a fever latent in his blood. Still young enough to hope that one taste held in common might presuppose a universal sympathy, he was drawn to a careful examination of Mildred's outline.

She had now that mysterious significance which anything may acquire if we look at it with sufficient intention. It distinguished her, as an aureole might, from all other persons afoot. It became imperative that he should watch her actions. He liked to feel that she was walking in front of him, unconscious of his attention; but presently she entered a little shop, and he was left to digest the slightly heightened picture of her personality which fancy offered him.

He saw her as he passed the door, buying tracing-paper and an H.B. pencil. The shop dealt also in firewood, soda, and other sordid necessities of the household. But Mildred thought that she detected a look of relief on the face of the proprietor when he turned from these things to the sale of 'artists' materials'; and feeling this to be a sign of grace, she endured smells of soap and tallow, and encouraged him.

Miss Brent was aware, without turning her head, of Willie Hopkinson's attentive glance. In women not yet possessed of a lover, this faculty of perceiving rearward admiration is often highly developed. She thus entered the bindery with his image pleasantly fixed in her mind, and spoke of him to Janet Vivien in phrases which a grammarian might have parsed as Conditionally Possessive.

Miss Vivien, however, was not sympathetic. She detested Willie. She had the cold virtues of the Vestal, and liked to exhibit them; but he had given her no opportunity. Few attitudes are more fatiguing than that of defence against an attack which never comes. Because he did not make advances for which she would certainly have snubbed him, she considered him to be an excessively ill-mannered young man.

Her father was a clergyman of uninteresting orthodoxy; she had been reared amongst grey proprieties. She knew that her hair was particularly nice—soft, and warmly flaxen, with a fascinating twist in it. The elder Mr. Hopkinson, on his preliminary visit to the 'Presse and Ploughe,' had looked at her—first judicially, and finally with approval. He liked girls of the deep-bosomed, slow-moving type; they made good wives and mothers. For these reasons Janet thought that she, rather than Mildred, should have wakened Willie's dormant manliness. Mildred's hair was sepia-colour, a lank and unpoetic mass. Her accent frequently annoyed Miss Vivien, whose own intonation was correct, even ecclesiastical.

'I should doubt,' she said, 'if that young Hopkinson meant anything by staring at you. It was probably absence of mind—unless it was impertinence.'

'It wasn't either the one or the other. In fact, now I come to think of it, I've noticed before—'

'You're always noticing things!'

'Oh, so would you,' said Mildred violently, 'if you felt like me! Anything to avoid noticing what's always under one's nose!'

'It's no use to be discontented.'

'Discontented? I'm starved! Is it discontented to be hungry? People who've got plenty seem to think it is. Don't you see that this place and all its pretences don't satisfy you if you want to live? It's like those patent foods that don't feed you—it keeps an ache alive. Oh, I would notice anything if it would make me forget to notice that! But I'll escape! I'll get to know the bright clever people, who know the difference between emotion and strawberry jam!'

'D'you think young Hopkinson does?'

'Well, he's not like us.'

'That's true. He's awfully queer. Sometimes he doesn't look altogether like a human being. Mr. Tiddy thinks he isn't quite right in his mind, and that's why his people have put him to bookbinding.'

'Nice compliment to us!'

'Isn't it? But there's something in it. It makes me feel positively creepy to be left alone with that youth—I keep expecting him to do something uncanny.'

'I'd rather feel creepy than feel nothing,' said Mildred slowly. 'But I know what you mean; it is the air he has of always looking at something that we can't see. Have you ever noticed his eyes? They are so strange—a queer pale blue, the colour that you see in the deeps of a moonstone, and black round the outer edge.'

Janet laughed sarcastically.

'You're half gone already,' she said.

During this and the succeeding days, she offered Mildred the insolent attentions which unimaginative propriety is so ready to bestow on more courageous, less conventional natures. Miss Brent was not happy. She knew her attitude to be superior to Janet's, and her understanding greater; but Miss Vivien possessed the knack of creating the opposite impression.

It is always exasperating to feel like a fool; and specially so when you know that you are not one. Before a week was over, the atmosphere of the workshop had become inimical to Mildred. She lived with the knowledge that two pairs of eyes—for Mr. Tiddy, jealous of his supremacy, had early caught the meaning of Janet's censorious glance—hourly accused her of desiring a flirtation with Willie. But she set her teeth, and deliberately sought his companionship. Being ignorant of love, she despised it: she had been known to say that it spoiled a good artist. She refused to sacrifice a friendship because others held more vulgar views.

The charm which drew her to Mr. Willie Hopkinson was no physical fascination. She was sufficiently perceptive to know that he was abnormal, but still too conventional to like it. His queerness lacked colour. He did not talk of it—a defect. But she felt the spell of his detachment, and looked to him, as a prisoner to S. Leonard, for the freeing hand which should hit off the fetters from her soul.

At this time, when Janet's point of view was painfully obvious and Willie's attitude as yet indefinite, Mildred sought refuge in her work, and chained her attention to the creation of a wonderful book-cover for a Christmas play, called by its writer 'A Masque of Marye's Childinge.' One copy—for the author—had been printed on large paper; and this she dressed in cloudy blue leather, whereon inlaid wash-leather sheep were kept by grey morocco shepherds.

Willie admired this work, and complimented Miss Brent upon it very kindly: he was acquiring some of his father's condescension towards women.

'Have you read the book?' she said.

She was quick to seize opportunities for congenial conversation.

'No; but I've heard it well spoken of.'

'Ah, by Intelligent Catholics, I expect. He is quite the poet of that movement.'

'What do you think of it?'

Mildred read the *Academy* and the *Outlook* at the Free Library every week, and knew what to reply.

'There is a great deal of spiritual feeling in it,' she said. 'And, I think, that combination of paganism and pageantry is very attractive. After all, few people are more truly and artistically Christ-like than the heathen.'

These remarks impressed Willie, already struck by Mildred's original methods of work—the despair of the bindery and the solace of her own spirit.

Bookbinding is the most conservative of the crafts, and originality in its apprentices is apt to be considered as a vice. It irritates the tender vanity of superiors. Mildred's wash-leather sheep hurt Carter's feelings and ruffled the temper of Mr. Tiddy. The idea had never occurred to them, and they were sure that it was wrong. Yet she was modest in respect of her performance, being easily deceived by the apparent excellencies of self-advertising craftsmen.

She worked hard; partly because her mother was poor, and she had never questioned the necessity of wage-earning, partly because of her smouldering ambition, which pointed to industry as a possible way of escape. But she found no peace. Heredity was disastrous to her happiness. Romanticism in her was crossed by a strain of obtuse convention. Her father, a brilliant and unpleasant man, early perceived that he could never hope to find a woman who was his intellectual equal. He therefore decided, with a denseness peculiar to the supercilious, that his best chance of serenity lay in marriage with a domesticated fool. He chose a type at once amiable and irritating. Mrs. Brent never learned that repetition does not add point to an argument, or that it is useless for the naturally dull to attempt to shine. Too stupid for intellectual joys, yet not quite stupid enough for unconscious content, she became a miserable compromise between parrot-house and parlour.

Her husband had said to her, whilst their married life was still young, 'My dear, you will never be wise. Pray God you may become more foolish.'

But she did not. She remained dimly perceptive, and was always wretchedly aware of her own denseness when she failed to see one of her daughter's infrequent jokes.

Mildred, blending the characteristics of both parents, often missed the best pathways in life for want of the mental agility needed to perceive them; as she spoilt the flavour of her friendships by lack of conversational sweetness. Subjective stupidity and objective cynicism do not make an attractive blend. To Willie, however, they suggested that aloofness from worldly interests which is so difficult and desirable. He thought that Mildred might possibly possess a soul. As the weeks went by he began to take notice of her, criticised her designs, and recommended books, and found this new patronage pleasant. She seemed grateful when he spoke to her, and never resented her own failure to understand his remarks. As a fact, she preferred that he should sometimes be incomprehensible. The higher he was above her now, the greater his power of leverage should he choose to exert it. She was not yet of the incorrigible company of dreamers, but knew that in that direction lay her hope.

This gentle and appreciative attitude won its way with Willie, so that he began to connect the bindery with the sugar of Mildred's smile, not any more with the salt of Carter's discourse. He was not in love with her. He imagined that she would resent and despise soft tendencies even as he did. He ranked her with Stephen and Elsa, as a person of intelligence whose society pleased him.

Gradually he discovered that he was more comfortable in her presence than in that of Mrs. Levi; more certain of his own identity. To Elsa, he would never venture to speak of his vision of the universe: he sometimes thought that she did not take him quite seriously, she baffled and distressed him, though he could not escape her net. Stephen, who shared his outlook, disputed its interpretation at every turn. Willie now desired a friend at once intelligent and subservient, to whom he could point out the hollowness of the scenery which they had learnt to call actual; the ridiculous seriousness of the society of men, gravely concerned with details of station and appearance on its little moment of respite between two deaths. Such a companion could be taught to share his moods, respect his knowledge; would help, not hinder, the real business of life—the journey of his soul toward truth. Mildred could be trusted to understand enough, but not too much. His dignity would be safe with her: he was sure that she would never laugh at him.

So two restless spirits drew toward one another; one craving for a wider, the other for a more peopled world. In each, the dominant motive was an egoism. Willie desired that the grey infinity in which he existed should contain at least one other being by whom he was admired and understood. Mildred saw Willie as a person from the outer world, who had stepped into the narrow circle which hemmed her in: and clung to his hand in the hope that he would drag her beyond its boundaries into an ideally interesting society where her work would be appreciated, her intellectual longings fed, and she could come to the growth which lack of nourishment now denied her.

But whilst Willie the dreamer saw no need to exchange these silent fancies for the awkward paraphrase of speech, Mildred became anxious and insecure. She believed herself to be possessed of intuition, but was actually unable to assure herself of any but concrete facts. She wanted a sign from this elusive and desired companion. Her imagination was only skin-deep; it beguiled, but did not convince her.

The word came; but, being long awaited, did not satisfy. They were walking together to the tram after a day spent in dreary forwarding. Willie's performance had not pleased Mr. Carter, who had expressed his opinion with unusual tartness.

'It's extraordinary how slip-slop a young chap gets once 'e starts on courtin',' he had said.

This speech had been very distasteful to Willie, and an occasion of confusion to Mildred. He said very coldly to Carter:

'I think I shall go now; I can't do any more to-day. I'm waiting for the green morocco to cover those books.'

But before he could get out of ear-shot, Mr. Carter's sarcastic gloss reached him.

'Ah, it's somethin' softer than morocco that's hinderin' you, Mr. Hopkinson!' he said.

As he walked down Titian Road toward the High Street with Mildred by his side, Willie felt upset, depressed, and lonely. He knew some explanation to be imperative. He glanced at her: she was looking straight before her, and holding her skirt with one badly-gloved hand. A sudden shyness had him by the throat. It choked him. He could not speak to her.

But presently an omnibus passed close to the curb. It was a day of liquid mud: he was obliged to draw back hastily from the ensuing splashes. In doing so, he touched Mildred's arm, and at once felt more at his ease.

'I am lonely!' he said abruptly. 'I want your friendship! We are in sympathy, I know. But there are things that I must tell you. I am not quite like other people.'

'Of course,' answered Mildred, 'I always saw that.'

She ceased on the expectant note, and Willie knew that his next words must be definite.

'Yes,' he said, 'I am—'

He stopped. It was absurd, but he did not know how to go on. He could not say, 'I am an immortal spirit,' and his condition as yet lacked other substantive. He thought a little, and then added:

'I live in two worlds.'

The phrase came to Mildred as a spark in darkness. It startled, but did not illuminate. She did not perceive that this was their moment of communion: she was a person who needed explanatory titles to the chapters of her Book of Life.

'How interesting!' she said.

CHAPTER 14

BUT THE ROAD BECOMES MUDDY

'How could he see what is hid
If it were not so, the lover?
How could he say, "She alone and no other"?
Maya, illusion!'

—ALICE HERBERT

MR. WILLIE HOPKINSON did not again offer his confidence to Miss Brent: his desire for sympathy was held in check by a wholesome fear of appearing ridiculous. He established her, very suitably, in the suburbs of his spirit, where she soon assumed a commanding position.

New factors were bringing unwelcome complications to his view of the universe. Each step of his road was now disputed by the varied powers within him—by a restless, poetic imagination, as yet scarcely conscious of itself; by a confused and unhappy soul fearful of all entanglements; by a body which age was ripening for assertion. Stephen's influence, which he distrusted but could not escape, urged love upon him as the sacrament of a spiritual reality. The unromantically robust Pauline, still unconscious of her conquest, maintained her inexplicable ascendancy over Mr. Miller's heart; and Willie was compelled to unwilling attention whilst Stephen described his sister's merits, and laid bare to him the very human transports which he mistook for illumination of the soul.

Stephen had a way of calling to spend the evening with Mr. Willie Hopkinson, thus placing himself, as he said, in Pauline's *aura* if not in her presence. As a matter of fact, like many tactful people, she did the wrong thing in a spirit of pure kindliness, and made a point of leaving the two youths together in the dining-room whilst she retired to do needlework in another part of the house. It was then that Willie's acid comments on Stephen's ardours would lure his friend on to explanation and defence.

'Can't you understand?' he said one day when the controversy had been specially embittered. 'It seems so odd, because you never lost the light; you have intuitions which ought to help. You're a mystic if you are anything, and yet you deny Love; and Love's the only mysticism that's any use.'

'Perhaps so, when two souls are created for each other. But Pauline!'

'You don't think, do you?' said Stephen, 'when I idealize Pauline; when I make her the whole type for me of woman in the world; that I imagine my own words to be actual and literal—think her other than a human girl?'

'No,' replied Willie; 'but you will before you're done.'

'I shan't. I shall always know that it is just because she is my girl that she means so much. Every man must find his Madonna in a woman—perhaps every woman may find her Christ once in a man. Can't you see that there's a sort of perfection, a nobility, in loving the imperfect? In giving yourself to something that can't really help you, that can only give itself to you?'

'No,' said Willie, 'I can't see it. It's a chain, a tie to earth.'

'No, it's a way through really; an escape. The power of your love, you see, is not exhausted by the earth-object, because that's partly illusion. But the love is real, and goes on far beyond: and in the end, perhaps, it finds the True Beauty.'

His known taste for literature obliged Stephen to speak like a book. He stopped now, feeling rather tired, and began carefully stroking Pauline's black Persian, which, feeling equal to a little conversation, had jumped upon his knee, and now sat purring with the assured condescension of an obliging archangel. Bertie Anthracite Hopkinson was a cat of intelligence and charm. His names, emblematic first of softness, secondly of blackness, thirdly of his position as a son of the house, excluded further description. Stephen, so alert in his sympathies toward all that was alive, had cultivated a mesmeric touch which made Bertie Anthracite his friend. They held long conversations, which irritated Willie as much as they pleased his sister; and went through dignified and ceremonial games together with a footstool and a ball of string.

This attitude of Mr. Miller in the house—an attitude at once amorous and homely—stirred dormant forces in Willie's subconscious self. It introduced into his attitude towards Mildred an element which he did not in his cooler hours desire. Stephen's exalted phrases stood like stained glass between him and the world.

They affected his outlook, and at times he dreamed that an ideal love might indeed be the Graal of his quest. Mildred's ardent mind and clever fingers pleased him; he imagined her always beside him, sharing his fears, his discoveries, his success. The idea had charm. He played with it. Then a sense of the Grey Dimension rushed back. He dreaded the chain of earthly interests; and came hastily to his old attitude of determined detachment.

But he could no longer look on Miss Brent as a Person rather than a Girl. His environment warred against this happy neutrality, and steadily pressed frank comradeship into more sordid paths. Mr. Carter, to Willie's disgust, still took the issue of the situation for granted. He watched his pupil's progress with a benevolent smile, and by persistent presentation of Mildred in the light of normal courtship, dimmed the idea of Platonic love which Willie struggled to keep in mind.

'You might do worse, Mr. Hopkinson,' he said. 'Miss Brent, she has ideas as I don't altogether 'old by as to design and such; but she's a rare 'and at the sewin' press, which is what you'll find useful in the future, and I'll allow 'er toolin's very nice.'

In Mildred's presence, however, Willie retained his remote, therefore interesting, attitude. His attentions were meaningless; he seemed content to drift without thought in the delicious tides which ebb and flow between friendship and passion.

'Young Hopkinson doesn't seem much inclined to come to the point,' said Janet; she had become more sweet-tempered since Mr. Tiddy's interest was concentrated on herself, and pitied Mildred's equivocal position.

'What a vulgar idea!' answered Mildred coldly. 'Can't you realize that friendship is possible without flirtation? Between cultivated people, sympathy is quite sufficient.'

She was happy. After all, a slight improvement, if it be unexpected, is enough to turn Earth into Heaven. She liked to think that her friendship was an intellectual one, and had nothing in common with an ordinary entanglement. It meant much that she should be preferred before Janet, whose fascinating hair was enhanced by a good complexion. Willie's self-control did not annoy her. He appreciated her, and she him. He lived in town, and brought the air of a larger world to the workshop. She, coming every day from her cheap and hideous home on the edge of a newly-developed building estate, envied and admired him. Much of Elsa's philosophy was now repeated for Mildred's benefit, and increased her respect for Willie's cultivated mind.

There came a morning, however, when a well-defined feeling of discomfort was noticeable in the bindery. Its happy atmosphere of security had gone, and the air was full of fretfulness. It was known, vaguely but universally, that Mr. Tiddy and Miss Vivien had been 'carrying on.' The fall of Propriety is generally more sudden than elegant. Janet's descent amused even Mr. Carter, a Puritan at heart. A less virtuous, more experienced maiden might have repelled Mr. Tiddy's onslaught with success; but she had allowed him to kiss her behind the door of the dressing-room, not knowing that her mother was waiting for her within.

Now Miss Vivien applied gold-leaf to her book-cover with a trembling hand; she was leaving next week. And Bertram Tiddy, at the opposite end of the workshop, made end-papers with sullen energy. Both were suffering from loss of dignity, and beside this the decline from virtue seemed insignificant.

These events reacted on Miss Brent and Mr. Willie Hopkinson, and caused them to realize their sex with some acuteness. Mildred, who was more receptive than perceptive, and found every passing emotion an amusement or a grief, suddenly felt it as an injury that Willie showed no disposition towards inconvenient passions. She forgot the superiority of ideal affections, and longed to be kissed. It was a demonstration in little of the psychology of the crowd. Willie was uncomfortable, depressed. He could not understand himself; an irritating condition. He had felt uneasy lately when away from Mildred, yet dissatisfied when he was with her; and his mind, which despised this weakness, could not control it.

For some weeks, his bad appetite had alarmed his mother, who was afraid that the gas stoves used for heating the workshop dried the air too much, and lowered his vitality. The only remedy for this, she knew, was good food; and, with a well-founded distrust of the local confectioner, she supplied him with lunches of meat-pie and homemade cake, and a patent medicated cocoa which nourished the brain without upsetting the liver.

At one o'clock Mr. Carter retired to the Sun in Splendour for a cut off the joint and a pint of half-and-half, and Mr. Tiddy and Miss Vivien vanished towards secret places where they fed.   Then Mildred, who took her poor lunch of buns and apples at the bindery, did illicit cookery upon the finishing stove, and shared Willie's cocoa in a spirit of pure comradeship. These picnics, when they sat together on the table and talked of Literature and Art, had developed a familiarity both innocent and delightful.   Once or twice he had called her his little sister, and she had pretended to like it.   It made Mrs. Hopkinson very happy to find that her son got through a quarter-pound tin of cocoa every week.

But on this day they were nervous, shy of each other.   A possibility to which neither desired an introduction had been forced upon them.   Mildred's manner was slightly frosty; there was an unusual formality in Willie's phrases. It was a grey day in February; he was miserable. Weather affected his outlook, and he felt earth-bound and hopeless. It seemed that their happy friendship was in danger, and he suddenly realized all that it had meant to him.

'Aren't you happy?' said Mildred abruptly. He had only eaten half a mutton-pie and one piece of cake.

'No,' he said.

'Anything wrong?'

'Nothing's wrong, but I'm wretched. Everything is so medium. When I try and look into the future, I see such a foolish, meaningless life ahead of me—no truth, no sincerity; everything sordid, earthy. I dread it.'

'I think, if I had your life to live, I should be happy. You have clever friends, you're in the movement, you can develop your powers. *You* haven't got to be always thinking about what sort of work pays best. Suppose you had to live down here, with nothing beautiful to see, no cultivated people to talk to, no one to understand you, no hope of escape?'

'If I did,' said Willie, 'where would be the difference? Only in externals, after all. You think I have more chance of finding myself than you have, a better environment, more freedom. I haven't really. We're both struggling in chains, you and I—silly, soft chains we can't break. My existence is quite as ugly, quite as dead as yours, if you only knew it. I sometimes wonder whether there are any real existences, any real meanings in life. I muddle along through a world of spectral nothings, and never leave them behind. I'm lost in them, they shut the light out, and yet they're unreal.'

'Oh, but I've often felt that too—that feeling that one is missing the real things. It's only in dreams I come near them—perhaps it's in dreams I live best. But it's horrible when one thinks that one has only one life, and it's going—going all the time.'

A passionate discontent shook in her voice. It did not occur to Willie that her idea of reality and of life might not correspond with his own. She was dissatisfied; she desired the real things. He looked at her with new interest, a kindness from which condescension had gone.

'Oh, do you feel that?' he said. 'I've been lonely all my life because I could never find anyone who felt just as I did about it. All the people I live with are so busy with the detail of existence, that it never occurs to them to look at its shape as a whole.'

His tone was sincere, agitated; a subtle flattery. It roused the woman in Mildred to the wounding of the artist, and prompted her to an effective and fatal utterance. At heart an actress, she could not bear to miss her cue.

'I've always been lonely too,' she answered. 'No one has really understood me, because my outside doesn't match my soul. It's horrid to look ordinary and not to be it. I seem to have been waiting and waiting, for the person who could help me to live my own life.'

A sudden vision of completed existence flashed upon Willie's inner eye. For one happy instant he thought of Mildred as a soul which shared his restlessness and his hopes. He was standing very near to her; and now he saw her radiant, transformed, the focus of his inarticulate craving.

He took one step nearer. It seemed to Mildred that he was staring at her with a curious intensity. Really, he saw nothing but a coloured blur before him. Then the connection between mind and action snapped. He became an automaton in the hands of a strong emotion, and words came to him so quickly that he could not arrange them in order, as he might have done in a quieter hour.

'Oh, don't wait!' he said. 'I want you! I want you! What does it matter about dreams of the future? That's nothing. I'm here, and you're here, and we can't do without one another. That's all that matters. Dearest! I'll make you live. I know you understand me. We shall find the meaning of it all if we look together. The heart speaks sometimes, and then one knows the truth.'

He took her in his arms and kissed her—a timid, inexperienced kiss. But Mildred, in spite of her rather mean ideals, was essentially virginal. The thing, coming with the violence of an accident, appalled her. She hated crude emotions. A natural horror crossed her triumph, and she drew away from him.

'Oh, what's happened?' she said. There was pain as well as amazement in her voice.

Willie could not answer her. The hot phrases which he had so suddenly let loose had lowered his temperature in their passage. He felt, comparatively, cold. Astonished reflection trod close on the heels of impulse: he had strongly the mysterious sense of being a stranger to his own actions; of standing aside and watching that ingenious machine, his body, perform a series of evolutions in whose direction he had no share.

In a mood of entire detachment, he looked on,—amused, critical, almost interested. He began to wonder what strange being had spoken by his lips. He noticed that his body was curiously excited by the attitude it had taken up. Its pulses raced, it trembled helplessly, its agitations almost disgusted him—he, the spiritual Willie Hopkinson, who had thought to find something very different from this in love. He wanted Mildred: he was pleased to have won her—for now she was passive in his arms, and he knew that she was won—he could not disassociate himself altogether from his sex. But he was secretly troubled and disappointed by the quality of his emotion. 'Is this all? Is this all?' the feverish soul in him cried out, whilst some other and irresistible impulse drew his trembling lips to Mildred's cool and steady ones, and found him the caressing words which the situation obviously required.

And Mildred, the idealist, had only one coherent thought.

'How awfully astonished Janet will be!' she said to herself.

At the end of an afternoon spent in simulating an elaborate unconcern, Miss Brent and Mr. Hopkinson parted with such emotional display as the publicity of Titian Road allowed. Each, for different reasons, was anxious to be very modern and collected.

But they could not help feeling agitated, even upset, by what had occurred.

Mildred, always verbally cynical in matters relating to love, came from her first encounter with it surprised and rather sad. Her official views had been unconsciously modified by the softer imaginations of her favourite novelists. These now invited comparison with immediate experience, and the vivid tints of the ideal brought out the greyer tones of the fact. The heart seldom wakes at the first touch. Mildred's had only stirred sufficiently to feel a drowsy disappointment in its own sensations. Hers was that spurious love founded on light fiction, which debases the currency.

The thorough training she had received in all branches of Ornamental Design made her capable, however, of appreciating the artistic possibilities of the situation. She felt that Willie's proposal should have been arranged with due regard to the laws of composition. He was the most abnormal young man she had ever met. He affected her like a Voysey wall-paper, and this alone proved how suitable he was to become the background of her life.

But his wooing, coming as the last term of an intellectual friendship, should have combined the emotional atmosphere of 'Wuthering Heights' with the spiritual platitudes of 'Middle-march.' Mildred was very well read. Willie's hurried onslaught had been on a different level from the passionate epigrams of her dreams. It was breathless and ungrammatical; its phrases were objectionably homely. She decided that it lacked the lyrical impulse. Considering the matter on her way home, she told herself with growing bitterness that she was not satisfied. She had been too hasty. The whole incident now struck her as tame: and its memory annoyed her the more when she remembered that for a moment it had contrived to make her lose her self-control.

She wondered now what blind impulse had forced her to return Willie's nervous kisses, and could find no answer to the question. She felt hot with shame as she thought of the wild moments when she had trembled in his arms—and their sudden, inelegant separation when they heard Carter's step in the corridor. He had entered with a specially benevolent grin, and had gone promptly to work cutting the edges of a large atlas, leaving them together at the finishing bench. Probably he had suspected. A sudden loathing of love and its vulgar accessories overcame her. It seemed to her that it was very like bookbinding—full of poetic charm when seen from outside; but made up, for those who chose to investigate its technique, of ordinary, sticky, even unpleasant materials.

But just as she reached home, a sense of comfort relieved her burning eyes, and softened the curve of her firm thin lips. She was Engaged; and only an emancipated woman can savour the full joy of that astounding knowledge.

The homeward soliloquy of Mr. Willie Hopkinson was not much more cheerful than that of Miss Brent. He too had suffered a certain disillusion, though the more romantic disposition of the amorous male kept him from the depths of his fiancée's cynicism. It had seemed to him in the moment before he kissed Mildred that a great light was about to break upon his life; that its local colour was going to be of an indefinite golden tint, instead of the disagreeable brown of the past. More than mere passion—the longing for an unknown beauty—had driven him to love. He could not tell himself that these hopes had been fulfilled. The afternoon's experiences toned in with the rest of his existence in an artistic but depressing manner: he would have preferred a more violent contrast. Grey World and brown earth were still with him, but the golden light refused to come. Willie had a pretty taste in metaphor. He told himself as he strolled away that he had thought to fit a key to the lock which shut him from a Burne-Jones country, and it had only opened upon a Dutch interior after all.

The engagement caused some stir, but little enthusiasm. Mr. Hopkinson said that it was infernal nonsense. Willie was only one-and-twenty, and juvenile marriages were bad for the race. Mrs. Hopkinson only hoped that Mildred was a thoroughly nice girl; but her inflection was sceptical. Fiction and France together have contrived to discredit the art-student, and Willie's friends were usually peculiar.

But Mrs. Levi, at whose altar he had so long offered a romantic incense, felt it as a personal grief.

'I had hoped,' she remarked to her husband, 'that he would have too much sensibility for this. Love is the most beautiful of the passions: but only when it has no ulterior object can it really minister to the higher life.'

She reflected on the superior habits of the Middle Ages, when young men were content to worship at the feet of married beauty without any hope of reward. 'In those days,' she said, 'life was really beautiful. An engagement, I think, is almost indelicate.'

She had some justification for annoyance. Hers had been the first hand extended to help Willie to escape the stagnation of family life. Now, with the callous ingratitude of intelligent youth, he left her on one side and deliberately framed his own career. She had taught him too well. He had learnt to appreciate women, and desired to possess one. He told her all about Mildred, sitting at her feet in the old confiding way, and holding her hand. He described her with some rapture, for he wished to assure himself that he was very much in love. Elsa felt that she was being treated as a favourite aunt.

Yet she still busied herself with his well-being, and appeared interested in the engagement. She even allowed him to bring Mildred to tea with her; endured her accent, her awkward manners, and her pretentious aestheticism; and told Mrs. Hopkinson that she seemed a sensible girl. She was absurdly kind-hearted for so handsome a woman; it seemed unnecessary, and Willie did not really appreciate it. But in matters of sentiment Mrs. Levi was an expert diplomatist. She had early divined the true state of his emotions; and, believing in the value of contrast, she hoped that the advantages of the connection might not all be on Mildred's side.

CHAPTER 15

A WAYSIDE SHRINE

'Now soone from sleepe,
A Starre shall leap;
And soon arrive both King and Hinde.
Amen, Amen;
But O the Place co'd I but finde!'

—L. I. GUINEY

IT was no impulse of inquisitive piety which drove Willie to enter the church of Our Lady of Pity. He had a love for London, his true mother, greater than that which he found for any human being. Child, first of her slums, and secondly of her suburbs, she held him tenderly but relentlessly in her great, grimy, yet strangely poetic hand. He found in her streets the mystical place-spirit which is seldom permitted to enter her houses; and it fed his soul. Seeing her as a dream-town set over against the city that has foundations, he felt that in her entity she knew herself so to be.

Now that his working hours were linked with Mildred, and so robbed of the quiet inward happiness they had possessed, an old craving for solitude returned to him. Miss Brent retained her power over his senses, and compelled a lover-like demeanour which he found wearisome, and she lacking in enthusiasm. This killed the peculiar fascination of the workshop, for the religion of labour is austere, cloistral; it may tolerate a high passion, but it hates an entanglement. That gate was shut: he was driven to look for some other resting-place.

Holiday afternoons, therefore, he spent alone when he could; on the pavements, or in museums looking at beautiful things which pleased him. He discovered that a bit of Limoges enamel, or a casket of old French ivory, may be the best of companions to those who can concentrate their attention and hear its thin faded voice. Education now helped him to appreciate exquisite handiwork; and the immortality of works of art, which, once created, outlive their fragile makers and take their place amongst eternal things, struck his imagination.

On one such day, when suggestions of blue in the sky and a dancing breeze in the west kept him out of doors, he first noticed, in a wide street of ostentatious shop-fronts veiling squalid tenements, a dark passage between the dingy houses. It was not a thoroughfare; a swing-door under an arch closed its farther end. Willie had a curiosity for doors; the never-extinguished hope of the adventurous that they may hide something worthy of discovery. This one seemed oddly placed. He was interested—walked down the passage. Then he saw that it was a church door, and paused. Churches had never attracted him.

But at that moment it opened, and a young man came out. He had a clever face, the thin, nervous hands of an artist, ardent eyes which shone with grave rapture, as of one who has been about a happy business. Willie had not imagined it possible that men should enter a church on a week-day. He was greatly astonished. Almost mechanically, he caught the door as it swung to, and went in.

It was a large church, with wide aisles, a high vault, transepts: but being ignorant of architecture he was not impressed by its plan. The first thing that he noticed was a faint aromatic smell which soothed his senses. He was nervous, not knowing the meaning of the things he saw, or what his own right of admittance; so that his perceptions were rather exalted, and he felt that there were mysteries very near. An influence, real though elusive, imposed quietness and respect. He had been of course in Protestant churches, but they had left no mark on his spirit, and gave him no clue to this experience—to the hush, the awe, the weight of a new form of life. The idea of a religious building as provocative of emotion was strange to him.

The place was so still, so remote from ordinary existence, that it seemed incredible that fifty yards away newsboys were offering the latest details of the Bootle Horror, and omnibuses full of cheerful persons were hurrying eastwards to matinées and exhibitions. He did not know what to make of this dim hall, and these quiet people who passed him. He had been accustomed to live with the sense of aloofness; but here his want of comprehension came from inferiority, not detachment. He had suddenly come upon a new country. He remembered old stories of people who had found an

open door, and walked through it into fairyland; and realized that
the door which shut silently behind him had cut him off as a prison
gate might have done from his daily world.

He looked down the long aisles. They were misty, half lighted
by coloured windows in the south. Far away, he saw lights burning,
and persons who knelt by them. It all seemed to him profoundly
unnatural. He felt as if he had penetrated to the home of a race of
beings not entirely human—an unsuspected world within the world.

A woman passed by him. In the street, he would have known
her for a very ordinary, well-behaving person, not to be suspected
of vivid emotions. Here she was remote, magical; caught up by the
strong love of the initiate. He watched her as she made the sign of
the Cross, and knelt very simply and without shame before an altar.
It seemed to him that she stayed there a long time: he dared not
move, because of the tension of her attitude. Presently she kissed
the feet of a statue that stood there, and came away. Her face as
she passed Willie was serious but very contented. No doubt she
would go out into the foggy sunshine and take a hansom or the
omnibus and go home: but her real life had been in the moment
when she kissed the image with a convinced sincerity which did not
belong to Suburbia and its gods. It was evident that great matters
happened in this building.

He had wandered now as far as the northern transept. The little
chapel which opened from it was empty of worshippers. Its altar
had a plainer look than others which he had passed—the shrines of
S. Joseph and S. Anthony, crowded with votive gifts. Willie looked
up, and his eye was caught by a mysterious invocation—words,
written in tall gold letters above the altar—*Veni, Creator Spiritus!* He
did not recognise its relation to the commonplace English hymn,
the clumsily-phrased 'Come, Holy Ghost.' It seemed a strange,
majestic utterance. He felt the full weight of its tremendous appeal.

Veni, Creator Spiritus!—this, after all, was what he had been
asking all his life. People, then, came to this place to find an answer
to his own tormenting questions; to gain an attitude, an interest,
above the petty illusions of visible life. They were living in an air he
could not breathe, amongst realities which he could not apprehend.

He looked back down the aisles. Everyone else was kneeling.
Evidently, it was right to do this. Willie, naturally aesthetic, valued

ceremonial and symbol. He also knelt. He disliked the sensation: it is not easy for an Englishman to kneel in a public place. He felt sure, as he bent his knees, that he was being observed; and felt hot, ashamed, desperately foolish. But with the deliberate humility, there came a new sense of peace. He felt a power near him; a touch, new and purifying as the Angel's wing which fanned Dante's forehead on the mount. I think that he was purged of the sin of pride in that moment.

He rose with a knowledge of his ignorance such as he had never yet possessed: aware that he, the unworldly person whose unique perceptions showed him the blindness of his neighbours, the hollowness of life, was himself without understanding, blind and speechless, when ushered suddenly into the presence of one of the spiritual secrets of the world. But he divined the beauty which he could not comprehend: it quieted him, gave him new hope. As he went out, and down the grey squalid passage to the street, he passed a little shop-window where statues and rosaries were for sale. There were some books, too. He noticed the name upon one of them—'The Garden of the Soul.'

'Why, that is what this place should be called!' he said.

He came back to the church again and again: fascinated, puzzled, always without comprehension of the charm which drew him there. Once he heard a High Mass sung, and was disappointed. It was ornate, dazzling, but it did not impress. He loved best the quiet moments of devotion, when the place was a home, not a court. When love outweighed ceremonial respect, and showed itself in a familiar simplicity, tears came to his eyes, and sorrow for his dumbness to his heart. He knew then that a beautiful reality wrapped him round and helped him; that this place, where invocation of the Invisible never ceased, had an existence in Eternity not granted to the hurrying City streets. But the music and the incense were no part of that vision; they confused the image and frightened it away.

A curious change was worked in Willie by this quaint access of piety. He came back now to books read in the past, and found in himself a new spirit of evocation. Phrases long familiar raised unsuspected veils and permitted him to look into their eyes, and there read messages and prophecy. These were old friends, loved for their verbal magic, now understood. From a prayer for admittance at another gate, he turned to find this door held open.

But Mildred had no share in his new radiance. Her eccentricity, cool, well-balanced, deliberately fostered, was at the opposite pole of idealism from Willie's dim intuition of beauty and holiness. The sun which lit his newly discovered country plunged her into a winter of shade. Caught up by the grave fascination of the sanctuary, he thought contemptuously of Stephen's remarks on the spiritual nature of love, and wondered what would be left of his passion for Mildred when once he had thrown off the shackles of sense. Already, he felt a change in the quality of his affection when she put off her working overall and came to meet him in all the fatiguing fluffiness of dressy blouse and home-trimmed hat. It was the fellow-worker, the comrade, that he loved; not the flesh-and-blood girl whom custom compelled him to kiss.

He realized that his old state of isolation had been very dear to him, and that now he had lost it. Stephen had made a fatal mistake. This was not the Companion who would lead him up the hill. He must climb that path alone; and Mildred, in the valley, would always be a drag upon his steps.

Divergent ideals soon became apparent. He told her of his religious intuitions, and she was vexed. Catholicism was fashionable, but had many inconveniences. She wondered how many more fads Willie would develop. As persons professionally connected with wall-papers end by decking their own rooms in whitewash, so Mildred's association with Willie induced in her a love of normal things. Engagement necessarily involved some readjustment of her point of view. Originality in a friend is often eccentricity in a husband. She was determined to manage Willie: she wished him to get on. There was in Mildred that strain of meanness which often goes with a sharp, shallow intelligence. She could sacrifice nothing of her hopes, nor weigh Willie's love and happiness against her own rebellious ambitions. Love, pleasant as an entrée, could never form the staple of her life.

But when she attacked him for his dreamy outlook, she met an obstinacy which she did not expect.

'What I want you to do, Willie, dear,' she said, 'is to take a more reasonable view of things. You get on so much better if you treat things as if they were important, even if they're not. And surely that isn't difficult.'

'Oh, of course not! Nothing's easier. All you want is that I should banish my sense of proportion; and after all most people manage to do that very early in life. Anything can be profoundly important so long as one is careful to look at nothing else. But once glance at the stars, once open the books of the mystics, and the game is up—the panorama can never deceive us again.'

'Yes, well. That's all very well, but it isn't the way to get on.'

'Get on! Who wants to get on? What does it matter about succeeding here? It's the afterwards that counts.'

'Oh, I never could get up any interest in religion.'

'Religion? It isn't religion: it's reality. Whatever you believe or don't believe, life's only a tiny snippet of existence; and it's not worth counting against the afterwards.'

'Well, you may think that, but you don't know it. I'd rather make the most of what I've got, not invest all my capital in a dream.'

'See here, Mildred,' said Willie abruptly; 'unfortunately for me, I do know it. You always say you understand me, but I see now that it was only a fancy of your own that you understood. You bathe your mind in a froth of mysticism because it amuses you and makes you feel clever, but you don't believe in it one bit. I don't have to believe it, because I know. It isn't a case of intuition or anything like that, it's a case of what has happened. I wasn't always Willie Hopkinson. I lived once—a street boy in the slums. I died once. I was ten years old then, and my view of life was rather like yours. But I passed over into the horrible country where the Dead, who made the most of life, as you wish to do, live for ever in empty loneliness—because they took with them out of this existence nothing that could subsist when the body had died. I'll not risk that Hell again. I saw the world you and I live in now, as the shadow and the dream it really is: yet I longed to get back into touch with it —back to the old pretences, the colour and light. It's not much, but it's all you have to hope for if you chain your ideals to earth-interests and earth-success. I've got back: but I've never lost that knowledge. The Grey World is with me all the time, and the voices of the miserable dead; who spent all their energies, all their opportunities, for the sake of a few years of " getting on."

Mildred shivered.

'Oh, don't be so horrible!' she said. 'Your imagination is positively morbid.'

'People with a sense of proportion—a sense of background —generally are morbid. Most prophets and truth-tellers have been called that—or something similar—at one time or another.'

'And quite right too. Prophets and truth-tellers, as you call them, are usually only dreamers who let their little fancies stand for facts.'

'Oh, no!' said Willie. 'Some are: but the real thing isn't to be mistaken. One or two have seen truth, and those who know can recognise that element in their vision, however they may wrap it up. Of course, the ordinary human creeping thing who never looks at the sky, is bound to think everything above his own head a morbid fancy. I've no doubt that if a blackbeetle ever conceived of human beings as they really are, all the other blackbeetles would lock him up, as a sufferer from dangerous delusions.'

'Perhaps you'll mention some others who had this knowledge that you boast of?'

'Well, look at the mystics, for instance. Look at Plotinus, Blake, Swedenborg, the Indian philosophers—contemplatives all over the world who have looked beyond the shadow of earth and seen another Reality, some as a dim reflection, some as a perfect truth. Look at Dante, at the poets. They all speak a different language, but what they are trying to say is substantially the same. It's an ineffable news, not to be put down in human symbols. I've only seen the dark side yet, but I'll find sunshine and safety before I die.'

'It's ridiculous,' said Mildred, 'to bring in Dante and people like that. They were artists, poets who tried to invent something beautiful. And it seems to me that's what you're aiming at.'

'Poets see further than most people. They don't get the dust of daily life in their eyes, as practical persons do. And as for Dante, you read him now, and call him a fine poet—he has no actuality for you: he lived too long ago. But suppose that any person came to you now, and said, "I—I, who stand here, have been over that frontier. I have passed out from this solid, ordinary, modern world,—the world of comfortable mahogany-furnished dining-rooms, and motor-cars, and milliners' shops—and I have wandered with the Dead in another dimension, which is near you now, if you would only believe it. And I have returned, holding fast by my knowledge." That has actuality, hasn't it? That is real? And Dante's dream must have been as real as that to his neighbours.'

'And a nice mess he made of his life!'

'No one who finds the Ideal as early as he did, and holds it all his life, can have the inner misery,' said Willie. 'It's uncertainty, not knowing what to aim at, helpless groping in dark places, which brings that.'

'It's all a dream.'

'You said once,' answered Willie rather sadly, 'that it was in dreams that you lived best.'

'Oh yes, in the pretty airy ones that made one happy—not in this. You may be right or not—how am I to know? If you're wrong, you've made life a horrible nightmare for nothing. It's awful to have to think about death—really think about it, not take it for granted and forget. And if you're right, you've got knowledge that we are not meant to have.'

'*Meant* to have? But I can't help knowing.'

'Well, I can help it, and I won't know! I won't have all my hopes and my ambitions poisoned, and made to seem not worth while. I've only one life as far as I know, and I claim it as a right to order it as I think best. I can't live it on your lines. You terrify me. I don't think you're quite alive in the human sense of the word.'

'Oh, Mildred,' replied Willie, 'if only you knew! If only I could make you see! It seems incredible that you shouldn't believe me. Can't you *see* that I'm speaking the truth?'

He went towards her in a sudden access of compassionate tenderness.

'Oh, poor little dim-eyed girl!' he said, 'don't be lost in the shadows! Why should the truth be dreadful? Can't you trust me? Can't you *feel* the Invisible Things?'

But Mildred drew back from him.

'No, no! don't kiss me!' she said quickly.

From her tone, one might almost have thought that she was frightened.

CHAPTER 16

DIFFICULT PATHS

'The singing of the office . . . was like a stream of water crossing unexpectedly a dusty way—*Mirabilia Testimonia tua*.'
—WALTER PATER

IT was at this time that the heart of Miss Pauline Hopkinson, long besieged, opened its gates to Mr. Stephen Miller. It was not to be expected that she could resist a lover at once so ardent and so unsuitable. At first disposed to despise him because of his friendship for her brother, she was caught at last by his freshness and sincerity. To a person of her temperament, his courtship was full of surprises. The ecstasy with which he kissed her well-developed fingers administered a shock to her theory of life. Even her fringe, waved twice daily and confined by a net, had its poetic element for him. In the intervals of playing hockey and making blouses, she found herself thinking of this odd, intelligent boy. His dark face, his fervent anxious eyes, haunted her. She was impressed by his writings. They were obscure, and seemed to her remarkable.

Pauline was a wholesome English girl—a good-tempered, self-reliant animal—Stephen told her that she made him think of the Valkyrs and of Juno. His flaming imagination, turning from transcendental things, fused sentiment and fancy in the crucible of desire. Finally, Pauline was trapped in the meshes of his passion, and for the first time in her life obsessed by an interest which was neither a game, a fashion, nor a food.

As was right in so muscular and well-educated a woman, she was ashamed of her emotion. She took to wearing veils, lest anyone should notice the new radiance of her smile. She walked in a delicious dream, and told herself hourly that she was an idiot. But the Hopkinson family, who found in this engagement an antidote to the annoyance of Willie's entanglement, saw other grounds than those of sentiment for hearty congratulation. Pauline was marrying well. She was a sensible girl, and had sufficient *savoir faire* to keep this fact well in the foreground. It veiled the unreasoning pride which she felt in her vivid, picturesque, and dreamy lover.

Mr. Hopkinson, not suspecting his daughter's secret aberration, was pleased with her. To him, Stephen was a repulsive young fool, but he gave his consent with astonishing cordiality. Mr. Miller's extreme youth was no impediment. The best of theories becomes untenable when opposed by an advantageous fact. The race had to take care of itself when an alliance with Miller's Sapoline was in question.

One may pity Mr. Willie Hopkinson, hemmed in by lovers, yet —in other than the Biblical sense—very sick of love. Universally accepted as a member of that happy fellowship, he suffered, as only a sensitive spirit can suffer in a distasteful environment. In the midst of the confusion to which he had now reduced his life, two spots alone remained where he might hope for peace. In the church of Our Lady of Pity—his constant refuge—his best, humblest, most hopeful-self trimmed its lamp and patiently waited for the day. In Mrs. Levi's drawing-room, where a flattering sympathy awaited him, his meaner personality plumed its ruffled feathers and regained its self-esteem.

His position was ridiculous. He should have lived with eyes wide opened on the ugly illusion which his fellow-men had made of life: indifferent to its claims, its little vexations and silly excitements. He remembered the hour when he first saw that Heaven and Hell were equally near his grasp—that all depended on the attitude his soul took up: when he knew that wonderful worlds, more real than the dusty earth, were his if he could but see them.

The attitude his soul had taken up was compounded of fractiousness and despondency. He had done nothing with his knowledge and his chances. True, he had tried to open the eyes of two persons to the true meaning and real dangers of life; but the experiment had scarcely been successful. One he had estranged,— for Mildred's altered manner was unmistakable—the other he had kept, but less as a friend than as a prospective brother-in-law.

It was Mrs. Levi's peculiar merit that, knowing nothing of these things, she did not perceive the discomforts and inconsistencies of his situation. She spoke pleasantly of Mildred at every opportunity, admiring her artistic taste, her intelligence. Miss Brent had recently decorated Willie's sanctum with a stencilled frieze of may-trees blown by the wind. Mrs. Hopkinson thought that the design made the room feel draughty, and had put up thick curtains of crimson serge. But Elsa admired it.

'Such a beautiful symbolism,' she said—'the blossom of life blown to your feet by the zephyrs of Love. Dear Willie! I'm sure you'll be happy together. You are both so very artistic.'

Willie listened to her rather gloomily. His dignity was comforted, but his irritation hourly increased. Mildred often snubbed him now, treating his fads as follies, not as the natural accompaniments of talent. She took her work to Bertram Tiddy for correction and encouragement, and only accepted from Willie those useful attentions and ceremonial gifts which ameliorate even the most tedious engagement.

Mr. Tiddy, who had suffered an eclipse since Janet's departure and Mildred's betrothal, began, under these circumstances, to recover his normal air of omniscience. He was lonely. The girls, in their earlier and simpler developments, had been much to him. More had been the consciousness that he was much to them. Miss Vivien was now placed beyond his reach. He met her occasionally in the public gardens, walking with a sister of repellent propriety. It was rumoured that she intended to train as a children's nurse. Miss Brent, whom he had once thought available but unattractive, was the acknowledged property of Willie Hopkinson. Mr. Tiddy, left without an admirer, watched them working together under Carter's benignant eye, and longed for the advent of some new apprentice on whom he could impose his view of Art.

So it was that when Mildred—bored, disappointed, pining for any excitement—again turned to him for appreciation, she met with an almost abject response. Mr. Tiddy came to her side stroking his bristly chin regretfully, and smoothing the soft collar of his canvas shirt. He had an inner conviction that he was a fine craftsman; its sacramental result, as expressed in his manner, reminded his enemies of an insolent shop-walker.

Willie was absent: Carter was selecting materials in the store-room. Bertram, smiling pleasantly, leaned over Mildred as she sat before her work. He missed the nervous flutter with which she had been accustomed, involuntarily, to acknowledge his presence. Mildred had known deeper emotions, and mere propinquity no longer moved her.

He considered her work with a flattering but critical attention. She was decorating the insides of a book-cover with a pretty fretful pattern of fish and sea-birds, painted in faint colours upon the vellum *doublure*.

'Very nice!' he said—'very nice indeed! So quaint and original. You are developing quite a style of your own, Miss Brent; it's New-Arty, and yet it's individual.'

'I'm sick of the old traditional patterns—all the borders and panels and dot-work.'

'So's the public, I believe. We want freshness in design, a return to nature, imagination.'

'Carter doesn't approve of that a bit; he says that my ideas aren't workmanlike.'

'Ah, yes! Carter! He's an excellent forwarder, of course; but one can't expect him to understand the artist's point of view.'

'He's so horribly particular about neatness and all that.'

'Absurdly so, in my opinion. After all, Art doesn't consist in minute finish, which is all Carter cares about. Look at the Impressionists! We're here to produce beautiful things, not abnormally strong ones. You want to be practical, not perfect, if you're going to succeed with Arts and Crafts. And I think, you know, that's where Hopkinson makes such a mistake—that is, if he wants to get on—'

Mildred moved nervously; she did not feel capable of conducting Willie's defence. But Mr. Tiddy left his sentence incomplete. Carter had come back to the next press, carrying a roll of cloth and the shears. He looked at Mildred's animated face, and noted Bertram's position.

'Beg your pardon, Mr. Tiddy,' he remarked, 'but your glue-pot will boil over in a minute, and then there'll be a mess.'

Bertram retreated.

'Get on! *He'll* never get on—not at what you might call a good class o' bindin',' said Mr. Carter. 'Very different from Mr. 'Opkinson, 'e is: always slip-sloppin' and chatterin', thinking about prettiness instead of mindin' his work. 'E calls them things he does Art; *I* calls 'em whited sepulchres, all messy within. Now your young gentleman, Miss, with all his little ways, he do know how to 'old a paste-brush or a paring-knife proper. Mr. Tiddy cuts 'oles in the leather, and then 'e makes another 'ole in his manners with the language as he lets out.'

Carter collected his tools quietly around him, and remained on guard near the indignant Mildred for the rest of the afternoon. He felt it his duty later to caution Willie against Mr. Tiddy's encroachments, which recurred at every opportunity. But though he hinted as well as he dared at the dangers of the situation, his remarks made little impression. Mr. Hopkinson was neither alarmed, angry, nor incredulous. Distracted between the difficulties of his outer and his inner life, he forgot, as thoroughly and often as he might, the nature of the chain which bound him to Mildred Brent. He lived in a state of dream, neglecting his work, often leaving the bindery early to enjoy an hour of meditation in Our Lady of Pity before submitting to the stifling influences of an evening at home.

The secret of the sanctuary still eluded him. He knelt before an Unknown God, and his prayer for light received no acknowledgment. Yet that the light was there he never doubted: and one day a sign renewed his hope and gave to him some measure of serenity.

He came into the church as a procession left the altar to carry the Host between the ranks of the kneeling congregation. Choir-children walked before the canopy with great baskets of flowers—all of the simple, homelier sort; as daffodils, narcissus, violet. They took out the blossoms one by one, and kissed them with the affectionate importance of solemn babies before casting them under the feet of the priest. He, a real and eternal Christopher, bowed down almost with awe of the monstrance he carried, trod carelessly enough upon that exquisite carpet. It seemed so small a sacrifice in the presence of the mightiest offering in the world. Willie felt all the majesty of that progress: that prostration of the loveliest in Nature before the humblest of the servants of God. He picked up a poor crushed violet, and placed it between the leaves of his book: it seemed a shield, an amulet, wrapped round with the peculiar powers of any natural object that has touched the fringe of another universe. But still, the passion with which he kissed its leaves was idle. His will refused to consent to his longing: he could not believe.

He left the church more than usually troubled. Outside, the street was dark with fog. He was tired out by his own sick sensations of spiritual aridity, his sight confused by long gazing at the glory of a painted saint. He blundered in the doorway and collided with some person also going hastily out: and they found themselves together on the threshold.

Willie looked up, apologized, and was ready to pass on: but the tall bent figure, the clever sensitive face which he saw, seemed familiar. He looked again, and met an answering recognition. It was the young man who, coming out with a convinced and happy expression, had determined his first visit to the church.

He looked now at Willie's pale despondent face, and smiled at him. His smile was illuminative. Behind his spectacles, one saw grey eyes of an extraordinary clearness and charity.

'I've seen you here before,' he said, 'haven't I? But I don't think you're a Catholic?'

'No.'

'I thought not. You have that anxious look of a person who is not quite sure of his road. But you will be.'

'I come here because it is so quiet, and one seems to feel the real thing near one.'

'If you've found that, you're on the way already.'

'Isn't it odd?' said Willie suddenly. 'I've often been in Protestant churches, and they never feel like this. They have the same atmosphere as the rest of the world; but here one's feet are not any more on earth.'

'Ah, no! this is a joint in the armour of the material world. Where there is a shrine set apart, you know, the other world presses through into this. The curtain of separation is torn: one may get a glimpse of the Vision. That atmosphere which you notice is faith —ecstasy—the knowledge of spiritual things, which overflows in the soul and affects everything which is near it. Catholic sanctuaries are charged with a kind of holy magic. They are so old, so venerable; their very walls are saturate with God. "*Raise the stone, and there thou shalt find Me: cleave the wood, and there am I.*" But Protestants discourage ecstasy. Theirs is the religion of common-sense. They turn their enthusiasm towards work, not towards faith. You will find their churches empty except at the hours of service.'

'Yes, I know.'

'Even then, you won't find any intimate sense of joy in the congregation. It seems natural to the Englishman to behave coldly and correctly to his God.'

'In this church,' said Willie, 'people seem to forget their bodies. They slip away from the grey, ordinary earth, and find an answer to everything in some heaven that's close to them though it's shut to me.'

'Yes, that's a secret the Church has never lost, even in these blind centuries. But the reformed religions knocked all the poetry out of Christianity. Extraordinary! One hopes that in the closet of the believer the prayer of passion is still raised and the rapt accomplished: but I'm afraid it's an axiom of the Puritan to be dour, even with the Deity.'

He looked at Willie carefully and slowly.

'But you'll find faith,' he said: 'one can see that. It's there, you know. And your soul is set at an angle which will catch the light, once you're strong enough to tear the Veil away.'

He smiled at him again as they parted—a very friendly smile of sympathy and comfort. Then he turned down a neighbouring street and walked away quickly. Mr. Willie Hopkinson watched the tall, thin figure and bent shoulders till they were out of sight. Then he realized that a new element of consolation had come to him: that a certainty had been added to his hope. His friend had spoken to him of faith with the quiet balanced conviction with which one accepts the ordinary and indisputable in life. To him it was not less real than sunshine or his bodily raiment and food. In his soul, lit up by an inner light, Willie saw for the first time a reflection of the Beautiful God.

They never met again; but he was stronger and happier all his life because of that instant of communion.

CHAPTER 17

A SHARP CORNER

'Romance . . . depends on the Soul and not on Upholstery.'
—JOHN OLIVER HOBBES

'THOSE clever little fingers,' said Mr. Tiddy, 'were made for success.'

Mildred smiled, and continued to glair the letters upon the back of her book with a steady hand. She wished that she knew how to blush. She found Mr. Tiddy's vulgarity restful. His slovenly work made her own seem exquisite: his attentions restored the feeling of power which Willie had rudely disturbed. Bertram now shaved three times weekly, and wore his hair short—a concession to prejudice which did not suit his style. But his conversation remained on Mildred's level, making Mr. Hopkinson's frequent absences from the bindery so many holidays for his fiancée. She could then, as she said, devote herself entirely to her art.

Mildred despised Willie, and she feared him. She could not forget the horrible confidences which he had made to her, although she had refused to believe them. His dreaming eyes, which she once had proudly described as 'not altogether human,' now filled her with terror. But he was her affianced husband; young men were scarce in Turner's Heath; she had not sufficient trust in a kindly Providence to bring her engagement to an end.

Mr. Tiddy, who possessed something of the cunning of an experienced fox-terrier, knew how to extract a double advantage from this state of things. He flattered Mildred. He spoke with vague grandeur of his theories of art, and hopes of their future success. Incidentally, he cast an unbecoming light on Willie Hopkinson, first as a man and secondly as an artist. Mildred, still at that stage of culture in which it seems clever to be contemptuous, was not disgusted by Bertram's hints. They amplified and excused her own thoughts, which were more critical than kindly.

Her attitude now suggested that she was willing to talk to Mr. Tiddy whilst waiting for her glair to dry. She was a girl who never wasted her time.

'I wonder,' she said, 'if I ever shall succeed. It seems so difficult to get one's work well known, doesn't it? Of course, advertising is horrid. But I've always longed to develop a style of my own, like Sidney Henders, or Miss Delmere, or the Little Gidding people; so that everyone could recognise my things, you know, and I could exhibit at the Arts and Crafts.'

'I bet you anything I'd make your work succeed. There's a tremendous opening for artistic novelties—*chic*, original, Japanesy things with plenty of colour. All the swell craftsmen are hampered by tradition; they're afraid of being eccentric. But the public expects artistic things to be eccentric; it don't understand expensive simplicity. If they have their books bound by artists, people want the price to be moderate, and the design not too artistic to be understood.'

'I suppose good work always succeeds in the long-run.'

'Not it! Quaint work does. And that's your line—and mine too, for that matter. In these days, one must look at things in a practical light. Dress artistic; talk artistic. That's all to the good, it impresses people. But don't you get taken in with all that stuff about the beauty of labour and reticence in design. After all, it's the public we've got to look to, and it's our business as artists to make the public take to Art. That's a good enough ideal for me; and the way to do it is to give people something a bit better than they would have thought of for themselves, not something so artistic that it won't live in a middle-class drawing-room.'

'I wish I could get Willie to see it like that—so much more sensible, when we've got to live.'

'You won't. Hopkinson's a different type from you altogether. You're a born craftswoman, Miss Brent. You'll do well if you get a chance. But he's got no push: clever, of course, only not in that way. I sized him up directly he came here: one of those dreaming impractical chaps, always worrying about perfection. He's a cross between Carter and a minor poet.'

'I'm afraid he doesn't realize how important it is to succeed.'

'No,' said Bertram; 'it's a pity. Seems such a waste. What I feel is, you ought to be in your own little bindery, don't you know? Somewhere West Kensington way to start with, moving into Bloomsbury when we—I mean, when you had got a bit of a connection together. There's hundreds a year in those ideas of yours, your inlay and designing and so on, if the thing was run on a business footing. But I doubt if you'll ever get Hopkinson to consent to it.'

'Oh, I can't let him ride rough-shod over all my chances. I'm ambitious. I must develop myself. Because I'm going to marry him, it doesn't follow we think alike.'

'Ah, but you wouldn't be able to manage it alone. You wouldn't like to be worried with all the commercial details. You want a man to look after you and take all that off your hands. My idea of a small business like that would be, just an artistic industrious fellow and his wife working together, don't you know, with one apprentice perhaps. And no flexible sewing, or revival of antique methods, or any rot like that. I know the swell binders talk a lot about it when they're lecturing to amateurs, but it's all bunkum. We'd get all the foreign art magazines, and introduce the new French and German fashions before they got common. That's the way to run a successful bindery—you must be arty, and you must be up to date.'

Mildred sighed. Mr. Tiddy had never appeared to her in a more attractive light. She forgot his sticky hands and her own high ideals, and remembered only the agreeable picture suggested by his words. A spray of almond-blossom tapping against the window-pane reminded her that she had now been engaged to Willie for more than a year. She looked back, recollecting her hopes. She looked forward, and saw no chance of their fulfilment. She desired admittance to an appreciative, artistic society. But Mr. Hopkinson's very ordinary family treated her with condescension—his irritating unworldliness forbade her to expect any considerable improvement.

'It sounds lovely,' she said to Bertram; 'and once one got known, I dare say one would get to know Sidney Henders, and the Battersea Press people, and even the Little Gidding Guild. It would be so nice, I think, to be in touch with other artists. In a congenial atmosphere, one develops one's highest powers. But I shall never get Willie to see that: I don't believe he cares a bit whether he's an outsider or in the swim.'

'Ah,' replied Bertram, 'I often think, if you won't mind my being candid, that it's a pity in some ways that you're engaged to Hopkinson. Best for you, no doubt, but one hates to see a good artist sacrificed. I used to fancy once, you know, that you and I might have done some good work together if we'd gone into partnership.'

'I'm afraid that would be impossible.'

'I know. I'm too late—just my luck. I was wrapped up in my work, never saw. But I can't help wondering, if Hopkinson hadn't spoken first—'

Mr. Tiddy leaned towards Mildred, and looked at her with anxious eyes. She had seen the same expression in those of a well-fed dog who hankers for yet another bone. But she remembered Janet. She could not be sure of his intentions. She drew back.

Bertram, however, was in earnest. Miss Vivien's enchanting hair might invite to dalliance: Mildred's talents made her desirable as a wife. He would not be rebuffed. He placed a questioning hand upon her arm.

It is interesting to notice how small are the instruments by which Providence often contrives to effect its ends. Mildred did not intend to behave treacherously towards Willie. She was in the act of telling herself that she had really gone far enough. But the draught caused by Mr. Tiddy's abrupt movement caught the sheet of uncut gold-leaf which lay upon her gilding-cushion, and sent it in a fluttering dance across the workshop floor. The traditions of the 'Presse and Ploughe' were economical. Bertram and Mildred, from force of habit, started in pursuit: he eager to be of use, she proudly unconscious of his assistance. Gold-leaf is a subtle, human, very aggravating thing. It has moods, it is nervous. This sheet, after settling upon a backing-board, where it seemed quietly to await capture, rose suddenly in the air as Miss Brent approached it, and fled to the cutting-press, under which it lay perdu for some minutes. But presently its edge, shining amongst the snippings of mill-board and paper, caught her eye. She rushed towards it, a large dab of cotton-wool in her hand, not noticing Mr. Tiddy's simultaneous approach from the opposite side of the room. He saw the gold-leaf, bent down, and stretched a long arm tentatively towards it. She stooped, dived under the cutting-press, and found herself on her hands and knees within a few inches of his face.

Miss Brent's natural fear of knocking her head against the press made quick retreat impossible to her. Her position was too cramped to permit her much liberty of action. There was a slight scuffle. Then she rose from the floor; flushed, confused, and without the gold-leaf. But she was not disgusted. She was a woman who admired promptitude and resource. Mr. Tiddy had vindicated his manhood.

'Give me another, Millie,' he said.

Mildred smoothed her hair and looked at him seriously.

'Oh, Bertram,' she answered, 'are you sure that it is right? I can't bear to be cruel to poor Willie. But it's very difficult to know what to do when one's duties conflict. After all, we aren't really suited to one another, are we? And I feel I ought to think of poor mamma.'

*   *   *   *   *

Miss Brent found no difficulty in making Mr. Willie Hopkinson aware that their marriage would not take place. Her love of delicacy in outline had not helped her to appreciate the same quality in human affairs. The luncheon interval seemed to her a fitting moment in which to reveal to him her change of plans. Her sense of design was satisfied by the idea that their engagement would begin and end under the same conditions of background and boundary. It was like a half-drop repeat pattern: circumstances had compelled her to lower herself a little, but otherwise her attitude was unchanged.

She glowed with womanly virtue as she made his cocoa, and saw that he had his lunch comfortably before dealing a blow which would certainly have destroyed his appetite. She arranged her tools ready for the afternoon's work, took away the cups and washed them. Finally, as he lighted his second cigarette, she came to the point.

'There's something I've got to tell you, Willie,' she said. 'But I'm afraid you won't like it.'

Willie started nervously. His father, in a sudden spasm of generosity, had that morning offered him an allowance which would enable him to marry immediately. Willie had not yet found a reason at once valid and diplomatic for refusing this inconvenient gift. It did not seem possible that any annoyance emanating from Mildred could equal this. He answered her rather indifferently.

'Yes, dear? What is it?'

'I think perhaps it's better to put it plainly—kinder to you. You see, Willie, I've seen for a long time that we weren't really suited to one another. I'm sure you must have noticed it too. And I have my profession to think of—and, the fact is, I've decided to marry Bertram Tiddy.'

'*Tiddy?*' said Mr. Hopkinson.

He had controlled with difficulty a spontaneous movement of relief and surprise when he perceived the origin of Mildred's embarrassment. His first feeling was gratitude to his deliverer; but this was overwhelmed by a natural disgust caused by Mildred's want of proper feeling. He thought that he could have trusted her to realize that his supplanter must, at any rate, be a gentleman.

'Oh, I know he's common and he can't draw. I shall have to put up with that. There's always something to put up with. But, you see, he's human. Your kisses make my blood run cold, they seem to come from such a long way off.'

'I quite understand.'

'Oh, do you? I hope you do. I wouldn't like you to think I had behaved meanly. You see, Bertram really requires me. He says I do him good. When I'm with you, you do all the improving, and that bores me. I didn't think it would, but that was my want of experience. Now I do feel that I shall be improving Bertram all the time, and as he's given me the opportunity it is no more than my duty to do it.'

'From your point of view, I dare say you're right.'

'Yes, well, my point of view, after all, is what I've got to go by. And when one recognises one has made a mistake, it's more honest to say so, isn't it? My temperament isn't like yours, and however much I might care for you, I feel we should never get on. I'm not a gentle doormat sort of woman. I must express myself. Art's what I care for really—Art and life. And I feel if I only get my opportunity I could do something at that, and so does Bertram. There's a great future in Arts and Crafts, but one must look at it from a practical point of view. And I've got poor mamma to consider. And, of course, I always saw that your people didn't really like me, and I have some pride—'

Willie was not listening. He was released with honour from an unendurable situation, and his one desire was for active flight. He stretched out eager hands towards air, light, freedom: towards readmission to the privacies of his own soul. Mildred's companionship had always entailed a certain spiritual stuffiness.

Miss Brent, watching his face, admired his courage. She was sure that he adored her: was surprised that he concealed his sorrow so well. She did not wish to be unkind, and attributing to him her own love of emotional garnishings, she touched him gently on the arm.

'Would you like to kiss me good-bye?' she said.

He started. He had been thinking of other things.

'No, thanks'—he answered shortly, and walked out of the place.

'Poor Willie!' murmured Mildred.

CHAPTER 18

INCIPIT VITA NOVA

'The Beautiful is essentially the Spiritual making itself known sensuously.'
—HEGEL

ALL things have their price. Mr. Willie Hopkinson paid in mortification for his freedom. Everyone pitied him—an insufferable thing. Sometimes, however, he pitied himself, for Mildred had preferred Mr. Tiddy before him, and this was a humiliating thought.

It had been his conviction that he was superior to his surroundings. They were impermanent; deceiving and deceived. His soul was eternal. Few of his friends appreciated the distinction; but that he attributed to the ignorance in which he chose to keep them. And though experience now compelled him to acknowledge the existence of forces, even in the time-process, which were greater than himself, these had formed no part of his relation with Mildred Brent. He had been superior to her, and he knew it. He had admired his own constancy, sometimes regretted it. She, in discarding him, had released him from a strain which he had long known to be unpleasant—even inimical to his spiritual growth: but approving the end, he found it difficult to justify means so wounding to his vanity.

Stephen and Pauline offered him a tactless and heartfelt commiseration which inflamed his already tender self-respect. They hid as well as they might their own raptures, not wishing to suggest painful parallels with his immediate past. Pauline, for the first time in her life, felt able to understand her brother. A broken engagement appealed to her as a solid and reasonable ground for mental distress.

'Poor old Will!' she said. 'It is hard luck! And you were so devoted to her. I can't think how a girl can be such a beast.'

Stephen, with real unselfishness, deprived himself of Pauline's society, and took his friend for long walks, encouraging him to talk of his grief. But Willie's very actual miseries were not those which Mr. Miller could best comprehend. His chief torments arose from a humiliating inability to grasp the principle which guided his devious career. Life seemed to lay traps for his spirit. One after another, hopeful paths failed him, and he came wearily back to the endless road. Elsa—Mildred—Stephen—each name brought the memory of fresh discouragements. These had offered comprehension and companionship, but they had failed.

To Stephen, perhaps, the Real World had some actuality. His love for Pauline raised him in some mysterious way above the sordid scamper after material success. He looked out on a dreamy earth with contented eyes, and breathed a serene and satisfying air. But the others only toyed with the symbols of transcendent truth, and their careless agnosticism clouded Willie's perceptions.

He had travelled far from the child who had prayed for a return at any price to the adventure of life: from the boy who had looked out on existence as a game to be played lightly, a pageant to be watched. The dark night of his soul was upon him. He felt spiritual realities slipping away, yet the pleasures of life seemed savourless and dull. All was unreal; nothing was worth effort. Even in the holy places he found no peace. He remembered the words of the young man of Our Lady of Pity, but told himself that faith was only one illusion the more.

It was to Elsa, long-suffering and secretly joyful, that he now poured out his mixed emotions. She had got her boy back again. She cared nothing for the twisted paths by which he had come. He was relieved—jealous—despondent. Her attitude towards each angle was correct. This was a part which she played to perfection, and she was delighted to have the opportunity.

'There is,' she said, 'such an exquisite pleasure in pain! Many of our greatest poets have noticed that. I could almost envy you your suffering. To suffer for love! Oh, believe me, dear Willie, this is much better than to marry for it. Yours is indeed the more beautiful part.'

'I'm so confused,' said Willie, 'so wretched! I don't know what's beautiful or what's real. It isn't love that makes me unhappy—it's the weary not knowing what to do. There must be some aim in life that's genuine, some experience that won't fail when one tries it.'

Elsa had one restful characteristic. She never asked for explanations. She accepted Willie's words as evidence of his abundant imagination, stroked his hair, and sent him to the National Gallery—her one prescription for agitations of the soul.

A subtle sense of the fitness of things had kept him from seeking the consolations of religion; Elsa's suggestion was a compromise which pleased him. He had a grateful recollection of those very silent rooms, watched by brooding Madonnas, by still gods, dream-portraits of personalities long ago released from the fret of life.

He went there—melancholy, feverish, impatient. He hurried through the turnstile, up the stairs, pushed open the door which leads to the great Tuscan room. But as it closed behind him, the healing process began. Something arrested him on the threshold—a restraining touch, a feeling that he was seeking with ungracious intention admittance to a company of friends. The quiet festival of colour on the walls seemed an invitation to some serious kind of happiness for which he was unprepared. The influence of beauty imposed its peace on him, as great communities always impose their etiquette: he felt that in such society one could not grumble of one's petty griefs. The place was full of the calmness, the ineffable hush, which belongs to transcendental things. It filled him with a grave delight. No sound of voices, no sense of human fellowship: only the repeated echo of footsteps upon the wide spaces of the polished floor.

There were other persons in the gallery, I think. A superior woman leading a meek, tired friend, and murmuring of L'Amico di Sandro and the Early Sienese. A curate, polite to the Madonnas, but coldly observant of the lesser saints. A pair of happy foreigners, for whom the place had all the glamour which the Uffizi and the Louvre keep for us. It did not matter. A great wall shut them from Mr. Willie Hopkinson. Only the pictures broke his solitude.

He sat down presently before that very lovely panel which is called 'The Madonna adoring the Infant Christ.' Its ceremonious beauty caught his eye; the ardour of its emotion held him fast. The peculiar fascinations of Florentine piety, at once so mystical, reasonable, and austere, come together in this picture—in its joyous purity of line, the intimate holiness of its atmosphere, the strange majesty of the rapt Madonna, who sits with hands folded in prayer and looks silently down on her Son. The wistful angels who lean against the sides of her throne are hushed by her intense stillness. They are spiritual persons, who cannot understand the earthly love which blends Mother and worshipper in one. One turns a dreamy face to her, asking explanation of the mystery: but she, in an ecstasy of contemplation, scarcely knows of their presence. She dreams above her child, lying very helplessly and gladly upon its mother's knee—as all that is holy in us lies upon the lap of Perfect Beauty.

Willie sat opposite this picture for a very long time, and looked; steadily, intently, without conscious thought. In the face of Our Lady was infinite promise, infinite peace. As he watched her, something unearthly, something remote from life, laid its quieting hand upon him. These things had not been conceived in the petty agitations of ordinary life. The Beyond had been at their birth, and left token of its presence. A door seemed to open: an unspeakable sensation warned him that he was lifted up past the boundary of grey illusion.

> 'Donna, se' tanto grande e tanto vali,
>   Che qual vuol grazia, ed a te non ricorre,
> Sua disianza vuol volar senz' ali.'

These words recurred to Mr. Willie Hopkinson, and brought with them new, undreamed significance. A master-key, it seems, may unlock the gates of many mansions. Those who have once prostrated themselves before Invisible Powers have gained a perception which is never lost. For the first time, he detected a truth behind the absurdity of Elsa's dictum that *prie-dieux* ought to be placed before the master-pieces of devotional art. The National Gallery, she said, always made her want to say her prayers. To Willie, now, there came that sensation of real worlds and unknown splendours very near, which had descended on him when he knelt before the Altar of the Holy Spirit. He discovered, as he had done when he wandered in the Grey Dimension, that one has only to turn one's eyes resolutely from Earth to lose its obsessing influence. It is the downward glance that anchors us to the world of sense.

Mrs. Levi's favourite catch-words came back to him—'Ultimate Beauty,' 'life-enhancing qualities of art,' 'spiritual significance of Italian Painting'—phrases to which he had never attached definite meaning. But this face, this picture which had worked a miracle in his tormented spirit, gave to them a sudden vitality. He saw, wondering at his past blindness, that it was above all things strange and significant that things should be beautiful at all. The ecstasy induced in him by loveliness had no relation to the necessities of human life. It was inexplicable. The ritual of light and colour veiled, as it adorned, inconceivable secrets.

He asked himself what indeed could be the spirit of loveliness if it were not a penetration of the Visible by the Real: the link between Truth and Idea for which he had been groping all his life. This thought he naturally imagined to be as original as it was profound, and pride of invention modified the crushing power of its truth. Beauty seemed to offer him an assurance of exquisite realities, to be given to those who desired them in faith and in love.

He looked at the quiet pictures—at the angels in their mystical dance before the manger; at the gentle faun who knelt by Procris, weeping that so much loveliness should have been taken from life. They seemed to him so many windows built towards heaven. He had a new vision of the world. He saw it as a shadow cast by Divine Beauty—a loveliness of which material beauty was the sacrament, the faint image thrown by God on the mirror of sense. In the Madonna he found the symbol of a reconciling principle, looking lovingly upon humanity, which it cherished and fed. Her manifestation was earthly enough: an illusion built up of paint and panel by some man held, as he was held, a prisoner in Time and Space. But her powers stretched into the Invisible. He wondered whence the vision had come which inspired the secret of her picture.

Then it occurred to him that the soul, in him conscious and perceptive, must exist in all men: obscure, mysterious, withdrawn from the squalid battle. Beyond the threshold of consciousness that unsuspected visitor sits, looking with steady eyes upon the eternal light. That light shone in these pictures. It seemed possible that in their creation the soul, which saw beyond the illusions of Time, had guided the artist's hand to some great purpose. Their message was the message of the churches, translated to a language which he could understand. He had found a religion. He recognised that the inarticulate ecstasy which came to him in the presence of all beautiful things was the same in essence as that emotion which he felt in Our Lady of Pity—another way of approach to the same God.

There are few more compelling confessors than a great work of art. Willie looked still at the Madonna, and the small details which obscure the issues of life fell away from him. He regained the power, long lost, of detecting fact in the midst of illusion. He looked back down the years, and was annoyed to find little in them that was worth notice. It was a petty record—a matter of drifting and discontent. That, too, had been the note of the Grey World: it seemed that his pretension of knowledge had not enabled him to escape its grasp. He remembered how he had broken the spell of that Dimension—the intensity of desire which had thrown him back again on life.

The will which had done that miracle was still with him. He asked himself how it was that he did not exert it, did not set it to the realization of reality, instead of stopping every moment to consider the chances of the road. He was twenty-three years old; a fully developed being. Yet he had allowed every influence to have power over his actions, had no dominant motive, no hope in his life.

There had been places, he knew, at which he had seen the faint outlines of happy countries, had caught a glimpse of the Delectable Mountains shining in the sun. For their sake he had set out upon his pilgrimage—a pilgrimage which might have offered him visions of beautiful landscape, and the bow of promise in the clouds, had he given his attention to the horizon instead of to the dust under his feet. He gathered up and compared the fragments of his knowledge. In the fret of work and passion, the old true outlines had grown dim. In the early years, terror of the after-death, of an eternity spent in the languid miseries of the Grey World, had driven him to search for truth. Now he fancied that Love might have been a worthier motive than fear, a better companion for the quest. There had been a certain meanness in his scramble after personal salvation, which sufficiently explained its non-success.

The adorable face of Our Lady shone as a favourable light at the end of a dark road. The reality at the back of the picture was speaking to him; telling him of exquisite places of the spirit to which he might aspire. He asked himself how he stood in relation to this universe, which strove towards Beauty as the realization of itself. In a spasm of self-knowledge, he saw his years in their petty ugliness, saw that he had done nothing with them, had not raised himself above the hopeless herd. He had stayed on the level, sneering at his equals. Now, with the clear sight of the newly-converted, he perceived how great had been his spiritual stupidity. He was disgusted with himself. The mountain road had been close to him all the time, and above him the austere majesty of the hill-tops.

'Oh, to climb!' he cried.

*   *   *   *   *

Mrs. Hopkinson heard him that night sobbing in his room very bitterly. She told Mrs. Levi about it.

'Quite hysterical!' she said. 'I nearly went in to him with the sal volatile, but I thought perhaps he wouldn't like to think I'd heard him—boys are so absurdly sensitive about those things. That horrid girl has evidently upset his nerves more than he'd allow.'

'A thorough change of scene,' said Elsa, 'is what he really wants. In contemplating the Beautiful, we forget our earthly griefs. And he can't go back to the bindery whilst that creature is there.'

'No, indeed,' replied Mrs. Hopkinson. 'Poor boy! I'm only thankful he found her out in time. She would have made him a wretched wife; full of modern ideas, and absolutely undomesticated. It's quite pulled him down, one can see that. I think we must really try if we can't send him away for a little change: all the doctors are recommending sunshine and fresh air for the nerves.'

It was Elsa who discovered the method of his pilgrimage—a personally conducted tour for professional men and others, 'A Fortnight with Saint Francis for £13 10s.' Taking its charges as far as Perugia, it there allowed them to wander at will.

'Nothing could be better for him than that,' said Mrs. Levi. 'Italy has such a wonderful effect upon the soul. Exquisite climate; and then the associations! Francis and Claire, and the beautiful wicked Baglione! And Perugino, of course. Florence is so hackneyed: and Rome—well, Rome is Rome.'

'Yes, you can't do Rome under £25,' said Mr. Hopkinson.
It was thus that Willie found Umbria.

CHAPTER 19

THE DELECTABLE MOUNTAINS

'What more beautiful image of the Divine could there be than this world, except the world yonder?'

—PLOTINUS

IN Umbria, where little hills reach up towards the kiss of God, bearing her small white cities nearer heaven: in Umbria, clothed with olive-woods where Francis walked, and crowned by turrets of the Ghibelline, there is a Peace of God eternally established. In this country, long beloved of the dreamy arts, spirits wearied by dark journeyings may still feel the quieting touch of Immanent Peace. Yet the soul of Umbria is as the soul of a very melancholy queen. The nostalgia of the distant descends on the hearts of her lovers, giving them a delicate sadness not easily to be effaced. Her very breezes seem to come from far off, charged with the murmur of dim memories. But the joy of a wonderful passion transfigures her regret. In her, the image of the Delectable Country, in whose likeness Earth was once made, is still to be apprehended.

On the walls of the city of Spello, high up on the hill between Foligno and Assisi, Mr. Willie Hopkinson sat, dreamed, and contemplated the world from a new standpoint. He looked down into the marvellous valley which has known the footsteps of so many saints. He enjoyed, with a vague but very serious delight, its exquisite cadences of blue and green, the magical light that hangs over it, the old dim roads that pattern its fields and vineyards into the semblance of some faded tessellated work.

Three hundred feet below him, the little Roman amphitheatre was a round shadow on the grass. Young and happy verdures had buried its ancient cruelties in the secret earth. The Etruscan blocks that he sat upon had been in their position perhaps two thousand years. They had remained for defence, as their dark-eyed, voluptuous builders had left them: had seen the Romans come and go, had watched the Northern emperors on their march to Rome, the Popes going up to Perugia. Finally, they had seen the patriot come, and the poetry of Italy fade under his fingers. In their old age they were very stately. Man, creeping under their shadow or perched upon their height, seemed some ephemeral insect.

Yet, under that vivid sky, in an atmosphere where all things are fresh and definite and the air sings the hymn of Brother Sun, Willie could not believe in antiquity. He felt that he looked out on a world which always had existed, always would exist, and he with it: for the only real existence was in Beauty, and Beauty was eternal. He had quite forgotten Mildred—Elsa—his home—the slow grey life he must return to when this happy fortnight was done. These things had never had a very real importance for him; but whilst he knew them to be illusion, he had not been able to shake them off. He had felt them as a shadowy net, confusing and confining. In the sunshine of Italy they seemed tedious accidents. She was real, potent. She completed for him the vision of life first dimly seen in Our Lady of Pity, intensely felt in the National Gallery when the Tuscan Madonna spoke to him of peace.

The Umbrian landscape is essentially religious. It fulfils the message of the Church, the revelation of the painters. He knew that it had symbolic import, some bearing on the transcendental life: that atheism and despair were impossible in its presence.

He looked back down the path towards the town and saw, through the little Roman arch which spans the road, a group of people coming up to him. He was sorry. He had enjoyed his solitary hour. But Mr. and Mrs. Finchley supposed that he was sight-seeing. They felt that it was their duty to miss nothing of interest, and they had followed him.

They headed a procession representative of the population of Spello: several unpleasant beggars; many children; a woman bearing a jar on her head, whose face, poise, figure suggested a Tanagra statuette. Mrs. Finchley was trying to photograph her; but an old man with no nose, and hands in an advanced state of decomposition, insisted on placing himself in the foreground.

The Rev. John Finchley, who had a fussy manner and no Italian, seemed unhappy.

'Horrible place, this,' he said to Willie as soon as he came within earshot—'a disgrace to the authorities! We found the frescoes, but they weren't up to much: and they were cleaning the floor of the church, which was most unpleasant. I'm afraid my wife's got her feet damp.'

'Yes,' said Mrs. Finchley. 'But still, I liked them better than those things at Montefalco—they *were* Bible incidents, not those everlasting saints.'

'Saints seem natural here,' said Willie.

'Yes, I suppose they are; one must expect that in Roman Catholic countries. But I can never get really used to them: they seem to me such wicked creatures! It's the way I was brought up, I suppose. And to think of praying to them!'

'It's a great pity,' said her husband, 'that the Protestant religion hasn't produced any great artists. They would have painted the truths of Evangelical Christianity, and prevented Popish art attracting so much attention. These Romanist subjects are harmful to weak minds; they promote idolatry. Of course, the reason is that our great thinkers have been engaged with the higher aspects of things, and had no attention left for outward display.'

'A spiritual religion scarcely needs pictures, does it, dear?' said Mrs. Finchley.

Willie sighed, looked at her figure—short skirt and Panama hat clearly outlined against the delicate Perugino landscape—and supposed his happy day was at an end. He had suffered a good deal from the Finchleys since leaving England in their company nine days before.

Now they would drive back to Perugia, Mr. Finchley speaking of the political condition of the country, his wife much occupied by the private history of her fellow-tourists at the hotel. He wanted so much another hour of solitude, of secret conversation with the spirit which Umbria had knit up for him out of loveliness and antiquity.

Mr. Finchley looked at his watch.

'Half-past two!' he said. 'And you wanted to photograph Rivo Torto on the way back, didn't you, dear? and I promised to hold a little service in the hotel drawing-room at six. We must be starting back. Perhaps, Mr. Hopkinson, you wouldn't mind telling the coachman to whip up the horse a bit more than he did coming: in Italian, of course. It walked up all the hills.'

It was at this moment that Willie discovered that an afternoon spent in the society of the Finchleys was impossible to him.

'I think, if you don't mind,' he said, 'I shall walk back. It's under ten miles, and you will go quicker with only two in the carriage.'

'Oh, do you think you ought, Mr. Hopkinson?' answered Mrs. Finchley. 'You look tired already, I'm afraid you do too much; and your mother warned me that you weren't very strong. It's no use over-exerting one's self, is it? and the mental strain of seeing so many new things is dreadfully exhausting.'

She was a thin, active little woman, like a brown grasshopper; very good-natured, and devoted to her husband and her camera. She and Mrs. Hopkinson had been schoolfellows, and both thought the coincidence which enabled her to take charge of Willie a fortunate one. But a week of travel had given a touch of decision to Mr. Willie Hopkinson's rather fluid character. He was polite but firm with Mrs. Finchley. These days were sudden jewels set in the dull circlet of his life. He dared not waste them. The white roads, the lanes that went between the olives, were sending him a mystic invitation. He would tramp with the Lady Poverty, as S. Francis did.

From the ancient market-place, where a twelfth-century Madonna stands above the Roman gate to bless her citizens, he saw the carriage start. Its occupants had no farewell to offer Spello; they were carefully shielding the camera from dust and sun. He looked back gratefully to the grey walls, the friendly clambering streets with their Gothic houses, and went down alone into the valley of the Tiber.

'The broad road that stretches' took him to its bosom. The symbolic attitude of the traveller on the highway set the tune of his thoughts. He walked firmly, steadily, with a growing exhilaration. Blue sky, white blossoming trees, were as wine to his heightened perceptions. He smiled happily as he caught sight of Assisi, folded pale against her hill like an angel at rest. He felt himself to be, not any more the man in the world, but the pilgrim soul footing it between the stars. He was walking alone, sturdily self-dependent, through exquisite landscape towards an appointed goal. That, surely, should be his life. That *was* life—a journey upon the great highway of the world towards an abiding city: a journey to be taken joyfully and in gratitude because of the beauty of the road.

He conceived now of the world, of the body, as momentary conditions in the infinite progress of the spirit. Used rightly, a discipline, an initiation; used wrongly, a peril whose deeps he had once known. His idealism had come to this; to a guarded, tolerant acquiescence in the queer distorting medium of his senses, a willingness within limits to accept their reports. But it was the holy, the beautiful aspect of things that he asked them to show him. That was significant, true. No illusion of time and space, but an eternal thing which it was the very business of matter to shadow forth, the duty of that pilgrim soul in him to apprehend. One must not arrive at the Continuing City deaf and blind to the music and radiance, obsessed by the incident worries of life. That was to have passed through the Great University in vain.

Willie was beginning to recover from the disease of spiritual self-seeking which had crippled his first years. He had seen at last the face of the Great Companion. He knew what he wanted; the constant presence of that mysterious guide, the constant assurance of a strange but enduring amity. He had come to the second, or illuminative, stage of the journey: for his way, after all, had been the old mystic's way. There is no other practicable path for those who are determined on reality, who have found out the gigantic deception we accept as the visible world, the gigantic foolishness of our comfortable common-sense.

The old formula came back to his mind: 'Purgation, Illumination, Contemplation'—the three stages of the Via Mystica, acknowledged by all the masters who had trod it, the explorers who had left notes of its geography behind. This trinity of experience seemed to co-relate in some way with the triune vision of reality —'The triple star of Goodness, Truth, and Beauty'—promised to those who attained its highest stage. In his wanderings, apparently so devious, he had followed the old lines very exactly. He looked back on his feverish years: his poor efforts to grasp some detail of the shadow show as it passed him, and make it real for himself. He remembered his terrified search for safety, the Mildred episode and its humiliations, the hope that his first meeting with Stephen had brought: lastly, the quest of security amongst the Mysteries of

Catholic belief. He recognised in the slow abasement of his spirit, the gradual renunciation of pride involved in each failure, a purging of the eye of the soul that it might look with understanding on a clearer prospect.

All, it was evident, could not tread the same road. The idealizing power of his love for Pauline had made a breach for Stephen in the 'flaming rampart of the world': the Secret of the Altar offered a sure and certain hope to its initiates. But for Willie the shadow of an Everlasting No was across those paths. His way of escape lay through another gateway.

Climbing the steep lane between the olive groves in the silent heat of an Italian afternoon, everything seemed rather supernatural in its loveliness. He came to a shrine, where a faint Umbrian Madonna held out her Child to the traveller: and stopped to thank the Unknown God who had framed for his joy this wonderful Rose of the World. Each moment brought its miracle, in the further opening of those mystic petals. He had glimpses of all the worlds, —the holy, elfish, dark, and terrible countries—which are folded together to form the bewildering appearance which civilized persons call solid fact. Some resolving power in him separated these aspects of things, and set his feet in a magical place where all he saw and felt had the glamour of a fairy land inextricably entwined in this. So that he was not very surprised when, at a bend of the road, he came presently on a wayfarer of another century, left behind by the ebbing tide of poetic faith.

A brown-frocked Franciscan trod the path very soberly before him, unconscious of the road and of company upon it. His eyes were on the open book he carried: it was evident that his thoughts were far away from the dust and the sun. Willie, easily touched by the subtle charm of the religious habit, said '*Buona sera*' very pleasantly as he passed.

'*Grazie, signore; e buon passeggio,*' replied the friar mechanically.

He continued reading, his lips moving busily as if in voiceless prayer. But as Willie's shadow fell across his book, he raised a brown, ill-shaven face, and looked at him. His eye took in the contours of Mr. Hopkinson's strictly patriotic dress, and rested approvingly on his hat. It seemed that, like most persons who lived a cloistered life, he was interested in small detail.

'*Teh! un' Inglese!*' he said joyfully. 'If the *signore* would have the goodness to assist me a little in the pronunciation?'

He held out his book. It was perfumed with garlic, and in general want of repair. Mr. Hopkinson, expecting a Breviary, observed the title with surprise, '*La Lingua Inglese in tre Mesi —Grammatica, Vocabolario, Idiomi.*'

The little friar placed an odorous and insinuating head close to Willie's shoulder, and fell into step with him. He pointed to a tired-looking page of characteristic English puzzles—'Bough,' 'cough,' 'bought,' 'enough.' Escape was impossible. Willie, half annoyed, half captivated by the oddness of the thing, said the words over slowly; and this queer little son of S. Francis, twisting his tongue into strange positions, parodied him as well as he could. He also offered for criticism several obscure sentences, recognisable with care as British forms of speech. Anxious not to lose an instant of this precious opportunity, he grew very hot and breathless in the effort to combine hill-climbing with irregular verbs. It was evident that he was much in earnest.

To Willie, the situation seemed a paradox; absurd enough, yet with a certain irony at its heart. This friar, marked with the ensigns of a religious life, was living there in the cradle of his Order an existence which could scarcely avoid the fringe of Invisible Things. Yet all his heart was put in a struggle to acquire the language of a people so far behind his spiritual ancestors in all that. The very life he led—that temperate, ordered life of the Franciscan Observant —must place him on a hill which was not very far from heaven. But his most ambitious dream was of a scrambling down from that quiet altitude into the busy, noisy valley of the world.

'Is it by command of your Order that you learn English?' said Willie presently.

'No, *signore.* I learn it because I wish to live—to improve myself —for the glory of the blessed S. Francis. But in the convent there are indiscreet ones, who would say "Fra Agostino wishes to make himself wiser than his brothers." So it is only when I go into Spello to get a newspaper for the Father Superior that I can study a little of the *grammatica* on the road.'

'I can't think why you should want to learn it. It isn't beautiful, like Italian—I would forget it if I could.'

'Ah, *signor mio*,' said Fra Agostino, 'one must study the world the good God has given us, must one not? And to know all the excellencies He has given it, one must truly know the English, for it is from England that now all the new things come. The more one knows, the more one will love; and S. Francis laid on us the duty of loving all things. So, to study the English language is a true opera *di devozione*. It is that I may daily thank the good God for all the interesting things he has placed in the world. The English are so strong, so modern. In Italia, all is old, nothing moves.'

'Oh,' said Willie, 'we may be modern, but we don't understand things; we haven't religion, and the sense of beautiful living, innate in us as you must have here. We have to come to Italy to find the real loveliness, the old spirit left over from the happy days of the world.'

'If the *signore* were Italian he would not speak thus,' said Fra Agostino. He was trotting steadily by Willie's side, a moist forefinger carefully keeping his place in the grammar-book. 'In Italy is only the old things, the remnant: in England is fertility, growth; and liberty—even for the religious. The *signore* is like the English *signora* who was here two years back. She loved our Italy. In Italy, she said, the soul lives. She was surprised, too, that I should wish to learn the English. She called it turning my back on heaven. She came here for beautiful thoughts, being an artist; for it is true that Italy is the mother of artists. In England, she said, she had no inspiration. But *veda, signore*, she returned home, and she has sent an Ancona for our chapel. She painted it, altogether in the ancient manner, in her cell in England. She lives there alone; she is an anchoress. In Italy, there is none who could have painted that picture. The English are great artists, a great people also. I will show the *signore*, and he can judge.'

They had come now to the gate of the convent. They crossed the courtyard, went into the little church. It was very bare—truly a mendicant sanctuary. Crude coloured statues of S. Francis and S. Anthony contrasted painfully with the white-washed brickwork, the rough wooden stalls of the choir. The cheap ornaments and artificial flowers of the altar, jarred senses which had come straight from the exquisite shrine of the earth where Nature offers her sacrifice. Fra Agostino walked up the only aisle, and Willie after him. The place seemed dark after the sunshine, and they were at the altar-step before he saw the picture that was behind the Holy Table.

It was not, as he had vaguely expected, a stigmatized S. Francis, or an Anthony of Padua dreaming on the Infant Christ. What he saw was a woman's figure; spare, simple, ugly almost, in its short torn canvas dress that showed the bare feet worn by long travelling. Behind her was the dim green Umbrian landscape, as it stretches out from S. Mary of the Angels. Round her head, a cloud of wheeling birds made a halo; and within the halo a vision of the Cross. But what struck him most was a reticence of handling, which suggested behind the plain lines of the picture an ineffable peace, the secret of a complete inward happiness. This woman held out thin delicate hands in a sort of compelling welcome to her lovers. Her personality was the climax, the essential charm, of the place: so that it really seemed as if all who approached that altar must come to her arms.

Fra Agostino saw Willie's bewildered movement of admiration.

'It is the Lady Poverty, whom the Blessed S. Francis loved as a bride,' he explained. 'He left her to the care of his sons. They lost her, some say, after his death: but the Government has given her back to us. It was a beautiful idea of the English *signora* that she should be placed above our altar. A fine painting, is it not? I show it to all the English, for we are very proud of it in the convent.'

'What is this *signora's* name?' said Willie.

'The *signore* may read it at the bottom of the picture.'

There, on a little scroll, were words indeed, in clear black letters. *'Hester Waring painted this Picture in the fear of God and for love of S. Francis. At her cell of S. Mary-le-Street, in the year of the Lord 1900.'*

'Is this *signora* in religion?'

'No, *signore*. She has not taken the habit. But she is a *visionaria*, a solitary; she spends much time in contemplation. It is curious: there is a look in your eyes, *signore*, which reminds one of her. It is not often seen: it is the look of the ecstatic. The *signore* also has had experiences.'

They went out presently from the church; Willie much possessed by the personality of this unknown painter who also had seen the Secret behind the Veil. The image of this woman, living happy in her solitude, placidly translating her vision of things into material beauty, fascinated him. He had an irrational conviction that she was his friend. He said over to himself her name and designation: 'Hester Waring, in her cell of S. Mary-le-Street.' From far off, her example beckoned him.

He thought of her still, when he stood in the garden of the convent, walled in on the brow of the hill and looking down on great, peaceful spaces. The austere silence of the place, its attitude of expectation, helped his dream. Leaning over the wall at the end of the little orchard, he looked out on a sky and hills which seemed to him to be bathed in holiness, and wondered how much of what he felt was Earth, and how much Heaven.

'The Father Superior,' said Fra Agostino presently, 'comes much to the garden for holy meditation, as the Blessed S. Claire used to do.'

'But are not the Franciscans vowed to works rather than contemplation?' said Willie. 'Does not the Father Superior have to occupy himself with useful things?'

'Ah, *signor mio*,' answered Fra Agostino quietly, 'there is only one rule for the good Franciscan—to live in S. Francis' spirit as well as he can. The *signore* will remember that it was not when he was about useful things that S. Francis received the great favour of the Stigmata; it was when he meditated amongst the hills. The good God gives us useful things for seventy years only; but to His lovers He gives beautiful things for ever. It would be a pity, would it not, if we were not able to recognise them?'

But at the gateway the little friar's mood changed suddenly. The approach to the road drew his thoughts from the charm of the cloister to the drama of the great world.

'If the *signore* desires to do a good action,' he said softly, as Willie bade him good-bye, 'perhaps he would send me an illustrated post-card occasionally, when he has returned to his family in England. Views of the great cities of England, and of the streets. The beautiful ladies also. If the *signore* will do this I will send him Italian post-cards; and, if he desire it, I will remember him in my prayers.'

Mr. Willie Hopkinson reached Perugia at the moment of sunset, when a radiant sky shut blue hills and white cities in a warm embrace. He felt alive, exalted, intimately joyful. It was the ecstasy which comes with first knowledge of the secret of Being, with the first dim apprehension of the Shadowy Friend. But the atmosphere of the hotel, so warm, British and respectable, checked the raptures of the road. In the corridor he heard the ungracious tones of a harmonium. Mr. Finchley's little service was evidently in progress. Twelve travelling spinsters and a tired schoolmaster were singing the last hymn.

Willie stood to listen as he passed the door. The tune, it seemed, was 'Lead, Kindly Light,' but the words were new to him—

> 'Too long we followed that misguiding light
>   Which points to Rome:
> Now Luther's torch illumes the Church's night
>   And leads us home.
> Far from Confession, Incense, Feast and Fast,
> Till in the Gospel we repose at last.'

These lines had been added to Cardinal Newman's poem by the orthodox muse of Mr. Finchley, who considered that they made the hymn peculiarly suitable for use in Roman Catholic countries. Mrs. Finchley's wiry voice could be heard leading the congregation: she sang the last line in an acrid *crescendo*. This was her favourite verse. 'It breathes,' she said, 'such a thoroughly Christian spirit.'

CHAPTER 20

THE RIVER

'The afternoon draws quiet breath
At pause between the eve and morn,
And from the sacred place of Death
The holy thoughts of Life are born.'
—ISRAEL ZANGWILL

MRS. HOPKINSON was ill—so ill, that she almost seemed interesting. It had begun with a cold, which she would have nursed carefully in others but naturally neglected in herself. Her family were accustomed to leave matters of health entirely in her keeping: they had therefore nothing to offer—neither sympathy, patent medicines, nor advice. It seemed so unlikely that she should be seriously ill; it would be too inconvenient.

But when Mrs. Hopkinson began to let the hours slip by without concern; when the news that the butcher had called for orders did not stimulate her sleepy brain; Pauline, in whom Stephen's love had opened the gates of sympathy, became frightened. She sent for the doctor, and telegraphed for Willie, who hurried from Milan to find the household in disorder, dominated by a shadowy but very awful presence.

Curiously, in all his brooding on the quick flitting of life he had never contemplated the deaths of his family; the unpreventable obliteration of faces which made up the actual landscape of home. And quite suddenly, without any of the solemn preparation which mankind never ceases to expect before a crisis, this shifting of the scenes had come.

The certainty of impending death was written up: a helpless feeling, the consciousness of a Destiny not to be evaded, had abruptly replaced the wholesome bustling atmosphere which was natural to the house. He felt the strange hush, as of fear, with which the unsubstantial side of Being waits for the great change. All the cheerful, indeterminate sounds of the home-life seemed muffled. A sharp noise struck on the tense waiting nerves with a kind of horror. Already, as it seemed to him, the Grey People of the Sorrowful Country were gathering, expecting a new mourner to be added to their companies. They jostled him in the passages. In silent moments, he thought that he heard their faint cry as they circled about his mother's bed.

Meanwhile, though there was invalid cookery in the kitchen, and a dark whisper in the air of heart failure and want of recuperative power, no one but himself quite realized that Mrs. Hopkinson was in danger; that few inches remained of the skein of grey wool—dull, but warranted to wash—which the Fates had apportioned to her homely life. Mr. Hopkinson could not believe that she was no longer able to take a personal interest in the airing of his linen on Saturday night. The thing fell so far outside the daily routine as to seem almost like a miracle: and Pauline and her father did not countenance miracles, even domestic ones.

All through her life, Mrs. Hopkinson had possessed the knack of doing things in an unimpressive way. Her remarks fell flat; her unselfish actions passed without notice. There is a slightly squalid way of handling the profound and essential things in existence, which is peculiarly British. It was this method, this secret, which had depoetized Mrs. Hopkinson's life. She had brought forth her children amongst flannel and stuffiness; now she was slipping from existence surrounded by the uninspiring perfumes of eucalyptus and camphorated oil.

For Willie, however, the illness had a certainty of issue, and that certainty a horror, which kept all his thoughts chained to the sick-bed. In its last stages of purgation, his spirit had dropped many of the petty arrogances and intolerances which had made him in the past a thorny if intelligent neighbour. He now vaguely saw a beauty in those undecorative virtues which before had only irritated his hyperaesthetic mind. Believing that all things exist because of the loveliness that exists in them, he discerned with a certain sad and tender love some beautiful meaning hidden under his mother's garrulous kindness; as a majesty lurks behind the homely features of a Rembrandt portrait.

Yet he could not doubt that she was destined to the Grey World; to an eternal, useless flitting to and fro on the edges of life, which would be torture to her busy spirit. By a horrible irony, those very qualities for which he might have been grateful were her ruin. That intimate carefulness for home, that selfless preoccupation with her children's external comfort, which had been fostered by education, approved by convention, by religion even; these combined to tie her spirit to earth. She was an admirable animal, but she had built no immaterial heaven for herself. Where should she go, who had never in all her life longed for anything but the health and success of herself, her husband, and her family? It is very clear that the Eternal and Imaginative world is for those with eyes to see and hearts to desire it.

Willie knelt by her bedside; held her hand; watched her face. The whole scene had a horrible fascination for him. The brightly lighted bedroom, with its white enamelled furniture, pink striped walls, cretonne hangings, made the idea of imminent death incredible. All seemed orderly, earthly, actual. The fire had been made up, and burned cheerfully. There was a table near it with the remains of beef-tea, and a novel, 'Lily the Cheiromant,' which only two days ago Mrs. Hopkinson had been reading with great interest. Yet now she lay on the bed, as he once had lain, and struggled, half unconscious of her extremity, to retain her hold upon life.

Two worlds, two powers, were fused in that little room, and she was the link between them. Body and soul had entered on the last assault of their long tournament. He remembered, with a shock almost of fear, that in this same place he had made his second entry into the visible world. 'The houses of death and of birth'—the terminals of the time-process—came together here and showed to him the sameness of their secret.

He wondered whether she felt, as he had done, the dreadful isolation of the dying. It suddenly occurred to him that he, of his experience, should be able to help her in this passage as no other could possibly do. They were alone together. Pauline had thought the patient better, and had gone for a walk. Willie, with an indefinable knowledge that the time had almost come, that the last chains were loosed, felt that no interest would be served by candour. There is a horror in vociferous grief. He let his sister go. He would be with his mother, to help her take an atmosphere of serenity as near the boundary as she might.

For more than half an hour she had lain quite quiet. Everything suggested a drowsy calm; but it was the stillness of an armistice, not of a peace. The April sunshine, coming through the muslin curtain of the window, cast warm lights on her shapeless homely face, on the faded shawl about her shoulders, the crumpled long-cloth nightdress underneath. The bright light and the silence, things so opposite in their tendency, strained Willie's nerves, made him sensible of the strangeness, the awful quality in the appearance of things.

There was on one hand the feeling of inclusion, of safety, bound up in the walls of a home. On the other, there was the knowledge that all this, this haven, was a shadow, a dissolving view; that one of those whom it now seemed to hold so securely would presently pass out of its boundaries, unhindered by its walls, unhelped by all its comforts. She lay on the bed—she, for whom in a few moments nothing should be warm or durable any more—knowing nothing of all this; adventuring ignorantly into the darkness.

Then he looked at her, and saw that a change had already come. There was a new tension in her hand as it clutched the sheet, a hunted look in her eyes. Willie felt sorry for her; he knew that she had reached the first stage of the terror. She was cut off now from the rest of humanity. She could not speak to him. She was afraid that he would go away and leave her alone on the brink. He moved the pillow to help her struggling anxious breath; moistened her lips, which were dry and parched; bathed her temples, where the skin was already curiously drawn. He wondered whether any knowledge of his presence could force its way to the inner place where her spirit was fighting for life; whether he had power to galvanize the sleepy senses and send her assurance that she was not alone. Remembering the agony of loneliness he had passed through, he felt very pitiful. He would have wished his mother's death to be a more beautiful thing.

Another barrier fell before the enemy. It seemed that her comfortable trust in the solid earth and its furnishings went. She sat up suddenly in the bed, reaching out terrified hands to grasp something which should reassure her by its reality and firmness. Willie took the poor hands in his own, and held them tightly; trying with all the force of his will to fight the horror now so strong in her spirit. It was the convulsed, uncontrollable terror of a frightened child; horrible to see on that sane elderly face, never since his knowledge of it given over to other than tepid emotions. Our decorously insipid way of living makes the great terrors and joys of the human soul seem almost indecent. Willie shuddered and felt sick before the agony of his mother's first look upon death. He knew himself in some degree guilty of her torment; felt that perhaps the cares of his nurture had been for something in the maiming of her soul. To their parents, children must always be either wings or weights: he could not remember that he had ever helped his mother to rise.

Presently her lips moved; she was trying to speak to him. He leaned to her, but the words were difficult to hear. Two only he caught—an intense and bitter whisper—'Help me!' an appeal as it were from behind the barrier to some potent but negligent saviour still on the remembered shore. She was on the edge now: had seen something of the grey and empty places towards which her spirit was hurrying fast.

That cry, almost inarticulate, raised a passion of sorrowful love in Willie's heart. Always till now a solitary, living in a self-contained universe which only in externals touched the lives of his fellow-men, in this moment he suddenly felt the inter-dependence of all human things in their time of discipline. He perceived the impossibility of any perfect happiness for himself in the face of this torture of another spirit. He longed, as he had never longed for anything in his life, for the release of Mrs. Hopkinson from the Sorrowful Country. He was ready for a supreme sacrifice, forgetting altogether his cherished safety. His own future peace seemed a small price to pay for some surety of his mother's salvation.

'Mother,' he said, 'be comforted! I'll find a way, I'll save you! There's a heaven here quite close, if only you would see it, only look at that.'

But it was too late; his words could not reach her. In her twisted lips, the fixed gaze of her stony eyes, he could see signs that the agony of the passage had begun. The sensual world had gone from her. The other, in its dreary monotony, momentarily became clearer. But as he watched, her face relaxed abruptly. A little hint of some glad surprise crept into her expression. Some mystical sixth sense was added to her endowment, and gave her a glimpse of unexpected things. She looked at Willie, and smiled. It was a mother's smile; the radiance of a quite unselfish happiness.

'*You'll* be all right, dearie,' she said joyfully.

The stress passed from her face then; it did not seem that she was frightened any more. In another moment, the hand that he held became limp in his grasp. The empty body fell back on the pillows. Mrs. Hopkinson had passed over.

*   *   *   *   *

It was done; but so quickly, with so little fuss, that it seemed hardly credible. Willie, versed in the fictions of Maeterlinck, the poetry of static fear, had somehow expected that the visible side of things would show a certain sympathy, a knowledge of the soul's crisis. Impossible, he thought, that so irrevocable a thing could come so simply.

But nothing happened. There was no knocking on the door of life, no sudden gust of wind, no vaguely symbolic bird fluttering at the window. It was difficult to realize that the routine of existence had been sharply broken.

The fire crackled as before. A tradesman's van went down the street. Someone at the next house whistled for a hansom. Willie heard all these things quite clearly, noting them as he sat gazing stupidly at the corpse upon the bed. The hansom came and went. After that, silence. In another moment, he knew, he must go out from the room and tell the news to the household; start the useless and elaborate machinery of grief. But suddenly a harsh clang broke the stillness. The abruptness of the sound drew a sob that was almost of fear from him; but its origin was normal enough. Only a piano-organ, very new and insistent, which had stopped before the door and struck up the 'Old Hundredth'—

> 'All people that on Earth do dwell
>   Sing to the Lord with cheerful voice;
> Him serve with fear, His praise forth tell,
>   *Come ye before Him and rejoice.*'

It was London's dirge for her citizen.

CHAPTER 21

WILLIE TRIES TO LEND A HAND

'Be not the slave of Words: is not the Distant, the Dead, while I love
it, and long for it, and mourn for it, Here, in the genuine sense, as truly as
the floor I stand on?'

—Thomas Carlyle

IN the days of studied and slightly hypocritical gloom which
followed Mrs. Hopkinson's death, Willie sank back into himself,
rearranged the disturbed images which filled his House of Life.

A new duty had come to the footlights, jostling the dreamy
hopes that he loved. Himself so certain of his road, though hardly
yet in sight of the Peaceful City, the state of those blind adventurers
who blundered thoughtlessly through their moment of life seemed
to have become his responsibility, not any more his amusement.
'Save me from my friends,' cries the Egoist. 'Save me from the
conviction that I ought to save my friends,' were a better prayer for
the Dreamer.

His secrecy, his aloofness, took on for him now a character
almost murderous. How different, he thought, might his mother's
death have been, had he always spoken candidly and with insistence
of the world as he knew it to be! Some criminal cynicism had
paralyzed his sympathies, made him profoundly unconscious of the
duties that belong to knowledge. The stifling, ostentatiously dismal
air of the house; the days spent behind closed blinds; the honours,
to him so ridiculous, which were paid to the decaying corpse; these
gave to his remorse an acid tendency. It bit into his soul, driving
out the guiding lines which he had traced there in the careful hours
of peace.

The life of a bereaved household is always full of petty
discomforts. To everyone but himself, this state of things seemed
natural—a fitting tribute to the memory of an excellent housewife.
The fact that the tea had been made with luke-warm water, that
there was a feeling in the air of charwomen and spring-cleaning of a
specially lugubrious kind, only drew their thoughts more tenderly to
the virtues of the deceased. Mrs. Hopkinson had been of so little

account during her life, that the peculiarly unpleasant emptiness she left behind her came almost as an agreeable surprise.

The family sat in the dining-room, vaguely aware that its odours and inconveniences were more suited to their state than gipsy tables and brocaded chairs. Pauline, red-eyed, worried by her own incomprehensible sense of desolation, was trying to find some interest in the choosing of blouse materials from a box of patterns. Her head was heavy with tears, but she attached no real meaning to her miseries. Grief had become automatic—a reflex action.

Bertie Anthracite sat on her knee, a sharp contrast to her fatigued wretchedness. The outline of her lap suited his figure, and he had condensed into a compact mound of purring happiness. His society gave to Pauline a certain comfort. At meal-times he was fussily affectionate, as Mrs. Hopkinson used to be; and his intense blackness—he had no white hairs—had its own mournful suitability.

Mrs. Steinmann, who had come in to see if she could be of use and had remained because no one worried her to do anything, sat in the largest armchair with her hands before her. Her thick and bead-trimmed dress looked dusty in the April sunlight, and seemed to Willie like a woolly epigram which epitomized the mental atmosphere of the room. Opposite to her, Mr. Hopkinson, balancing his weight on the edge of the sofa, stared moodily at the fireplace. He wanted to read the new number of *Science Gossip*, and wondered whether anyone would think it an act of disrespect. Always more sensuous than emotional, an abstract grief bored him: but he stood in awe of Mrs. Steinmann, who was expert in the etiquette of death; he was anxious to do the right thing.

Willie, near Pauline, watched her idly, focussing his gaze upon the table-cloth on which she had spread her bits of voile and silk. Its red surface, covered with a pattern as black and shapeless as the nether world, had an air of hateful actuality which seemed to involve its owners in a small and satisfied materialism. He wondered what was at the root of this subtle antagonism between crimson felt and the spiritual world.

In a little while, Pauline gave up her attempt at occupation, pushed the box away, looked wearily at the clock. It was only half-past three. Mr. Hopkinson shifted his position slightly and began to clean his nails with a tooth-pick. The life of the room was stagnant, airless. The boredom of sorrow was weighing heavily on it—that attitude of weary unconcern towards life which lingers in the neighbourhood of death. Mr. Hopkinson and his daughter felt it the more because they were not sufficiently intelligent to understand it. Mrs. Steinmann felt it too, but it did not trouble her nerves. She recognised it as a normal accessory of bereavement.

Willie also was oppressed: drawn in spite of himself very near to the borderland of unsubstantial things. He could not remember Italy, or call back the knowledge of reconciliation that had come to him there. A cloud lay across the Beautiful Land. In that happy place, all the world had seemed strange and symbolical, the medium of adorable secrets. But beyond that, in the Dreadful Country, the shadowy side of the circle of life, it showed itself to be emptiness and illusion. To this plane of perception some force was drawing him now. He felt that unless the strong silence of the room were broken, the activities of daily life brought back, he should step over into the Grey World, and renew all the old vanquished fears.

Looking so closely at death had put the vision called Reality out of focus. He seemed to see the world-process as a great pendulum, swinging silently and incessantly through the seen and the unseen spheres. Always, on its journey and return, it carried the helpless, semi-conscious human soul. How casual and trivial, after all, was his short tenancy of the body: no more than the moment of rest before the return swing began! The magnetism of the Dead fought with him, as if demanding an interpreter in this deserter from their ranks. His mother was having her revenge.

He got up abruptly, went to the window, looked out between the slats of the closed Venetian blinds. In the presence of death, he still turned instinctively for relief to the poor little assurances of diurnal existence. But even the street gave back an inert image to him. There was something monstrous in the impassive stare of the houses. The sky, his great refuge, was vacant; it seemed immovable, as if the Earth had ceased to dance on its way through the heavens. He received the impression that the whole world was dead, and life itself a rare and confusing accident. He saw that the souls which filled the Grey World were really dead—had in fact never lived; and

that this deeper and more terrible death, of which the extinction of
the body is a symbol, was the source of all their miseries.

'Can't we *do* something?' he said suddenly. The sense of
suspended life was becoming unbearable.

Mr. Hopkinson looked at him dully. 'One must respect the
dead, my boy; it's customary,' he answered.

'This sort of thing isn't respect of anything,' said Willie. 'It's
awful. We might almost as well be dead ourselves!'

'I wish I was!' murmured Pauline. 'I shall never be happy again.
Poor mother!' The sound of her own words reminded her how
wretched she was; she began to cry.

Mrs. Steinmann got up. 'You're a little bit overwrought,
Pauline,' she said. 'It's not to be wondered at. I'll just get you the
salts off your poor mother's dressing-table—ammonia and eau-de-
Cologne—I noticed them when I was arranging the wreaths.
They'll do you a world of good.'

She went out of the room. Pauline choked, swallowed her sobs,
but could not control herself. Willie looked gravely at his sister.
Her outcry had startled him, for he had a superstitious feeling that
standing so near to the edge of things, even the spoken word was
dangerous.

'Oh, hush!' he said. 'You shouldn't speak so. Never ask for
death. Life, even if it's lonely, is less terrible than that.'

'Perhaps mother's lonely now. Perhaps she wants us!' wailed
Pauline. Her tears fell on Bertie Anthracite's head and ran down his
ruff, making damp and unbecoming streaks upon the fur. Bertie
got up, sniffing reproachfully, and went to look for drier quarters
on the sofa.

'My dear Pauline!' said Mr. Hopkinson very kindly, 'you are
distressing yourself without cause. The dead cannot be lonely. It is
impossible for emotion to survive the destruction of the brain-
cortex. To the biologist, remember, consciousness is inconceivable
without protoplasm. You know that quite well, but you are rather
upset. Calm yourself. Death is a most distressing phenomenon,
but unfortunately it's the rule of creation. No getting out of it, you
know. We must resign ourselves. Mustn't expect Nature to
preserve outworn material.'

Mr. Hopkinson blew his nose, and seemed more cheerful for his own explanation. 'Let us be thankful,' he added, 'that we live in a scientific age; and don't let us confuse ourselves with any mediaeval nonsense about future states.'

Willie, to his own surprise, began to speak eagerly and imperatively.

'Oh, but it's Pauline who's right,' he said, 'and it's we who talk nonsense, not the old wise peoples who made allegories of Heaven and Hell. The dead *are* lonely, when they die as mother has died, without seeing the real meaning of life. Listen, father! Oh, you shall listen because it's the truth. Why will you take the shadow for the real, and the veil for the limit like this? Can't you see, on your theory, what a senseless, unreasonable performance existence is? Isn't it arrogance to think that there's nothing more beyond the little scale of vibrations your senses and your instruments can pick up? That's what your view seems to lead to; and on the face of it, it looks a silly lie.'

'My dear lad!' replied Mr. Hopkinson, still preserving an admirable good temper, 'conclusions founded on Causation and Experience cannot lie. Modern science is as sure of its results as double entry. No room there for chance and fancy. What's put down on one page is bound to turn up finally on the other.'

'Oh, yes!' answered Willie. 'But not as you think, father. It's the invisible things, all the unnoticed forces, and the real critical events of life: they turn up again in death and make the future. All the steps the soul has taken, and all the loves and hates it has—those are the causes which have effects that count. I must tell you. You must listen. You're wasting your life on meaningless acts, living in great danger every minute. You've got to die, and you never think of that, never notice the real proportions of things.'

Mr. Hopkinson became annoyed. He felt that his son's remarks were in bad taste. He could not conceive where such silly notions came from. He was listening anxiously, too, for Mrs. Steinmann's returning footsteps. But he could not sneer as he wished. Willie was in earnest; and real earnestness, though it is generally grotesque, always shames its tepid audience into attention.

This it was, together with a complete uncertainty as to what he ought to do, which set Mr. Hopkinson's teeth on edge. He was in the state of wrathful discomfort to which any polite person may be reduced when an earnest missionary suddenly suggests a word of prayer in the drawing-room.

Willie noticed the expression of respectable disgust which came over the dull pink oval of his father's face. It did not astonish him. He went on.

'This world you think so important and trustworthy,' he said, 'is only a shadow, an imperfect way of seeing something that is very different in itself. Everyone seems to hate that thought; but why should they? When it fades for you to a colourless mist, as it has for me; when the dead become more real than the living, and Time and Space only empty words, modern science won't be much good. You're disgusted, of course: you think I'm mad: but I daren't let you die without saying the truth. Mother's gone, lost, and I never helped her. I'll not easily forgive myself for that—'

At this point, Pauline cried out quickly, 'How can you be so wicked, Willie? How *dare* you say mother's in Hell?' But he went on.

'Listen! your senses only know one world, and that the cheapest and most obvious; but there's world after world, and mode after mode of perception, wrapped behind it: only you will look down all the time, not up, to where the real things are written. And what will be the use, when earth's gone from you, of all the earth-powers you fuss about so much? It's the strong soul you will want then; and your soul isn't any further now than when you were a baby. All you will do, if you die like this, will be to hang about on the fringe of the old earth-life, just out of reach of everything you care for. That's the real Hell, and it's kept for those who have never been born in the spirit.'

He left off speaking, and no one answered. But Bertie Anthracite, awake, somehow conscious of a strangeness in the room, raised a black nose from between folded paws and looked at him solemnly. There was a remote and dreamy fellowship in his great amber eyes.

Otherwise, Willie's attempt to the breaking of barriers had resulted only in a stronger isolation. Mr. Hopkinson felt insulted —always the first reaction of a mean soul in the presence of truth. He had the comforting conviction that the boy was either off his head or playing the fool, but he did not know what to do. He missed his wife, who would doubtless have removed Willie on some convenient if undignified pretext. To Pauline, the whole scene seemed a puzzling aggravation of the general wretchedness of things. Only to Mr. Willie Hopkinson were his own words sharp and pregnant.

His speech, indeed, had been rather an incantation than a confession; for of his actual intention his father and sister had understood nothing at all. They were left with the impression that he was uncomfortably queer, and that his remarks had an obscure and undesirable bearing on religion. But his words fell back on himself, and the Gates of Horn, for him always on the latch, swung open. He lost the visible and the obvious, and won back his old sense of the extreme naturalness of unseen things.

The Grey World, in fact, rushed back on Willie, and he met it almost gladly as a relief from the suffocating limits of his home. It brought with it the colourless landscape of infinite space, and space was what he needed as an antidote to the littleness of life. He did not feel any more the terrors which it had used to hold for him. The crying of the dead filled him now only with a purging sadness. Their Hell had become his Heaven—a place of great clarity and peace. Beyond them, he saw all things reconciled and made good. Knowledge gave him faith; he looked out on the desert of death very steadily.

He knew now of nothing at all but the grey endless fields of that other Dimension. There, among the crowd and confusion of its populations, he was aware of the spirit of Mrs. Hopkinson, lonely and anxious, struggling to communicate with her children in the world. It seemed that his own spirit was being dragged back from visible life by her imperative longing, and met her on some intermediate plane. Her soul sank into his. She spoke to him; not coherently at first, but with the inarticulate hurry of a garrulous person who has been deprived of opportunity for chatter. There was nothing, it seemed, to be said. Their planes of being were too far separate. Only she rushed with relief on this unexpected gap in the barrier, took up the homely intercourse which had been the whole life of her soul.

She was overflowing with all the old, human sympathies which he had despised until she had taken them from him. She was still one with her children, and in some sense vicariously happy through them. He missed the note of boredom and despair which was his one sharp memory of the Other Side. Otherwise, he felt her presence to be absolutely natural. He lost with it the sense of something missing in the household which had worried him since her death. This force in the Grey World, loving him and leaning out to him, gave him a new feeling of unity and content.

'Dear mother!' he said suddenly. His voice was low but very penetrating, as if it had come from a great way off. It was not, in fact, his voice at all; but like that of a stranger using his lips. It caught Mr. Hopkinson's attention.

'Eh? What?' he said.

Willie, all his attention turned to another dimension, saw the sensual world uncertainly, through a distorting haze. No doubt he had a vague knowledge of the room, and of people in it, but their personalities did not affect him. He answered his father automatically, as one may answer questions given in a dream.

'Mother's here,' he said, 'watching us. Of course one knew she must be, but it's nice to feel it. And she's not so very unhappy; aren't you glad? She wants to get back to us, of course; but she'll find out presently that it's impossible.'

'Don't be such an infernal fool, Willie,' said Mr. Hopkinson very sharply. 'We've heard enough of your morbid fancies for one day. Besides, this is no time for ghost stories; you're upsetting your sister.'

Pauline, in fact, had turned very white. As Willie paused, she burst into loud harsh sobs of terror. But her brother was now beyond the reach of hysterics or reproofs: he did not hear or see anything of what was happening in the room. Mr. Hopkinson, as he realized this fact, was seized by an uncontrollable fear which he knew to be unreasonable, and which made him feel a great dislike for his son. He attributed it to the religious views of his semi-human ancestors; but this did not mend his damaged pride.

Willie had slipped from the visible world as completely as in the first years of his childhood, before his communications with the earth-life were solid and complete. He was now established on the other plane; recognised its misty landscape, the texture of its life. He was puzzled. His mother seemed to be happy—incomprehensibly happy for that empty and desolate place. She had so long been accustomed, it seemed, to find contentment in the well-being of her children, that now their existence on earth made a little Heaven for her soul.

Love that was not love of self appeared to bring its own reward —an arrangement which struck Willie as extremely odd. It was in this that Mrs. Hopkinson lived, secure from the loneliness of the self-centred dead who hunt forever for their lost happiness. But her life was not firmly established. She was uneasy. As his spirit was driven against hers by the tide of his thought, or drawn back by the drag of the world, he knew that all was not secure with her, that there was something she had to tell him. He remembered what a friendly listener would have meant to him when he was amongst the Dead, and turned his whole will towards the understanding of her message.

'Mother, what is it?' he said. 'I'm here. I know. I can speak for you.'

The answer came like a voice within his own mind. He knew at the moment of speaking what it was that she wanted. She was afraid. Not afraid of the place where she was, but of being forgotten, seeing her place filled, her memory in the world overlaid with living interests. When that happened, he saw, she would be quite alone, would have lost her anchorage to earth. Love gave her a part still in the home that she had cared for, but it was a reciprocal love, a magnetism in which the living had to do their part. Only in their remembrance she retained her hold upon visible things. The forgotten die, as the loveless die: except those happy dreamers who have found the Heart of the Rose, and pass from the Earth-sphere to the Absolute. He saw suddenly and unforgettably the one great duty of the living, in the loving commemoration of the dead.

'It's all right, mother dearest,' he said. 'We shall never forget you. You shan't be forsaken. We love you, and there's no barrier. You'll always be with us now.'

He felt then her personality enfolding him—the affectionate, deprecating being whose constant timid questions 'Anything you want, dearie? Are you sure you're feeling quite the thing?' had filled so great a space in the tissue of his life. Now the irksome guardianship was over, and he, instead, was made the keeper of his mother's happiness. He seized on the new duty gladly. He stood up, held out his arms—irrationally, but with an utter conviction, as if he were indeed going to hold her to safety. He said nothing. He seemed to have gone past speech to the place of pure thought.

Mr. Hopkinson, watching him uneasily, decided that he was going to faint. As a matter of fact, he was acutely but narrowly conscious; blind to the sensual world, but with eyes wide open to an inner secret, the holiest that he had known.

His mother was his to care for, and he was her son. He knew, for the first time, that he loved her.

*   *   *   *   *

He came back with a violent sense of physical shock to a roomful of startled persons: Pauline in hysterics on the sofa, Bertie Anthracite standing fascinated and rigid at his feet, ears forward and fluffy coat nervously erect. Mr. Hopkinson, red-faced, awkward and angry, patted his daughter with a helpless hand. Only Mrs. Steinmann stood triumphantly upon the hearth-rug, undisturbed by anything more exciting than her own promptitude and common-sense. She had just thrown a large glassful of cold water in Willie's face.

'Just in time!' she said joyously. 'You'd have been off in another minute. Still feel giddy? I thought you'd been looking poorly all the afternoon.'

'Neurotic young ass,' growled Mr. Hopkinson. His shaking hand reminded him that he had passed through a very creepy ten minutes; but Mrs. Steinmann's sensible attitude reassured him, and he was now only uncertain whether Willie's display meant illness or folly.

'Nothing like a sharp shock at the right moment!' Mrs. Steinmann continued, as the wrathful Willie, suffering from the insecure sensations of the recently anaesthetized, hastily dried his face, and tried to check the rivers which were running down his back. 'Only over-excitement with a touch of liver in it, most likely. You never can tell what form bile will take. I remember, Willie, you had an attack something like this when you were quite a little boy. It made your poor mother very anxious at the time: she thought it was your brain.   I told her she was wrong, I've had so much experience with boys: and as a matter of fact it turned out to be nothing but stomach.'

Mrs. Steinmann's tone was full of cheerful authority: but she raised her eyebrows in a knowing manner as she glanced at Mr. Hopkinson, and he touched his forehead with one finger and nodded gravely in reply.

CHAPTER 22

CROSS-ROADS

'Quand on veut noyer son chien, on dit qu'il a la rage.'
—*French Proverb*

STEPHEN, in the double capacity of Willie's friend and Pauline's lover, was forced into a family consultation. The situation was serious. Mr. Willie Hopkinson had neither repented nor explained his outburst. Knowing that explanation between the ignorant and initiate must always be a paradox, he had chosen an attitude of smiling unconcern which strained not only his own nerves, but also the understanding of his relations. It seemed to Mr. Hopkinson irrefutable evidence that his son's conduct proceeded from disease rather than conviction. But a medically inclined cousin, invited to lunch in order that he might pronounce on Willie's mental state, had been disappointing. He found, he said, nothing organically wrong with the boy. A nervous temperament, which wanted taking out of itself. He advised his disgusted host, who longed to discuss the question of neuroses, to give his son a good tonic and let him go to the devil for a bit.

'He's wrong,' said Mr. Hopkinson. 'I'm convinced of it. Symptoms are everything in these cases, of course, and he couldn't judge in a short interview. But that attack the other day; the simulated voice, and the hallucination, and all that false excitement —distinct traces of a lesion there, to my mind.'

'In my opinion,' said Mrs. Steinmann, 'Willie's never been quite the same since his trip abroad. I put it down a good deal to the sudden change. Many constitutions can't stand it. All his usual habits altered; and then foreign food. That alone was almost bound to upset him. So oily.'

'Yes,' replied Mr. Hopkinson. 'Your daughter meant kindly when she recommended that trip, but I always thought it a foolish plan myself. I've no belief in these changes. Oxygen's the same all the world over, and after all there are few places where the comforts of life are so well understood as in this dear old England of ours.'

'Oh, Elsa's a fool when it comes to questions of health. She seems to think a course of bad hotels and old churches will cure anything. But as I say to her, what on earth's the good of this rushing about Europe nowadays, when you can buy all the same things in London? It's silly as well as expensive, and I'm afraid it's had a good deal to do with Willie's queerness—that, and his mother's death on the top of it.'

'I think,' said Stephen, 'one must not expect Willie to be quite normal. He has unusual gifts, and his own way of seeing the world—'

He was wondering, as he uttered these facile phrases, how best to solve the equation of which Willie, Mr. Hopkinson, and his own convenience, were the principal terms. Stephen at this time hung in the balance between solid interests and spiritual hopes. To be engaged to be married to a wholesome young woman, must in the end prove a sobering influence. He was growing older and wiser in the strictly useful sense; approximating the texture of his dream to the texture of life. His sharp intellect, as little content with the isolation of the mystic as it had been with the gregarious greyness of common life, sought incessantly for compromise. He was not deceived by appearance; but many of its aspects pleased him, and he refused to give them up.

Toward Willie, he felt respectful but impatient; wanted to help him, was irritated because he showed himself so little ready to be helped. His visionary strength, flung into his love and his profession, still gave him a glamour that was not quite of the world. It explained his hold upon Pauline's heart, as his restless, critical mind explained the gulf which broadened between him and her brother.

Stephen wished to succeed both as the lover of the Ideal and the husband of Miss Pauline Hopkinson. This programme called for a tolerant spirit best developed amongst persons unfamiliar with the flaming visions of his youth. Hence, he did not care to be thrown too much in Willie's company. It made him uncomfortable, like living opposite a church that he had ceased to attend. He had now so disciplined his mind, that he had become something of that ideal spectator of life, who is willing to accept everything, and even to be credulous when the play demands that exertion. He could turn without any disagreeable emotion from the writing of a sonnet on the Virgin to the designing of a Gothic hall for political meetings. But he knew in his soul that Willie, the tedious fanatic, remained spiritually superior to himself, the intelligent taster of life.

Gratitude, of course, should have had some place in the matter. This consideration troubled Mr. Stephen Miller in his better moments. Willie had once opened for him a treasure-house at which he had long been knocking. But he had walked through it to another which lay beyond, and now he was sure that the first one had been not a treasure-house, but a dream.

In substance, therefore, Stephen leaned to the view that Mr. Willie Hopkinson's elimination from the family circle was expedient, if not inevitable. He foresaw constant collisions between Willie and his world, only to be avoided by his own permanent employment as buffer. But to succeed as an architect, pose as a Platonist, and manage a commercial father-in-law, seemed vocation enough for Stephen. He told himself that Willie would be happier away from home. He knew that everyone else would be happier without Willie, for it is horrible to live in the constant presence of something which you know that you do not understand. Mr. Hopkinson and his daughter had been nervous and irritable since the afternoon when the Unseen World was brought into sudden and confusing proximity with their dining-room furniture.

Loyalty, however, was expected of him. It was the mere duty of friendship to break the impact between Willie's idealism and his father's well-educated mind. Remembering with terror the unpopularity of his own early beliefs, he entered delicately upon the defence.

'I think,' he said, 'you must make allowances. You were startled the other day by Willie's behaviour, but he has a curious way of putting things—always has had. It's quite likely, too, that he sees much that we do not see. You don't believe that, perhaps, Pauline; but Mr. Hopkinson knows as well as I do that it's a scientific possibility. Our senses are not perfect agents by any means—'

He looked carefully at Mr. Hopkinson. He desired to confuse, without offending, his future father-in-law. A bold excursion into the enemy's country seemed his only hope.

'I don't think,' he continued, 'that because Willie's brain reacts on experience rather differently from yours and mine, Mr. Hopkinson, it's necessary to say that he's insane.'

'No—no,' replied Mr. Hopkinson. 'Possibly not.' He regretted this admission immediately, and hurried on to get out of sight of it before it could be recognised. 'But he's a deuced nuisance in the house. Transcendentalists, and seers of ghosts, and so on are out of date. He ought to conform to modern notions. It's an atavism —about a century behind the times. Reminds me, Stephen, you were rather taken up with the spook business yourself at one time.'

'That was before I knew you and Pauline,' said Stephen hastily.

'Ah, nothing like a bright, sensible girl for settling a young chap. But the question is, what's to be done with Willie? Bookbinding no go, thanks to that love-affair; business no go, he's no head for figures. Can't have him loafing about here all day.'

'If you like,' said Stephen, 'I'll speak to him.'

He found Willie in low spirits. The sunshine of Italy had faded. Much of the old misery had come back. Those deeps of experience in which his mother and he had found each other had ill prepared him for the squalid questions and strictly pathological sympathy of the following days.

'What on earth am I to do?' he said. 'I can't stay here. They look at me suspiciously. They think I'm mad. Funny, isn't it? but it doesn't amuse for ever. This life is stifling me. I'm not strong enough to breathe through it. When I'm here, I lose the holy strangeness of the world.'

'That's true. You're all out of key here. Something will have to be done.'

'Oh yes, I must go. It's no use to stay. I thought it was my duty to tell them the truth, so I tried. They saw I meant it, too, though they'll never acknowledge it. I made them feel for a minute that there *is* an invisible world, and father won't forgive that; people are so tenacious of their own little lies. And anyhow I can't stay. I've seen the road, and at the end the Beautiful Gate; but here I drop back to the grey, I can't follow the star.' He stopped. 'But it seems wrong, wasteful,' he said slowly. 'I ought to help someone else to see it. Won't anyone ever believe me, don't you think?'

'No,' said Stephen—'never. Haven't you learnt yet, my dear old chap, that no one is convinced of anything second-hand? The idea of it must be in their minds first, or you can't wake it up there. You've had a try, and you see the result. Everyone takes you for a lunatic. Conform, or clear out. It's the rule of the world, and you'll be happier if you give in to it.'

'As you've done,' said Willie. 'And live round the trivial almanac of games when I might be in touch with the Real.'

'Well, suppose I have done that? It's no good to sneer about it. Your way can't be my way ever; give that idea up. My existence is run on quite other lines than yours, but I think and hope that there's more than one way home. You're too arrogant; why should your vision be the only one? Your knowledge of things is the determining fact for you, but it's not for me. It's I, as I stand in the world, that counts in my own life. If I live purely and with all my might, and react to every object in my world,—the simple things, like love and work and home—I can't be far wrong.'

'I feel that about work,' said Willie. 'I must work, whatever happens. Somehow, this week has made a difference in that— seeing a death-bed, and the grave silently filled up. Why, already her memory is beginning to fade; isn't sharp-edged any more. It's awful to fade out of life like that, as if one were some painting washed from the wall. I feel now, I must leave a mark in the world, some *patrin* to show that I've passed.'

'But don't you see, that's just the root of my life? The world put its impress on me, I want to leave my impress on the world. It needn't be work; life will do it. If I only leave children that I've trained behind me, that's something. The fault of your sort of life for me is just its aloofness from things. I hate that detached feeling. I feel now, I've got a poise, adjusted myself to every part of existence. It's a compact, temperate happiness. I've developed my powers all round—'

'But you've lost the Vision,' answered Willie. 'Oh, Stephen, and you nearly had it once! Remember the old days, how clearly you saw then.'

'I persuaded myself that I did, because it was so amusing. No one can get your conviction unless they're born fey.'

He spoke sharply, remembering a night when he too had been fey, and dropped for an instant his birth-right of belief in the solid earth.

'This,' thought the intelligent Stephen, 'is the worst of letting one's self be run away with by other people's ideas. There's nothing like an old belief for making one feel awkward and foolish. One should keep one's creeds upon the literary plane.'

'Perhaps,' said Willie, 'I am fey. If so, it's a happy fortune. But not here. The weight of all these people that refuse to see life as it is, presses me into a sort of insincerity. I can't love here; I can't hope. I must be alone, where there's a space. Here, I always remember the Illusion, but I only see its miserable side.'

'Then go,' said Stephen.

Willie knew that he was glad. He had already hinted to his sister that he would like to leave home, and the suggestion had been well received; and Pauline, whose engagement took precedence of her intellect, might always be trusted to echo, without editing, Stephen's opinions. It was humiliating, but natural enough. At close quarters, Willie was an element of uncertainty. At a sufficient distance, he might be counted as an asset—'clever, but peculiar.'

'If you'll think,' Stephen continued, 'you'll remember, those who had intuitional truth were always solitaries. It's always been the same; they never could mix with the rest. You've got your truth in a different way, but it comes out the same in the end. You can't be a citizen when you've ceased to believe in bricks and mortar.'

'*She is a visionaria, a solitary; she lives as an anchoress.*' Willie heard again the voice of Fra Agostino, saying as a very ordinary thing these words. They mixed themselves with Stephen's last remark, 'You can't be a citizen when you've ceased to believe in bricks and mortar.' The idea of that artist, working in her cell, had never gone far from his mind. To think of her was to feel the cool fragrance of the cloister, the quiet yet busy air of some ideal working-place.

Work, he knew, he must have. Contemplation had brought him peace only whilst his troubles came from within. Now that death —the death of friends—had become a fact for him, nothing but the anodyne of manual labour would bring him back the poise from which he saw the joyous mystery of things. He began to understand something of the feeling of the hermits, whose refusal of the world, he thought, had been more a development than a denial of self. He too longed passionately for silence, the clean contours of the country. The restless *ennui* which he felt could only be abated there. For him, impure influences hung round the life of the City. He could not pray in her churches, remember the holy Dead, work under her sky. Yet he knew himself able to recognise the cadences of the great Song. Should he not go to the place where they were audible?

Because many persons liked to herd in cities and bargain with their neighbours, and had grown into the idea that this was of the essence of life, that was no reason why he should do so. It was just as possible now as it ever had been to withdraw from the crowd and live quietly. He was set for a while on a great round world, tumbling through space. It was clearly in his right to choose for himself that part of it where his probation should be passed—the place that could offer him the one thing he wanted, that ecstasy of knowledge which he had felt for a moment or two. Not stones and slates, but the intangible world of sordid personalities, shut him in. Their dream must always be unreal to him, therefore useless. Stephen, in spite of his vivid intelligence, was really a groundling. Once he had reached a hand to his friend through a window in the wall of sense; but now he had drawn back with merely a grudging remembrance of the landscape he had seen. Love has more than one way of anchoring a soul to earth.

But Hester Waring in her cell: she, it seemed, had built herself a world from the happy difficulties of her art and the silent spaces of the earth. If she could so throw off the clogging habits of the crowd, he could too. He longed for freedom. But he was lonely; wanted flattery, encouragement. Now as ever, at the last resort it was a weakness not a strength that determined him.

'I'll go and speak to Mrs. Levi about it,' he said.

CHAPTER 23

THE VALLEY OF HUMILIATION

'I have talked once or twice of the Shadowy Companion, but one must
not forget that there is the Muddy Companion also.'

—ARTHUR MACHEN

WHEN Willie came in to her, Mrs. Levi was sitting with her back to
the window, and in becoming proximity to a group of daffodils,
arranged in the Japanese manner in a Wedgwood soup-plate. She
received him on the plaintively expectant note, which her admirers
were intended to mistake for cordiality. He was welcome. Elsa had
been dull during his absence. Mr. Levi had recently taken to golf; it
affected his conversation, and the passive contempt which she had
always felt for him was rapidly changing to active dislike. One
cannot speak, even cryptically, of the high lights and values of life,
to a person who replies in terms of tees and niblicks.

Willie came to her in the mood of a world-worn warrior
returning to the kindly nurse of his youth. He wanted advice,
practical counsels for the future. He did not know as yet what to
do with his new freedom, how to act so that he might not lose the
light he had gained. Elsa, who pointed so persistently the way she
did not go, might solve the problem. He longed for an
environment in which he could talk truthfully and without fear.
This, perhaps, were too much to hope for. But he felt that he had
in her a safe and comfortable feather pillow for his weary soul: and
his first impression, greeting eyes that were fresh from the
schooling of Italy, pleased his taste. In the soft secretive folds of
her mauve white and gray tea-gown, she looked like an inky
rainbow set for promise in the cloudy skies of his life.

But he noticed a change in the room. Its atmosphere, always
very personal, did not any longer agree with the quiet lines of its
decoration. There was a sense of insecurity. Elsa had a restless
expression, unexpected movements: some unfamiliar attribute had
been added to her.

Mrs. Levi, in fact, was unhappy. At forty years of age, she found
herself with a vulgar family, a vanishing figure, and few resources

beyond her unimpeachable if shallow taste. A handsome woman dissatisfied with her husband is at best a percussion cap—at worst a bomb. Her explosive power, increasing with maturity, varies at last in inverse ratio to her charm. Elsa had passed her perihelion: now she was retreating from the sun. The last stages of her inflorescence had been accomplished with the violence peculiar to her race. With advancing years, the circle of her waist grew larger, and that of her admirers correspondingly decreased. She became eager, nervous; lost the assured pose of the divinity and took on the subtleties of the huntress, as Diana when she left Olympus for the woods.

Willie's engagement to Mildred had been the first check in a career at once virtuous and successful. He had worshipped her, and she had ceased to be enough for him. It was astounding, but so obvious that she was obliged to believe it. But the breakdown of his passion had restored her self-esteem. Evidently, it had been a temporary aberration. She allowed herself the pleasure of forgiving him for a crime of which he was unconscious, and supposed that as consolatrix she had regained in full her old power over his mind.

Now that he returned to her—cool, cured and free—she felt that the time had come to drive firmer rivets into the loose chain by which she had bound him. She did not want love. That was often inartistic and always dangerous. She wanted subservience. Her husband had never given it to her, and she still supposed that it was worth having. Willie's desertion was a sign, unmistakable if unexpected, that her charm was no longer sufficient to hold all the allegiance of a man. Who shall describe the spectres that wait upon fading beauty? Elsa saw long dreary years of respectable nonentity ahead, when her title to consideration would be that of wife, not of woman. Even whilst Willie kissed her fingers and called her his only friend, this vision wrecked her peace. At all costs, she was bound to forget it; for her self-respect was hinged on more delicate matters than her knowledge of Italian Art. She knew that ideal loveliness would give her no consolation in the moment when it became her only hope.

She set herself now to a careful flattery, a judicious condescension. But she found a change in their relation. Willie was older, more manly. He no longer sat at her feet. This new air of independence, this assumption of equality, pleased Mrs. Levi. She perceived that her prize, could she secure it, would be something better than the charming, neurotic boy of the past. She was placed on her mettle. This was a man who could, if he chose, dominate her, rather than be possessed. As she looked at him, she felt again the delicious weakness, the happy helplessness of sex, which she was afraid that she had lost with her youth. She thanked Providence for this unexpected mercy: it took ten years off her age.

She leaned to him, held his hand, spoke of their long separation.

'But it has been good,' she said. 'I find a change in you. You are happier, stronger, are you not? Oh, I know your trouble. Death is terrible always, and a parting. But your soul, I think, is more quiet?'

'Yes,' said Willie. He spoke meditatively, as if reasoning with himself. 'Yes, I think I begin to understand. It's not all so simple as one thinks at first; there's more gradation. Italy helped; I owe you the thanks for that. I shan't be confused by the ugliness and artifice now. But I've thought lately that Stephen was partly right when he spoke of love as the real key.'

'Yes?'

'But only so far as it's a sort of beauty. It must be a mystic unfettered love; an ardour, not an instinct. An attitude of rapture towards something outside one's self—beautiful things, or exquisite emotions.'

He seemed to be gazing at Elsa, reading her, wanting her. But really he was seeing in a far-away vision Umbria, and the Franciscan chapel, and the picture which had filled his heart with a humble and a passionate desire. Mrs. Levi, however, met and claimed that brooding look, and a pleasant excitement possessed her.

'Ah,' she said, 'I so thoroughly agree with you. Ultimate Beauty is not to be found in conventional passions, is it? It is the strange and the obscure in love, the panic rapture, that feeds the soul I think. So few understand that! Modern love seems always to lead to the altar or the divorce court. In either case, the advertisement is a profanation.'

She had slid into the dreamy, rhapsodic tone; the tone that had always held her fascination for him. But he no longer found her entirely convincing. He had made the inevitable progress from a general love of the lovely to a passion for simplicity, rightness, and distinction in Art. Elsa lacked the touch of austerity which was necessary to the satisfaction of his taste. She had developed, too, that dangerous tendency of brilliant women, which leads them to parody, when they intend to accentuate, their own charms. She was tempted to add artifice to art, and the effect was disagreeable. Her languid voice was a little too slow and precious; the delicate perfume which hung about her possessions was a little too strong. So that a suggestion of the panther crept in to mar Willie's admiration; he thought of the subtle claws; and a memory of the mouse-like Mildred rose gratefully before him, as of something brought forth indeed of the earth, but sane and temperate.

Elsa had intuition; she saw her influence in the balance; and an appealing, baffled look, veiled the assured vanity of her beautiful eyes. She wanted his unqualified devotion. It had soothed her as nothing else could do. She could not be aesthetic without an audience.

'How lonely we are, you and I!' she said. 'How absolutely lonely! I sometimes think that because of that there should be more than a common communion between us. We felt it from the first, did we not?'

'You were always most kind to me,' said Willie.

He moved uneasily: Elsa frightened him. It is uncomfortable to owe a debt of gratitude to an idol whose clay foundations you have just found out.

'If I have been kind, it is because kindness is so easy, so natural, when one spirit is in sympathy with another—'

She crossed over to the low divan where he was sitting, dropped her voice to a lower and more tremulous key.

'You and I,' she said, 'alone amongst all these domesticated animals, these human machines, trying to extract sweetness and light from the comfortable squalor of things! How could we help turning towards each other? It's strange, but from the beginning I knew that we should think alike about all that really matters—the sadness and the glamour of life. We both look at existence so thoroughly in the Botticelli way.'

'It was you who first taught me to do that,' said Willie, rather nervously. Some form of civil thanksgiving seemed safe.

'You would have found it for yourself sooner or later: one cannot deny one's temperament. Sometimes, I'm almost tempted to wish that one could. There are moments when I long for human intercourse, and the warmth of things. But I'm too fastidious. I cannot care for kisses unless they are the medium of a spiritual embrace. A husband's caress, I fancy, must always be a very desolate thing.'

'You're bound to be lonely,' answered Willie, 'if you care for loveliness at all, I think. People don't understand it just now, whatever they may have done once. When the soul wakes, it sees that it is really shut off from the others who still sleep, can never communicate with them. One must find one's own happiness, and no one can help anyone else.'

'Ah, we are each so truly alone upon the road, are we not? But now and then, a miracle may happen, as it has between you and me, and two spirits understand one another. I often think, as I look at lovers, at husbands and wives perhaps, What use is this appearance of comradeship between your bodies, when your souls can never be companions? With us, how different! It is a joy to take the hand of a friend when there is no conventional glove between. There must be something beautiful, something emblematic, I think, in the material touch, the caress perhaps, which is born of a mystical friendship.'

'Oh no,' said Willie. 'It's the material part of life that spoils everything. You begin by trying to be fair to your body, and it turns round on you and stifles your soul. It's a danger. One must keep it down if one wants to see the Vision.'

'But I have felt sometimes,' she said, 'have not you? that material life has a use, perhaps, that is not inimical to the Higher Beauty of things. It should be the symbol that interprets the needs of the soul, its communions and its revulsions. What else, indeed, can it be for? Our physical acts, in that way, may become the paint upon the canvas of life.'

'Perhaps. I'd never thought of it like that. Of course, all sensual things must be the shadows of some great Reality—'

'Yes, yes! That's what I mean. And the outer and visible signs that are enough in themselves to satisfy the lower, denser natures

—they might become for us the symbols of a transcendental mystery.'

Very suddenly, and without in any exact manner defining to himself the meaning of her words, Willie felt frightened. Some power on watch within his spirit trembled: he became coldly, numbly afraid, as if he were a small animal waiting for the spring of an evil beast.

'We, who have courage, who are independent of all the silly regulations of the world,' said Elsa, 'why should our lives remain incomplete?'

He did not answer. He was dazed by his own vivid intuition. A dreadful silence sprang up between them. It was like the slow droppings of cold water. As each second passed, and each drop fell, Willie, knowing that Mrs. Levi watched him carefully, felt her personality come round him like a cloud. At first, he was passive under the influence: then, as the silence took shape, and weighed more heavily on him, he perceived in himself quite suddenly the birth-struggles of a new individual.

It seemed to be called into existence by the strained atmosphere, in which he could hear Elsa's quick breath calling to him. Her eyes, wide open, tried to meet his. In her, too, there was a change. Both had dropped to some dark, elemental plane of existence. They were dominated by a force much stronger than the tidy conventional Self of daily life.

The heavy scents that hung about the room dulled Willie's brain. Something tremendous had happened; he did not quite know what it was. The unknown powers which lie at the back of Silence and constitute its danger and its charm, seized hold of him. He recognised in himself a dark personality, now fully born, of which he had known nothing in the past. It was hideous, yet it had a horrible fascination. It lived, he perceived, in some black and unsuspected world to which he had never penetrated; yet it was as truly a part of his Ego as the soul that he watched over so carefully.

Still in silence, he saw a monster rear itself up in Mrs. Levi's spirit, look at him through her eyes with a horrible longing. And the creature that was hidden in him said to him insistently, 'Seize your prey. It is yours: why do you wait?'

The silence seemed now to have lasted many hours. It was this that had loosed these prisoners upon them. The chatter of daily life shuts down many terrible captives, which struggle to the light in the rare moments when the tongue is still. This silence was strong and dangerous: more dangerous than all the subtleties of speech. There was distilled from it some violent impulse; morbid, evil, unspeakable. Willie knew now of pleasures more piercing than the common things of sense, and of the obscure temptations which come to those who have tried to live altogether in the spirit.

The inner enemy was creeping upwards. The stillness and that strange glow in Elsa's eyes seemed to be crying 'Shape your dream as you choose. Matter means nothing. It is only the clumsy vehicle of soul.' He began to tremble. She saw it, and her excitement increased. She would not move. She wished to taste the full intoxication; and for that it was necessary that he should be the captor, not the slave.

One must suppose that the gods were not on the side of Mrs. Levi; for it was at this moment that the sun came from behind showery clouds and shone brightly. It foiled the hastily drawn curtains, and laid a beam of strong clean light across the room. It struck Willie's eyes with a sharpness that was almost a sound: he turned to the window and saw blue sky, and the innocent loveliness of a flowering laburnam-tree against the drab stucco of the opposite house.

The sky stood between the dingy roofs and chimneys—the same immaculate purity that had vaulted in the magic of Italy. Below it, the tree tossed its sacrifice of yellow blossoms, in a gay revel of perfection which was piety and daintiness in one. It drew his thoughts abruptly to the ordered and exquisite places unsullied by human grime, where life could be beautiful, temperate, ideal. He looked back at Elsa and the elaborate artifice of her setting. The creature whom she had roused in him knew nothing of the heavens, and only the baser secrets of the earth. It shrank back, like a germ of disease, unable to bear the sunlight. The dark magic had vanished. Everything, after all, was sane and normal.

Mrs. Levi seemed to have faded, become ordinary. He had thought of Lilith: now he saw only Eve. The horrible things that he had learnt in the silence retreated to a great distance. He came back from the dark dimension and looked about him: first with a sick disgust, then in a puzzled, doubtful way.

As the image grew less distinct, he began to question his own perceptions. Finally, Elsa sank back to her old easy careless attitude, smiled at him with the old assured condescension. Then it came to his mind that he had wronged her: her words could not have carried the weight which his nervous fancy had supposed. He had been betrayed into the last meanness of male vanity. He felt hot, ashamed: wondered how much she had read of his thought. He dared not speak. But he withdrew the hand that she had kept between her fingers. Her touch burnt it.

Elsa, perceiving her mistake, behaved well. To shock Willie would be to humiliate herself: she set herself to the saving of his modesty. Fortunately the conversation had been metaphorical from the first. One dexterous touch from her would be enough to make it entirely unintelligible.

'The legend of S. Catherine,' she said, 'puts the idea of a spiritual union so exquisitely, does it not? A ring given in a dream! What symbol could be more appropriate?'

Willie's instant and obvious relief was perhaps the greatest of the afternoon's cruelties. Elsa drove back the unbecoming tears from her eyelids, and saw for one hateful instant the gulf which her years of maturity had placed between them. Then she pushed him a little from her and looked at him, almost in her old, kindly, patronizing way. Perhaps there was a new glitter in her eyes had he seen it, but he was glad to avoid them.

'Why weren't you my son, Willie?' she said. 'I often think the fairies must have changed you with Geraint. There is something in you that appeals to me so strangely, makes me feel almost that you are mine.'

Willie received this idea gratefully, and discussed it in all its bearings: so that the phantom which lay between them was pushed out of sight, seemed unreal, impossible. It is really quite difficult to believe in the evil elemental things, when one is eating thin bread-and-butter in a pretty house rented at £250 a year. The tense expression, the wildness, had gone from Elsa's face. Willie began to wonder whether it had ever been there.

But as he was leaving, her acting broke abruptly. She caught his arm and looked into his face. He felt the fingers shake upon his sleeve.

'I'm a fool!' she said. 'Oh, what a fool! But I thought for a minute that it could have been beautiful: oh, indeed I did. With us, because of the artistry we could have put into it. And all my life, I've wanted something beautiful and secret. Glamour—even a wicked glamour. Anything to break this neat, stucco existence! And there's a strangeness in you, Willie; a magic. With you, it could never have been the sordid thing.'

She forgot her pose and her reservations. She came closer to him, showing in her carelessness the loose folds of tired skin on her neck; the peevish lines of unwilling age about her mouth. Her lips were almost on his cheek: his soul felt suffocated. It was horrible. He broke away, found himself blundering down the stairs, came into the street.

But once in the air, he had a sudden sense of liberty and exhilaration. It seemed that he had left a part of himself—a baser part, unnoticed, none the less existent—behind. He knew himself now strong, free, a Man. In her clumsy effort toward binding him, Elsa had loosed the last of his chains.

Willie had led a white life, kept chaste by the shining quality of his dream. Curious innocencies were mixed with his thoughts about things. That Elsa, for him the first priestess of the Higher Beauty, should actually seek as pleasurable and rare this debasement of their intercourse—this made him rock with the violence of the impact, as it came into collision with all his past hopes of the world. For the first time, his light contempts of matter turned to hatred. He perceived some positive principle of evil—venomous and aggressive—in the body. It confirmed in him that latent asceticism which is natural to the contemplative mind.

He stood on the pavement, outside the door—that door where he would never again ask for admittance. All the words of their interview passed across his memory in endless procession; over and over again, with a firm tread not to be stilled. They made a horrible and tuneless noise. But for them, his mind was silent. Their steady tramp drowned the rushing trebles of the street. It is so hard for a man, if he be of pure life, to realize that there is anything of the animal in his woman-friend. Elsa, clever and absurd, kindly and affected, always restfully appreciative—he had felt so safe with her! Now he should never forget the evil thing which had brought a quick savagery into that placidly artistic drawing-room, and roused with its stealthy touch some unnameable creature latent in him. Half the anger he felt was for this: that he had found an actual temptation where he had thought himself invulnerable. There had been a 'beauty of ugliness' in the morbid forces which Elsa had loosed between them; and another, unexpected element was added to the tangle of life.

When the tidy vestments of social intercourse are torn, it is generally that we may see how necessary is their presence: even for our immaculate selves.

CHAPTER 24

THE PATH RUNS TO THE WOODS

'Then he went on till he came to the house of the Interpreter, where he knocked over and over. . . . Then said the Interpreter, Come in; I will show that which will be profitable to thee.'

—JOHN BUNYAN

LOOKING into the depths of the woods, seeing against white sky strong trunks and wandering branches laced together in a mysterious friendship, nothing is easier than to believe in nymphs, dryads, elemental presences of the forest. They stand shadowy upon the paths; they laugh and sigh; and sometimes the soul hears them with a sudden terror.

Paganism is thrust upon one in the country; a whole invisible, immemorial population walks upon the lonely heaths and makes the brushwood tremble. It cries, 'You come with your new beliefs; your religions, dragged from the East and seated in the heavens; your science, and your blinded common-sense; and deny us. But we—we looked out on Arthur's knights, to us the old Romans came in fear and in secret; we are of the Earth, all-powerful and intangible. You cannot touch us, and we cannot die. All is of the Earth; the teeming spirit-world is her breath, pervading all and seen of none. You speak to us of a Christ who came from the Heavens. We say no, He came from the Earth. The sum of her pure impulses and poetic forces, her power for a magical righteousness, reached their term in Him. He is the Fair Brother of whom the dark creatures of the forests know dimly; as Jacob and Esau, so Pan and Christ. Both live. But do not fling back the terrible birth on Earth's bosom, and deny her—her Beautiful Son. Look back, and see how many times she has strained toward the ideal which He perfected; see the Buddha births, the fair god of the Norsemen, Phoebus Apollo, and the rest. The Incarnation was an incarnation of Earth-holiness, which God gave her with the breath of life when she was made.'

In such a way the voices of the woods spoke to Mr. Willie Hopkinson, as he trod a path between the trees. He gave them a willing attention. He had developed the sense of adventure; that power which differentiates the romantic from the prosaic world. He felt that everything was possible, and to one who is in this disposition the impossible is sure to come. Want of faith in the improbable is really responsible for all that is deliberately dreary in our lives. Those who go whistling down the road, eyes raised to the sun and hope waiting round the corner, seldom find the excursion of life a disappointing one.

Memory of Fra Agostino, his altar-piece and its painter, and the finding on a map of the woody hamlet that is called S. Mary-le-Street, had set him upon these travels. He looked for a happy termination; for some beautiful surprise, and the discreet discovery of a friend. The whole world seemed smiling, helpful, and unexpected. So that he was not astonished when the turning of a corner, as the trodden path wandered through the pine-wood, brought an abrupt change in the scenery.

From the moment when he left the open country for the forest, he had felt himself to be in surroundings that were charged with romance. Now he thought of the background of some old picture —stiff, quaint, definite. The trees stood up straight and high on each side of him like sanctuary candles, their upper branches shining where they were caught by the sun. Between the austere ranks of their brown and purple trunks and dark network of their crowns, the sky, very blue, peeped in. But where he stood, trees fell away suddenly for a little glade of vivid mossy grass. It seemed to thread its way far down into the heart of the wood, as if searching for a treasure-house hidden there; and ended where a small white red-roofed building stood solitary, giving to its surroundings a touch of un-English magic.

He had strayed into the country of Dürer's etchings, or the legendary landscape of Benozzo Gozzoli. He expected that at any moment he might see a white hart flash past him, and follow it till it reached the cave where S. Giles was praying. He wondered which would be the most likely encounter—Snow-white and her dwarfs, or the Three Magi with their camels and their gifts. The background demanded pretty miracles, and he did not care whether folk-lore or piety supplied them.

But the centre of the picture was that little building, delicately withdrawn and gardened amongst the trees. The afternoon sun hit its roof, which flamed rosily against an emerald background. It looked oddly self-conscious in that very sombre solitude. Willie walked towards it; he was curious. It was like nothing that he had seen in English woods. He did not know what it could be.

Then he came up to it, where it stood guarded by two great larches. And it was a shrine that he saw—a whitewashed shrine, with red-tiled roof deep-eaved to keep it from the rain. There was a picture, painted with direct, affecting simplicity of the primitive masters; clear flat tints, firm outlines, a minute and loving finish of detail. It was charming and appropriate in this place, where a pretence at realism in art would have declared itself vulgar against the eternal simplicity of the woods. One saw the Madonna, very tall and grave, standing in that forest. Behind her, stone-pine and larch, dark and solemn, like the pillars of a temple against the sky. At her feet was all the population of the wood, come out to welcome and worship her; rabbits and weasels, badgers, squirrels, dormice and birds, sitting together in friendship. She raised a veil from her face and smiled at them; she was the Mother of all simple and delightful things, of natural happiness and pious gaiety. One black-cap had perched on her lifted arm the better to sing his *Venite*; two fluffy white rabbits, painted as Pisanello might have painted them, were against the hem of her blue dress.

It was a quiet picture, full of the kindly sorcery of the forest. In front of it, a plain silver lamp was alight; it gave that suggestion of a mysterious cult which lamps burning in the sunlight carry with them. Two dishes of white violets in moss stood on the red-tiled step; behind them and beneath the picture, a painted scroll was nailed up. It was there that Willie read these words: '*Of your charity think kindly on the soul of Francis Waring, for whose remembrance this place has been made.*"

The mystical air of the place was explained to him then. He had come upon a spot set apart for the recollection of the Dead. At such, he knew, one is more than ordinarily near the Eternal Thing.

He knelt down. Again, as when he saw the Lady Poverty, he felt that some great invitation was being offered to him; that there was here a new, simple, wholly satisfying reading of life. He found the attitude, if not the words, of prayer; and with it the solemn happiness which waits for the spirit that has strength to abase itself in the heart of the woods. All the natural and delightful sounds which are thwarted by mere active human presence, rush in on its stillness then. It is the saints in their open cells, the artists alone with their work, who know what magic of suggestion goes with the murmuring leaves and delicate movements of the earth.

All these things came to Willie as he knelt, and raised up in him the Pagan passion of the soil. It was one of those moments, for him so rare and precious, when his dream wrapped him round closely and he could not believe in ugliness. So that he stayed there, not in any serious meditation, but merely enjoying his own visionary idea of the absolute unity of things, till the sound of a footstep amongst crisp pine-needles raised his head and crimsoned his face with the ensign of an entirely common-place shame.

It was a woman who stood by him; a woman whose hair ran away from her face in interesting ripples, and twined itself into an umber coronet for her head. Willie's first thought of her was that he had never seen anyone before who had so much of the thirteenth-century in her look; and indeed Nature, hesitating between a grotesque and a Gothic Madonna, had given to her a quaintness which was the quintessence of all charm. One almost missed her features—delicate and irregular, with a sort of knowing, elfish purity stamped on them—because her smile seized the eye first and held it. It was the delightfully naughty smile of a fundamentally good person; an angel up to mischief. It was evident that she was the child of humour and holiness, a rare and very splendid ancestry.

She stood beside Willie for some moments. He had conquered the first impulse toward flight, and knelt still on the step of the shrine. Human life, be what it may, seems dream-like and elusive in the forest. He had no very direct sense of her nearness, for two things only were now real to him—the picture of Our Lady, and the sombre ecstasy of the pine-trees where they flung their branches to the light.

But she meant, it appeared, to bring him within her atmosphere.

'What are you doing?' she said.

Willie did not look at her. He wished to keep what he had got, undisturbed by external strangeness.

'I am trying to pray,' he answered.

'At any rate,' she said, 'you are honest; and that is the first step toward success.'

He glanced at her then, and knew her for a friend.

'It's hard,' he said. 'Dreadfully difficult. And yet prayer ought to be the easiest thing.'

'It's easier in the woods, or should be. There are no discords to interrupt. Perhaps you've come from a city. That's so suffocating. But you'll shake it off; the whole of life is a sort of prayer in the forest, and a language grows to suit it.'

Then, for the first time, he thought whom she must be, and saw in this quiet meeting in the woods the Event that his spirit had waited for. But he doubted, because she moved with such a gay liberty; more, he thought, like a pious squirrel than a person vowed to the religious life. There was nothing cloistral in her air.

'You cannot,' he said, 'be Hester Waring, who lives here as an Anchoress?'

She laughed.

'Can't I?' she answered. 'Why not? Am I too healthy? Or perhaps not solemn enough? But when you've lived alone with the sky and the forest, right away from the squalor of things, you can't be solemn. Everything's right. Life goes with a dance—' She stopped. 'But it's a dance before the Altar,' she added.

'But,' said Willie, 'does no one ever find you here? Have you really freed yourself?'

That, he thought, was the great matter.

'Yes, really! It's the loneliest place. One of those bits of solitude that's been waiting for its Crusoe. I'm as unknown now as when I came. The owner doesn't preserve, so there are no keepers; no other murder is done here than the natural law of the wood. Jays may live as well as pheasants, and sometimes pussy-cat owls look in on me at night. My friend, who possesses all this forest, has never stirred out of Italy since he came into his own. He is one of those happy visionaries whom the North lends to the South.'

'I've come from Italy to you.'

'Of course you have! It's where all the mystics come from, first or last. The Holy Land of Europe! The only place left, I suppose, which is really medicinal to the soul. There is a type of mind, you know, which must go there to find itself.'

'I was only there for thirteen days.'

'Days? What are days? It's the spirit, not the hour, that counts. One may live through a year of experience for every moment that Time sends flying into the Infinite. And specially in Italy. Time's torch burns slower there than in other places.'

She rubbed her eyes with a little impatient movement, as if she wanted to see something beyond the picture that they showed to her mind. Far down in their depths, a sombre angel sat and weighed all that he saw. He was considering very gravely the case of Mr. Willie Hopkinson, whose freckled face and careful clothing scarcely agreed with the attitude of his soul. Mrs. Waring loved an adventurer, but hated an affectation. Who, she wondered, was this rather second-rate young man, who had thrust himself so suddenly between the tight branches of her home? He looked less the Fairy Prince than the Commercial Traveller. She said to him brusquely

'Why have you come?'

'There seemed nowhere else. Fra Agostino told me. He showed me your picture, and I knew that you understood.'

Willie looked round him. The hush of the woods seemed like an invocation. He felt an intruder, small and mean in the midst of the enduring forest; but it gathered him up without effort and folded him in the general peace.

'Here,' he said, 'one could recollect the Dead.' He looked at the shrine as he spoke.

Her face lit up with a sudden friendship.

'Yes,' she said, 'you can; and if you've got that, you're never lonely.' She stooped and trimmed the silver lamp. It had flickered. 'When Francis passed over,' she said, 'it seemed that there was only a great darkness left. But I said to myself "*Pazienza!* I shall die too. It is a regrettable accident that he should go first, but why be inconsolable for a temporary loneliness?" And I settled down for the long wait. But I found that other people blurred the image that I had of him. I did not wish that. So I came here, to be alone with the wild clean creatures. I thought that I would like to pass the time

as beautifully as I could. It would be a pity if I met him with a
sullied spirit; he went away before life had time to tarnish and finger
his soul.'

'And you found him?' asked Willie.

She looked at him sharply.

'How did you know that?' she said.

'I know it,' said Willie, 'just as I know that I shall never be sure
of the Secret whilst I live in the crowd. I've got two things to do: to
remember the soul of my mother and live the Imaginative Life.
You are on the same road, and you're at peace; so you must have
found him.'

She considered him very gravely.

'I wonder,' she said, 'how far you have got.'

'Oh, not far. In Italy, I just began to see. But my life's been
passed in ugly places, and I wasn't strong enough to pierce through
that.'

'It's difficult, isn't it? It seems so much easier, in these days, to
live morally than to live beautifully. Lots of us manage to exist for
years without ever sinning against society, but we sin against
loveliness every hour of the day. I don't think the crime is less
great. Beauty, after all, is the visual side of goodness: it is Christ
immanent in the world; and its crucifixion still goes on.'

'Oh, I've seen that, too,' said Willie. 'I've seen Heaven and Hell,
and the light at the back of things. But I lose it all so quickly. I
daren't live the conventional life; it makes me forget the real things.
And it seemed that you'd found a way to live rightly, and do work,
without shutting your eyes on reality.'

'I think that I have,' she said. 'But it's a very old way, you know.
The way of the hermits, and of Blake, and Thoreau: and of all the
men who have wished to possess their own souls and be still. It's
only a shaking off of the idea that you must live like the rest; an
exchanging of the world Man mutilated for the world God made.'

'It's hard to do, all the same.'

'Oh no. It's childish to think that. All the great things are free,
aren't they? Sun, and water, and air—all the everlasting symbols?
Well then, why can't you take them and enjoy them in simplicity?
You haven't got them for long, you know. And afterwards, if
you've only ugly years to look back on, you'll regret. Here, one can

be absolutely happy. I can be a saint or a baby or an artist, just as I wish. Yes, a baby! Haven't you ever noticed that there's a sort of divine babyishness about people who are really at peace, just as there is about people who are really in love? They get back to the elemental stage, and express themselves through a simplicity that seems childish because children, as a rule, are the only creatures pure enough to have it.'

She showed him her cottage, of a shining order. He saw her books, her little cooking-stove; in one corner, a demure work-table, in the other a shelf with her tiny store of china, and a knife, fork, and spoon laid out. Everywhere, the neatness was so satisfying that it verged on actual beauty. There was a cot folded sailor-fashion against the wall, and behind it a cast of Michelangelo's stern and impassioned Mary with her Child. Hester caught Willie's look as he saw it.

'That goes deeper than a crucifix,' she said. 'It's the essence of the offering.'

He said to her: 'It's perfect here; one could live in the right kind of dream. But doesn't the solitude turn evil sometimes, don't the days ever seem tedious?'

'No, not now; there's such heaps to do. The painting, and thinking things out, and keeping the cottage and the shrine perfect. And then I've generally some creatures in the infirmary to look after; and in the winter, when it's stormy, I can always cook, and that never bores me.'

'*Cook?*'

'Oh yes! there's nothing so absolutely satisfying. It's a sort of triumph of art over the most animal part of us.'

She opened a cupboard door, and he saw pans and dishes of fire-proof china, moulds, pastry-board, and things to sift and grate with. There were groceries in their little labelled jars.

'My toy-cupboard,' said the Anchoress.

A ladder led to the sky-lit attic where her work was set out: panels and gesso, tempera colours, and all the fine careful apparatus of the water-gilder. Willie, one part craftsman, felt his heart going out to those clean, well-tended tools; knives, brushes, size, and colour-pots, all disposed with a loving touch which spoke of happy and deliberate labour. He felt himself in the midst of a diurnal piety, which made an anthem of the meanest acts. Outside were the sheltered hutches of her infirmary. Two maimed rabbits, a broken-winged pigeon, a damaged field-mouse, were convalescing very tranquilly.

'When I came here,' she said, 'some people talked to me of the selfishness of a secluded life. But *is* it more selfish, do you think, more recluse, to live here with the natural creatures instead of with the distorted human ones? We are all alive under the sky. The Spirit of God is in the woods as well as in the churches; He broods over the sheep-folds as well as over the hearts of men.'

'I never thought,' said Willie, 'that it was possible to live such a reasonable, unentangled life as this. It's all so right. And because others won't come with you to live in the open, surely that's no reason why you should go back and live in the dark with them.'

'That's just what I think. If only one could make them believe how satisfactory this is! The civilized, scramble-after-illusion people always remind me of a harlequinade. They spend all their time in bustle and hitting one another. And the joyous, significant life is so easy to get! so cheap! It's only to live beautifully, laboriously, and austerely: in the air, with the light and colour to remind you of the hidden Beauty behind. And to work with your mind, soul, and body; face difficulties; accept the discipline. That's life. Live so, and in the moment when you die you'll flame up towards the other side and live there vividly and eternally in a happiness that's all your own because you will have built your own heaven. But one must be detached, keep clear of the games and the gossip: they glue you to the earth. But I think you've learnt that. What you've not learnt is that only love can give you your liberty.'

'Oh, I know all about love.'

She laughed at him.

'You delicious infant!' she said. 'You don't think I mean passion, do you? Oceans of bathos peppered with islands of desire! That's no use, but Love is. You must love everything, don't you see, because everything in the whole world is being offered to you as a symbol of an adorable Idea that is beyond. It's only when you've entered into loving alliance with the Universe that you are making the most of life. Because flowers and trees live beautifully for you, it's your duty to live beautifully for others. That's the only law. You've got your moment of self-expression, and if you use it for ugliness you will die. You know that, and you fear it. But you mustn't be afraid, you must love. You've been hunting all your life for initiation, haven't you? But initiation and love are all one. And don't worry. Worry's the negation of God.'

He went away from her; thinking her wise, charming, enviable. Her manner to him had been so gentle that he never noticed that she was clever too. Yet, with light touches, she had helped his discontent to pass from the sensory to the motor region. She knew very well that he was one of her company: made for quiet journeyings, not for that frenzied rush to catch a hypothetical train which is called the strenuous life. As he left her, she said:

'Go back by the right-hand path. It is better for you.'

The path pushed its way by winding stages from the old forest to the new: then wandered by open glades where rows of baby spruces stood fresh and prim. Finally, it turned outwards, passed through a gateway, lost its firm outline and became grassy and uncertain of itself. In another moment it was gone; and Willie checked his stride with a sudden catching of the breath. He seemed to have stepped abruptly to one of the edges of the world.

He had burst, in fact, from the woods to the downland; from inclusion to infinite space; from a home-world to the very far country which stretches to the Hills of Desire. The downs went away from him; green, grey, mauve on the horizon. One could not conceive that they would ever come to an end. There was something religious in their austerity. Far away, on a ridge in those lucent distances, a flock of sheep spread fanwise. He saw no other living thing. But the silence was benevolent; there was at once an entire loneliness and a very intimate sense of consolation. Earth, undisturbed, took up her maternal rights: showed him, in a flash of vivid insight, the Imaginative Universe shining dimly through the Vegetative World. The mesh of Time had broken. Eternity was here and now: and he, wondrous, immortal, saw through the glassy symbol which is Nature the glory of the spiritual flame.

Willie flung himself upon the grass and kissed it. Hester had divined him well: he felt like a wanderer come home.

CHAPTER 25

COMMENTARIES

'I feel for the common chord again.'

—BROWNING

'MY dear,' said Mrs. Steinmann, 'have you heard?'

'I hope not,' answered Elsa languidly. 'Judging by your expression, it seems likely to be vulgar.'

'On the contrary,' replied Mrs. Steinmann, 'it's more your business than mine. That wretched young Hopkinson, whom you made such an absurd fuss of—'

'What, *Willie?*' said Elsa with some eagerness. She had heard nothing of Mr. Willie Hopkinson since their last interview. She missed him. His presence might be embarrassing, but his absence was insipid.

The involuntary propriety of her life, and Mr. Levi's cheerful confidence in her virtue, combined to irritate and depress her. There are circumstances in which an unsuspicious husband is an insult as well as a convenience: Elsa longed for a breath of scandal to stir the stagnation of her home. To be interesting and not to look it, is the hard fate of many intelligent women. As Mrs. Levi lost her slender outlines, her friends spoke less than they had done of her soul. Their wives began to call on her, and showed by their friendly behaviour that her reign was at an end. Charm is a matter of corsets as well as of culture: it is not picturesque to murmur spiritual secrets into the ear of a stout matron, however well-read. To a small mind, such an occupation may even appear ridiculous: and the minds of Elsa's confidants, though perfect in detail and often uncommon in shape, were rather restricted as to size.

All this made her look back regretfully to the time when the obtuseness of her relations only threw into sharper contrast the intelligent comprehension of her disciples. Destiny seemed determined to annoy her. Even her children refused to feed her vanity. Geraint she detested. Tristram had written from Paris of his engagement to an American student of voluptuous charm, and she saw the future in a horrid vision. She had longed for a lover, but

Providence, it appeared, was inclined to give her a grandchild instead.

Religion might have provided her with a refuge both natural and artistic; for she had always been a sentimental Theist, finding God so poetic a background to existence that she was careful not to blot Him out. But now she became impatiently atheistical as the morning sunshine faded. She could not believe in a Deity who was rude enough to permit her to suffer in such an uninteresting way.

Mrs. Steinmann—whose dislike of her daughter's anaemic insolence was tempered by her passion for imparting unpleasant information—now brought to her the news of Willie's withdrawal from civilized life. It had long been her belief that Elsa had made a fool of him: a work of supererogation not to be classed amongst the duties of a wife and mother. The discomfiture of their erring relations is an act of charity which few good women would willingly neglect. Having noted Mrs. Levi's excitement, Mrs. Steinmann kept her waiting for several minutes, took off her gloves, re-tied the strings of her bonnet, and then condescended to speak.

'Well!' she said, 'of course everybody could see that he was bound to do something foolish sooner or later: but no one imagined that it would be anything so idiotic as this. It seems he went off into the country the other day by himself—quite suddenly, without a word to Pauline, who went on ordering in his extra milk just as usual. Young men are so selfish; no consideration for the housekeeper. However, when he came back, he said he'd only come to fetch his things, as he was going to live down in this place in future—some little hamlet in Sussex, miles from a railway-station and altogether as inconvenient as you could find: it's called S. Mary-le-Street. He'd seen a cottage on the downs that he liked, and nothing would do but he must live there alone and do bookbinding.'

The blow was sudden. Elsa, unable to pretend gratified interest, leaned back in the shadow and contrived a becoming languor.

'How strange!' she said, 'and how courageous! I am not entirely surprised; it is the true expression of his temperament, I think. Alone with Nature and Art! He can scarcely fail to find peace.'

'Wait till you've heard the end of the story, my dear. Of course, he's his own master, being over twenty-one; and Mr. Hopkinson allows him £100 a year, so he can't starve. But he's going, if you please, to do his own cooking and everything, just like a common working-man. Think of the discomfort and the mess! And no one will take any notice of him. You know what County people are —they'll think he's a Socialist.'

'That,' said Elsa, 'must console him a good deal.'

'And what upsets me,' continued Mrs. Steinmann, 'is the risks that he must run. He was always delicate: and out in all weathers, with no one to see that he changes his boots! Cooking for himself, too; and one knows what that means—chronic dyspepsia for a certainty, if not gastritis. It's really a mercy that his poor mother died before this happened; it would have killed her, for he was always her favourite. And then, as I said to Pauline, what sort of a place do people of that kind live in? Some horrible little hovel, I suppose, with windows that won't open at the top: and ten to one the drains have never been inspected.'

'Nevertheless,' said Elsa, 'I can imagine being happy in such a life. It appeals to all that is best in me.'

'The risk of typhoid, and the constant society of earwigs, don't appeal to me,' replied her mother. 'Willie doesn't know what it is. If he had consulted those older than himself, instead of rushing away so hurriedly, it would have shown more common-sense, as well as being more respectful. What I quite intended to suggest to him was, that he and Geraint should take a little flat together— somewhere towards Hammersmith, or Chiswick. That is the right locality for Willie, with his fancy for Arts and Crafts; and Geraint could have come up by the tram and tube.'

'I don't think they would have agreed very well together; their temperaments are so diverse.'

'Oh, but Geraint's such a good-natured fellow; he could have put up with anything. And Willie needs a cheerful companion: he is just the one person who ought never to live alone. I could have found them a nice cook-general, and they would have been very comfortable indeed.'

'For a permanency, I should prefer the society of the typhoid bacillus to that of Geraint,' said Geraint's mother pleasantly.

'You never appreciated that boy, my dear. He has got more sound, robust common-sense, than all the rest of you put together.

Mr. Hopkinson thinks great things of him. Only the other day, he said to me "Young Levi will do well; he knows the smell of money."'

'What,' said Elsa quickly, 'is Mr. Hopkinson going to do about Willie?'

'Well, he's really behaving most sensibly; not but what he always was a very reasonable, intelligent man. He says that he considers Willie isn't quite right. Such an unbalanced mind must mean organic mischief. If he were a little queerer, he might be a genius; but as it is, he's only a fool. Of course he isn't dangerous; but being like that, naturally it isn't any use putting him into business or anything, so he'd just as well be in the country as anywhere else. It's cheap, and not so exciting for him as town life; and the main thing is to prevent him from making a nuisance of himself. A terrible thing, isn't it? I can't think where it can come from, for poor Mrs. Hopkinson was quite normal. It's lucky Pauline shows no signs of eccentricity. Mr. Hopkinson says that Willie is a waste product of our civilization.'

'Ah, well,' said Elsa, 'from the point of view of material life, he may be so perhaps. But his soul had powers that were not of this age. I shall miss him. The companionship of a mystic is like a pool of water in a sandy land. But I cannot blame his decision. His environment was not congenial, and solitude is better than boredom. As Meister Eckhardt so beautifully said, "A crowd is often more lonely than a wilderness." But still, I should think he may feel the want of comrade souls, of sympathy, after a time.'

Mrs. Steinmann laughed. Her daughter, who was trying to feel exalted, thought the noise unpleasant.

'I didn't think you were so innocent, Elsa,' she said. 'A woman of your age! It isn't want of sympathy that Willie will suffer from. I should have thought you might have guessed that there was a young woman at the bottom of this ridiculous plan of his.'

'That,' replied Mrs. Levi, 'is most improbable. You do not know him as I do. It was his peculiar charm that he combined the ardours of a mystic with the cold purity of a cloistered life.'

'Ah, that was because he hadn't found what he wanted, my dear. He's got it now, and we shan't hear much more about the cold purity phase. An artist, I understand, who lives down there entirely unchaperoned. She gives herself out as a widow, but there's nothing to prove it. Willie's infatuated: told Stephen Miller that she had "raised him to the plane of the imaginative life"—whatever he means by that.'

Elsa received the shock with a fortitude which she usually kept for her cold baths.

'Ah, I understand so well!' she said. 'It is an illusion, of course, but for the time being it will probably obsess him. It was bound to happen—life is so difficult. But still, it is very disappointing for those who took an interest in his soul. No doubt, he has been deceived by an ingenious simplicity: a picturesque and rustic woman, I expect, who milks a cow and talks of the poetry of motherhood.'

'I hear she has no family,' answered Mrs. Steinmann, 'and to me that looks all the worse. No means of proving her age, which is the one hope in these cases. Pauline told me all about it, and I said to her, "Well, my dear, of course he thinks that she is immaculate at present; but in six months time it will be a very different tale." Those moony boys always fall a victim to the first adventuress they come across.'

Mrs. Levi changed the conversation.

*   *   *   *   *

Stephen had been down to visit Willie: an ambassador from the outraged proprieties of home. His mission included an inquiry into the sanitation of the cottage, and the investigation of Willie's flannel shirts, Hester's morals, and the cost of living in S. Mary-le-Street. He came back with a sort of wistfulness in his face.

'To see them,' he said to Pauline, when he had tersely mentioned the result of the visit to Mr. Hopkinson—'to see them, is to feel that one has somehow missed fire in life. They have everything, I think, that matters—health and innocence and hope. Willie is transformed. He's got a little cottage there in a hollow of the downs, about a mile from the shrine in the wood. He's set up his presses and his finishing bench, and he works there binding books, as she works at her paintings. It's all so simple and joyous; whilst one is there, one feels it's the only possible life. Just that one example seems to have taught him what he wanted. It shames me when I think of our drawing-office, and all the inefficiency and ugliness and fuss.'

'Oh, but Stephen dear! you wouldn't like to be a failure, like poor Willie?'

'What *is* a failure?' said Stephen. His dark intelligent face had a discontented look. 'I couldn't help thinking, when I was with him, that the sort of thing we call a successful life is very paltry after all. Of course, it's amusing: but it's rather the type of amusement supplied by a comic paper. I don't know that providing burlesque for the Deity is a very high destiny for a man.'

'You are very profane,' said Pauline stiffly. As her marriage-day approached, she began to treat Stephen with the firm common-sense which she usually kept for her relations. 'One has one's duty to consider; and of course Willie has shirked all his responsibilities and buried what talents he had in the most disgraceful way.'

'Well, I don't know. He's responsible for himself in the first place: and as for talents, he is doing beautiful work. I saw some of the bindings he had finished. They had a sort of distinguished rightness about them. He's found himself, that's the truth; and he's lost that look of grasping after something out of reach. I felt that he couldn't have worked like that in London. It's the great spaces and quiet influences that are turning him into an artist. I asked him if he were sure he'd made a wise choice: and he said "I don't want to be wise. The Wise Men had no peace, they journeyed after their Star; but my Star is carried and hidden."'

'How perfectly ridiculous,' said Pauline with decision. Much as she believed herself to love—even admire—Stephen, she felt that it was only right to check him before these objectionable ideas took root. 'I'm sure people who are any good can work just as well in town as they can in the country. I never could bear it myself except for the holidays, and then it had to be a place where the cycling was good.'

'Oh, it would never do for us,' answered Stephen rather sadly. 'But he and Mrs. Waring—' He stopped: Hester had charmed him, and he knew that it would be better not to speak of her. But Pauline was curious.

'I hope,' she said vaguely, 'that it is quite—all right? She's fairly young, isn't she?'

'Yes, but she has the active innocence that's invulnerable. And I believe she has Willie's queer ideas about dead people: she loves her husband now in exactly the same way as when he was alive. I noticed that she sometimes looked sad when she was talking, but her face was always happy in repose. She smiled then at something she saw, which was not visible to other people.'

'Still,' said Pauline, carefully balancing herself between purity and knowledge of the world, 'it seems a little risky. Willie must admire her, to go and model his whole existence on her like that.'

'Yes, but then, they are so exactly suited to each other that it's perfectly safe. Men don't fall in love with their stronger selves; it would be too appropriate.'

'Did Willie talk about her much?'

'No. He talked about his work—our work—making beauty. He seemed as though he still wanted to help me to see what he has seen; trace out the Divine in the world. As I came away, he said to me, "*I think the honest artist is very near to God!*"'

'What rubbish!' said Pauline. She was thoroughly exasperated. It was too humiliating that she should have to fight with Willie for the possession of her lover's soul.

Stephen remained silent. He was thinking out a little poem which had been suggested to him by Willie's words. It should be, he decided, a *canzone*, and he would call it 'Heaven's Atrium.' His sadness vanished—'few sorrows can outlive a little song.'

Presently Pauline recovered her temper. She perceived that Stephen's appreciation must have been poetic, not personal; and reflected that remarks which might seem irritatingly foolish if made by a common-place person, are often clever when they come from a literary man. Stephen's vagrant views were sometimes tiresome; but what did that matter, so long as they were not sincere? All men, she knew, required management. She took his hand, and rubbed her cheek against it.

'Darling!' she said contentedly, 'how nice it is to think that *you've* never let yourself be taken in by any of those morbid ideas!'

THE END

———

August, 1902 — *July*, 1903.

CPSIA information can be obtained at www.ICGtesting.com
Printed in the USA
LVOW012139150213

320406LV00012B/456/P